Critical acclaim for Geoff Nicholson

'It is a measure of Nicholson's increasing maturity as a novelist that he manages to weld this unlikely rogues' gallery of characters into a strong and convincing whole' *Daily Telegraph*

'Ingenious . . . earns top marks for originality and puzzlement'
Literary Review

'Nicholson juggles with breathless skill, and an enormous sense of enthusiasm' *The Times*

'Evilly exuberant satire' *Observer*

'Nicholson's writing is rife with deadpan wit, a style that brings both warmth to his characters and a chill to their obsessions' *Arena*

'Filled with weird sex, arbitrary violence and obscure threat . . . making you laugh out loud' *New Statesman*

'Nicholson's London has the power to provoke and enthrall'
Sunday Times

'I couldn't put it down. This ingenious, maddening and provocative novel explodes like shrapnel in the mind. Highly recommended'
Wendy Perriam

'A focus-juggling act of considerable dexterity . . . entirely satisfying'
Guardian

'Nicholson pulls things together with such audacity that you feel like applauding' *Time Out*

'An excitingly inventive novelist . . . a comic tour de force' *GQ*

Geoff Nicholson was born in Sheffield. His novels include *Hunters & Gatherers*, *Everything and More*, *Footsucker*, *Flesh Guitar*, *Female Ruins* and *Bleeding London*, which was shortlisted for the 1997 Whitbread Award. His works have been translated into French, German, Japanese, Italian and Spanish. He lives in London and New York.

By Geoff Nicholson

FICTION

Street Sleeper
Still Life with Volkswagens
The Knot Garden
What We Did on our Holidays
Hunters & Gatherers
The Food Chain
The Errol Flynn Novel
Everything and More
Footsucker
Flesh Guitar
Female Ruins
Bedlam Burning
Bleeding London

NON-FICTION

Big Noises
Day Trips to the Desert

THE FOOD CHAIN

GEOFF NICHOLSON

PHŒNIX

A PHOENIX PAPERBACK

First published in Great Britain in 1992
by Hodder and Stoughton
This paperback edition published in 2001
by Phoenix,
an imprint of Orion Books Ltd,
Orion House, 5 Upper St Martin's Lane,
London WC2H 9EA

ISBN 0 75381 263 0

Printed and bound in Great Britain by
The Guernsey Press Co. Ltd, Guernsey, C.I.

THE FOOD CHAIN

'*Tho' the Promotion of Trade, and the Benefits that arise from Humane Conversation, are the specious Pretences that every Tippling-Club or Society, are apt to assign as a reasonable Plea for their Unprofitable Meetings; yet most Considerate Men, who have ever been Engag'd in such sort of Compotations, have found by Experience, that the general end thereof, is a Promiscuous Encouragement of Vice, Faction, and Folly, at the unnecessary Expence of that Time and Money which might be better imploy'd in their own Business, or spent with much more comfort in their several Families.'*

Ned Ward,
The Secret History of Clubs,
London, 1709

Something creeps in, an awareness, a gut feeling, something felt in the heart, in the bowels. Something moves in the shadow, outside the glow of the candlelit table. The waiters smirk. The glasses are smeared with lipstick. The menu is written in a language you cannot read, and the prices are uncertain, but certainly not negotiable. There is cork in the wine, a fly in the soup, the waiter's thumb on your windpipe.

You feel light-headed but your stomach is leaden. Could it be something you ate? Something that disagreed with you? You feel for your wallet and it has gone. You tell yourself not to panic. You're known here. Your credit is good, at least it used to be, unless things have changed; a change of policy, a change of management. You need a drink, some iced water. You need some air. You experience heartburn, nausea, indigestion, seasickness.

The sea kisses against the shore, soothes the beach, crashes against the shingle, encircles and caresses. We open our hearts, then our mouths and bladders and bowels. We open the floodgates. We open the sewers. It all pours out and lies around us like gravy. We get out more or less what we put in. But this is not simply a question of ecology.

This is not the only possible world. There are others: Third Worlds and lost worlds and dying worlds. Some of them survive on scraps, on the waste and garbage from others' tables. There is a world of modest proposals, of bloated bellies and death. But that's the way the cookie crumbles. That's hard cheese, old man. The men with the money will tell you it isn't a question of money.

The metaphors crowd in; sex and death, hard meat, ravenous hunger, appetites to be assuaged, the flesh trade, the body economic, who we are and how we eat. And God drifts in too; holy bodies, holy blood, bread and wine, flesh and ghosts. 'Waiter! This isn't what I ordered. I wanted the loaves, the fishes, the water turned into wine,

1

the wafers, the pork. I demand to see the chef, the owner, some higher authority . . .'

Some diners pick at their food, or eat like birds, or are so hungry they could consume a horse, or a nest of sugar mice, or a candy mountain. The anorexics and the bulimics peer in at the restaurant window; the obese and the lean and hungry, the raw and the stewed. Some say hunger is a fashion statement. Some say eat the rich. Blood suckers and werewolves; they lean against the groaning board, these consumers of surpluses, of food mountains, failed harvests, essential commodities. Inside every starving peasant there's a fat bastard trying to get out. Just give him the opportunity. Just give him the means.

We search for new flavours, new blood, that mystery ingredient, something to tickle the fancy and the jaded palate. A healthy mind lives behind a healthy face. A sick mind lives in a body bag of flesh, sugar and red meat, white bread and saturated fats.

Eat that, it'll make a man of you. It'll put hairs on your chest, it'll help you see through the fog, it'll make your hair fall out. These are acquired tastes. The prices are high to keep out the riff-raff. A certain standard is expected, certain standards of service and decorum. These things do not come cheap. Free trade has its price.

We are civilised men. We do not eat because we are hungry any more than we copulate because we want to procreate. This is the pursuit of pleasure, not of knowledge. No fruit is forbidden. We always pay our way. Big fish eat little fish. Dog eats dog. There are things that money can't buy but those things do not appear on our menu; bear's paw, eye of newt, the gingerbread house, the frog in the throat, long pig, praying mantis.

ONE

He sat in first class breathing the dead air. He slumped in the big padded seat. He could see only clouds through the window. He asked for more champagne. When the hostess brought it he said to her, 'Do you know anything about the praying mantis?'

'No sir,' she said smiling.

'Well, the deal is this. The male and female praying mantis meet, like the look of each other, talk about what star sign they are, what their favourite movie is, then they go back to her place, some little woodland retreat, nothing too showy or expensive. Then they have a couple of drinks and talk about their childhoods and at last they start to make love. The male praying mantis is feeling pretty good now, he feels like he's made a conquest, and everything goes pretty good for a while, he touches her, she touches him, the passion builds and builds and finally, and this comes as a surprise to the male praying mantis, the female bites his head off. But as he dies at least he comes and a little while later the female gives birth to about two hundred eggs. I mean I've been on some bad dates and I've met some ball busters, but still . . .'

The air hostess was still smiling, but the smile had become thin and fragile, and she said coldly, 'Why are you telling me this?'

'Oh, it's just my clumsy way of asking if you want to fuck . . .'

'Don't act like a piece of slime, sir,' she said.

'Hey,' he said, 'no need to bite my head off!'

He rolled around in his seat with self-inflicted mirth, spilling drink and salted nuts down his trousers. It was a long time before he stopped laughing. The next time the hostess passed, amnesia had set in and she said, 'Any more champagne, sir?'

These were the joys of travelling first class. There was plenty of arm and leg room, the food was more or less edible, the drink was free, and you could talk dirty to the air hostesses and they would carry on smiling and serving and continue to call you sir.

He tried to settle. He tried to get interested in a magazine.

He failed. He brushed debris from his Armani suit, worn with a Jackson Pollock-style T-shirt, and espadrilles without socks. He put on his headset. Nothing suited him. He signalled that he did want another drink.

Virgil was in his late twenties though he looked and acted younger. He might have been mistaken for a certain kind of all-American rock star; nocturnal, dangerous, lean, hungover. He was badly shaven, his hair greasy, his hands dirty. There were some women, as Virgil knew very well, who found this sort of look irresistible.

He had been to England only once before, some years ago on a summer vacation from college, and then only to London. He remembered it as a complete disaster. He'd stayed in a cheap hotel in Bloomsbury. He was there a week. In that time he hadn't managed to work out the Tube system, and he hadn't been able to understand anything the locals said to him, and even though his tastes in food had been a lot less demanding then than they were now, he hadn't been served an edible English meal that whole week. After a couple of failures with roast beef and steak and kidney pies he stuck to imported fruit in the days and ate at Italian greasy spoons at night. He had planned to stay in England for a month, but after seven days of non-communication and bad food, drizzle and slate-grey skies, he'd headed for Greece. That was more like home, more like California.

His drink arrived. The air hostess smiled at him one more time. He guzzled the champagne. He got out his wallet and checked the invitation. It was classy looking; heavy white card, bevelled edges, handwritten in italics.

You are cordially invited to attend the Everlasting Club, London, England. You may arrive at any time of the day or night and be assured of a unique experience of fine food, drink and congenial company, all furnished at our expense.

He thought it was kind of strange that the invitation didn't give any address for the club, and there was a peculiar logo embossed at the top of the card. It showed a snake swallowing its own tail. Virgil found that a little unusual, but not as unusual as all that. And it had come with a first class return ticket and a hotel reservation, so he hadn't asked too many questions. He had nothing better to do, nothing much to do at all, so he caught the next plane. He had never heard of this Everlasting Club but he wasn't surprised they'd heard of him. He was the kind of guy some people had heard of.

He had set up one of Los Angeles' hippest restaurants. He had been described as the *enfant terrible* of L.A. gastronomy. He was the kind of guy who received a lot of invitations. He was the kind of guy who always accepted.

Virgil breezed through customs and immigration. The passport man asked, 'Here on business, sir?'

'Do I look like a businessman?'

'Here on holiday?'

'Well, I guess somebody's probably going to try to sell me something somewhere along the line, but I'm not buying. I'm here strictly for pleasure, know what I'm saying?'

The man waved him through. Down the green channel and through swing doors out into the real world. He saw expectant faces, a crowd kept behind barriers, chauffeurs and taxi drivers holding up signs with names on them: Da Silva, McLennon, Marchesi, Foo. And one of them bore the name Marcel, his name.

The driver holding his sign was a black man in his forties; solid, dignified, but a little hesitant. His face wore a puzzled, quizzical expression. His hair was flecked at the temples with grey and he wore, not a uniform, but a shiny blue suit with mustard-coloured brogues.

'I'm Mr Marcel,' Virgil said to the driver, 'but you can call me Virgil.'

'Right you are, sir.'

Everyone was going to call him sir today.

'And *your* name?'

'Butterworth, sir.'

'Yeah? You don't meet many people called Butterworth where I come from.'

Butterworth did not reply.

He led Virgil to the car, a black Mercedes saloon, not a limo; no cocktail bar, no TV. Virgil sat up front with Butterworth.

'What's your first name?' Virgil asked.

'Vince, sir, but they prefer it if you call me Butterworth.'

'Just trying to be egalitarian.'

'That won't be necessary, sir.'

He drove easily and with his full attention, a man who took his work seriously. The car was heavy and stable on the road. Virgil watched the other cars. They seemed small, vicious, rat-like. So this was England. He felt tired and hungover. He was suffering from jet lag. He reckoned he needed another drink.

'So where are you taking me, Butterworth?'

'To your hotel, sir, where you'll have the chance to wash and brush up, or even to sleep if you'd like, and then, any time you want to go, I'll take you to the Everlasting Club.'

'So we're not working to a deadline here?'

'No sir. The Everlasting Club is always waiting for you.'

'Hey Butterworth, who are these dudes?'

'Dudes?'

'The Everlasting Club; it sounds like a religious group or something.'

'No, there's nothing religious about it as far as *I* know.'

'What is it then, just another night-club?'

'Oh no. Not that.'

'Then who are they? What do they do? Why did they invite me?'

'I really don't know. You know, I'm just an employee.'

'I'm just supposed to sit back and enjoy the mystery tour, that it?'

Butterworth almost smiled then concentrated on the traffic.

'That's okay by me,' said Virgil. 'What the hell. I'll go anywhere for a free drink.'

'There is one thing I have to mention, sir,' said Butterworth. 'The Everlasting Club will expect you to be wearing black tie.'

'That's tough. I didn't bring my tux.'

'That's no problem. There'll be a dinner jacket hanging in your hotel room.'

'Yeah? They know my size?'

'They have ways I think, sir.'

Virgil said, 'I've never understood why people need to put on special clothes before they eat. Like I don't understand people who need to put on special clothes before they have sex. Do you, Butterworth?'

'I think the idea is it gives the event a sense of occasion.'

'I'm sure you're right. Why not? It's their party. I'll wear the fancy dress.'

They were soon in central London. Virgil recognised nothing. They arrived at the hotel. Virgil was shown to his room; considerably better than standard issue, with a leather sofa, a lot of egg-and-dart moulding and flounces, everything in cream and pale grey. There were flowers, a vast bowl of fruit, and a waiter arrived with more free champagne as Virgil was testing the bed for size; king-size.

He called room service and asked for gravlax, some quail eggs, a radicchio and chicory salad, olives stuffed with anchovies, rye bread, guacamole and nacho chips. He regarded this as a test. He was amazed they arrived at all, even more amazed when they arrived so fast.

He tried on the dinner jacket. It fitted perfectly. Yep, someone had done his homework. The bow-tie baffled him but he felt sure Butterworth would be able to help with the tying. He considered taking a shower but no, that would waste time. He wanted to get out there. He wanted to see the Everlasting Club, whatever the hell it was. He wanted to see what this whole thing was about.

He phoned Reception and asked the girl to tell Butterworth he'd be down in a couple of minutes. Butterworth was waiting patiently downstairs, seated stiffly in a high-backed armchair. He was prepared to wait all night if necessary, until the very moment when Virgil was ready. Virgil descended. Butterworth tied his bow-tie for him and they went out to the car.

'There's another little formality,' said Butterworth, embarrassed.

'Huh?'

Butterworth handed him an airline sleep mask.

'What am I supposed to do with this?'

'Put it on please, sir. I'm afraid you have to be blindfolded for the journey.'

'You're shitting me? You're serious.'

'I'm afraid so. It's so you don't see the route we're taking. It's a rule.'

'But I wouldn't know where I was going. I don't know London at all, wouldn't recognise a thing except maybe St Paul's, Trafalgar Square, and one or two Italian restaurants.'

'It's just a rule, sir.'

Virgil snorted in sneering disbelief, but he put on the mask. He sat in darkness in the car. It was at this point he wondered if he was about to be kidnapped. The invitation and the hotel room and Butterworth could all be a front disguising some arcane, say Middle Eastern, say Fundamentalist, interests. Virgil's old man was well-known in certain circles for being loaded, and Virgil liked to think he'd be prepared to dig fairly deep to save the skin of his only son and heir. Virgil only hoped there wouldn't be too much humiliation and re-education inflicted on him while negotiations took place. But of course he didn't really believe that. And just thinking about it was enough to make sure it didn't happen.

He sat listening to the car's engine and the sound of tyres on

the road. He felt the solidity of the seat under him. He felt surprisingly safe.

He said to Butterworth, 'Hey, what kind of voice have you got?'

'Voice?'

'Like is it upper class or lower class or what? I know that's real
important to you Brits. And with you being black and all . . .'

'Well, you know sir, I'd like to think that these days what a man
says is more important than the accent he says it in.'

'I'll drink to that.'

'But I suppose,' Butterworth continued, 'I've got a very ordinary
voice, sir, your basic London accent with a bit of Jamaica in it.'

Virgil said, 'Well, all you Brits sound like Prince Charles to me.'

He realised this wouldn't be much help if he really *was* being
kidnapped and at some point needed to describe the terrorists who
plucked him from the civilised streets of London. 'Well, officer, they
all sounded like Prince Charles to me . . .'

The car stopped after a fifteen-minute drive. So they were still in
central London. Butterworth turned off the engine. He got out of
the car and went round to open Virgil's door. Virgil stepped out, still
blindfolded, and Butterworth took him by the arm. They walked
across the pavement, passed through an iron gate which Butterworth
opened and closed, up a short gravel path, no more than four paces,
and up half a dozen steps. Butterworth rang the doorbell. The door
opened. 'This is as far as I go, sir,' Butterworth said, and Virgil took
a couple of steps forward, over the threshold and went inside. He
could smell polish and distant rich cooking; garlic, tarragon, game.
The door closed behind him.

He removed the sleep mask from his eyes. He blinked in the
artificial light. Butterworth was gone and Virgil was standing alone
in a small panelled entrance hall. Several doors led from it; big,
solid, wooden doors with brass fittings, but they were all closed.
He could hear male voices behind the doors, some engaged in
quiet conversation, others further away shouting and whooping
with laughter. Virgil thought, what the hell, he'd take the plunge
and open one of the doors, burst in and say, howdy, but before he
could decide which door to go for, one of them had opened a foot
or so and a fat, round, bald head popped out and smiled warmly
at him.

'Virgil Marcel!' said the owner of the head, enthusiastically. 'Welcome! Good to have you on board.'

The man stepped into the hall. The baldness and fatness were deceiving. In fact he was probably no older than Virgil. The face was smooth and very pink and unscarred by experience, though it was fleshed-out and coloured by too much food and drink. He looked simultaneously old and young; a baby-faced blimp.

'My name's Kingsley,' he said, 'John Kingsley, Chief Carver of the Everlasting Club. I'm jolly glad you were able to accept our invitation. We all are.'

'Free hotel and air fare,' said Virgil. 'How could I refuse?'

'Rather. Well, come in. Let's get you a drink.'

Virgil took an instant dislike to Kingsley. It wasn't only that he was fat and bald, although in some of the circles Virgil moved in that would have been enough; it was more the air of wealth, ease and assumed superiority, the glibness, the charm, the old school tie. Hell, he was just too *English* for Virgil's taste.

Kingsley led Virgil into the club. The hall had been small enough to have belonged to a private house, but the room into which he now stepped was bigger than any domestic room. It was a bar of sorts, a club-room, some sixty feet square, high-ceilinged, panelled again, dimly lit, not immediately welcoming. The bar ran half the length of one wall, and directly opposite on the other wall was an elaborately carved stone fireplace in which logs were burning. There were a few tables and chairs scattered unsystematically around the area, but not nearly enough for the number of men who were in residence. The men all wore evening dress. There were no women. The men were of all ages and were all enjoying various degrees of drunkenness.

Without consulting Virgil, Kingsley ordered two pints of bitter. The barman pulled the beer. No money appeared to change hands. Virgil wasn't very familiar with English beer, but he was familiar enough from his last visit to know he didn't like it. He took a swig of the warm, heavy bitter and then he remembered precisely what he disliked about it. His tastes hadn't changed so very much since his last visit. Virgil and Kingsley stood with their backs to the bar and surveyed the scene.

'Cute place you've got here,' Virgil said.

'We like it,' replied Kingsley.

'And what sort of gig is this? Is this what you call a gentleman's club?'

'Hardly,' said Kingsley.

'Well, how the hell should I know? I've never been to a gentleman's club. Not sure I've ever met a gentleman.'

'The Everlasting Club is something quite singular,' said Kingsley. 'But perhaps you're unfamiliar with our activities.'

'How did you guess?'

'To be brief,' said Kingsley, 'the Everlasting Club was founded in the mid-seventeenth century, immediately after the Civil War. It was a drinking club and dining society, high-living, sybaritic, anti-Commonwealth, that sort of thing. Members could arrive at literally any time of day or night and be sure to find festivities in progress. Members sat eating and drinking all the hours God sent. As certain revellers became incapacitated, new, sober replacements would arrive to continue the fun. The fire was never allowed to go out. The idea was that from the moment of the club's inception until the end of eternity there should be men gathered together, carousing, celebrating, indulging in excess.'

'An infinite party,' said Virgil.

'If you like.'

'I could get into that.'

'The Everlasting Club was founded in 1651 and we've been going strong ever since.'

'Not bad,' said Virgil, somewhat overcoming his antipathy to Kingsley. 'You mean you've been partying night and day for about three hundred and fifty years?'

'Exactly. At any moment since 1651 you might have come into this room and found a party in progress, the same party. You might have found the Earl of Sandwich or John Caius, or the Marquis de Sade.'

'Wow,' said Virgil. 'That's class.'

Kingsley smiled contentedly. 'Yes,' he said, 'it has a certain intellectual appeal, doesn't it?'

'Yeah, I like it. Not bad, Kingsley, not bad at all.'

'There's a book I could let you have, a sort of club history. It lets one or two of our little secrets out of the bag apparently. Can't say I've read it myself. Never was much of a one for books. Wodehouse is about my limit.'

'You don't say,' said Virgil.

He surveyed the room again. In one group a man was demonstrating a golf swing, another group had begun to sing about cockles and mussels, and elsewhere someone was massaging what looked like eggnog into one of his companions' hair.

'Who are these guys?' Virgil wanted to know.

'Oh, we're a diverse and glittering crew,' replied Kingsley. 'Barristers, men of property, Members of Parliament, sportsmen, senior civil servants, ship owners, actuaries, entrepreneurs, executives of all sorts, movers and shakers, wheelers and dealers, achievers, high-fliers, risk takers. They all enjoy the good things in life, and without exception they're very good chaps.'

As Virgil was forcing down the last of his beer a white-haired man of aristocratic bearing and wolfish good looks came casually to the bar.

'Virgil Marcel I presume,' he greeted and shook Virgil by the hand as though it was a great honour for him. Virgil was not aware of ever having seen the man before.

'My name's Radcliffe,' the man said. 'Charles Radcliffe. I ate at your restaurant when I was last in Los Angeles. It was an experience not to be forgotten. I hope you won't find our fare a little humble by comparison. What are you having?'

Virgil hesitated for a moment, looked at the rows of bottles behind the bar and felt spoiled for choice.

'Not beer,' he said.

'Ah,' said Kingsley, 'that's just as well. We have a club rule that a chap can't ever have the "same again". Not only in the philosophical sense, but in the sense that we insist you drink something different every round.'

'Sounds like a Frat house,' said Virgil.

Kingsley and Radcliffe smiled, either not feeling insulted or not knowing what a Frat house was. Virgil asked for vodka. It appeared promptly. Radcliffe wished him good health and returned to his own group, carrying with him a tray of drinks: tequila, pernod, peppermint schnapps and black velvet.

'That was Charles Radcliffe,' said Kingsley, a note of awe in his voice. 'He's the chap who wrote the club history. Brilliant man.'

Virgil refused to be impressed. 'Where do I fit into all this?' he asked.

'Oh,' said Kingsley, 'you're going to fit in perfectly.'

'You think?'

'Certainly. You're a bon viveur. You have a certain expertise in food and drink, both personally and professionally. You are, I have no doubt, good company. We think you'll be an adornment to the Everlasting Club.'

Virgil considered that answer. He wasn't convinced.

'Okay, so I'm an all-round great guy. So what do you want from me?'

Kingsley made a face as though offended.

'We don't want anything specifically,' he said. 'There are the club fees, which aren't cheap, but well within your budget, I'm sure. And we'd expect you to put in an appearance at the club every so often, but that shouldn't be too onerous.'

'But you expect a few favours, right?'

'No,' said Kingsley, in a way that tempted Virgil to believe him.

'See,' said Virgil, 'the trouble with you English is I can't tell when you're bullshitting and when you're not. See, what I worry about is you think I can do something for you, some favour you have in mind for the future but you're not telling me yet what it is. Everything goes along fine until one day you tell me what it is you want and then you find that I can't deliver. And then what happens? I'm in trouble, right? Concrete overcoat time, yeah?'

'Really Virgil, that's hardly our style.'

Virgil couldn't see much future in pursuing that line any further. They had a few more rounds of drinks; bloody Marys, brandies, and something that confused Virgil, called a milk stout. From time to time Kingsley introduced Virgil to other members. A few seemed to know who he was. They were all friendly enough. They said how good it was to see him, and they exchanged gossip about food and drink. They seemed to be mostly assholes. A few jokes were told. Virgil didn't understand them. They were English jokes. Virgil pretended to be amused, wondered why he was bothering to pretend.

'And how come there aren't any women here?' he asked Kingsley.

'I'd have thought that was obvious.'

'No, Kingsley, it isn't obvious. I'm a simple guy, maybe too simple for this joint, and when I've got a few drinks under my belt I often start to feel the need for a little female company. I like the kind of club where you can sidle up to a girl at the bar, buy her a couple of drinks, and before you know where you are she's telling you what you need to do to give her multiple orgasms.'

'We do have female members,' said Kingsley, 'but they need to be very special women indeed.'

'Hey, this isn't some kind of hangout for English faggots, is it?'

For a moment Kingsley looked as though he might challenge Virgil to a duel.

'No,' he said with finality.

When enough time had passed to diffuse this slur, Kingsley said it was time to eat. They stepped into the candlelit dining-room. It was dark in there. There was a long refectory table with perhaps thirty place settings around it, about half of which were occupied. The diners were scattered unevenly along both sides of the table. Most were eating so heartily and with such enthusiasm it looked as though they were putting on a show for somebody's benefit. Virgil's? A few had eaten so heartily they were unable to keep up the performance. They sagged in their chairs, stuffed and red-faced and unable to force any more down. Two or three of them had passed out, heads down on the table. Others belched and farted and picked things out of their teeth. It was easy to believe that all this had been going on for a very long time.

Waiters moved swiftly, if a little obtrusively around the table, delivering dishes, spiriting away used crockery, brushing away crumbs and wiping up spillages; a stately ritual or dance based on complex principles.

The table was decked with candelabra, vases of flowers, wine bottles, decanters, condiments; and in the very middle of the table, as a sort of elaborate table decoration, was a woman. She was on her back, her arms neatly by her sides. She was garnished here and there with clusters of fruit and bunches of herbs, but otherwise she was completely naked.

Virgil did a double-take. He thought at first it might be a mannikin or a pop art sculpture, but no, he could see her ribcage rise and fall, muscles twitching in her cheeks, her eyes blinking. She was a good-looking girl but Virgil didn't know what the hell she was doing on the table. If it was a way of asserting that they weren't a bunch of English faggots it seemed a little clumsy.

'Really tacky,' he said, but if Kingsley heard he ignored the remark.

They sat down next to a man who had passed out. There wasn't going to be any table-talk coming from that direction. Virgil found himself adjacent to the naked shoulder of the girl.

'Fortunately,' said Kingsley, 'we're able to drink wine with our meals. The "same again" rule doesn't apply here in the dining-room.'

'Thank God,' said Virgil. The mixture of drinks he'd consumed was fizzing uneasily in his normally highly resistant stomach. Kingsley poured two glasses of wine from a bottle set before them. Virgil caught only a glimpse of the label but he thought he saw the word 'Elderflower' on it. Virgil had never heard of elderflower. It tasted terrible.

'I guess it'd be dumb to expect anything so simple as a menu,' Virgil said.

Kingsley confirmed that it would.

'At the Everlasting Club,' he said, 'we eat what we're given. Perhaps that's a habit from public school.'

Virgil drank his wine and waited for some food to arrive. He watched the others eating. There was a manic, compulsive quality to it. They filled their mouths so full they could barely chew. The strain made their eyes water. Some didn't even seem to be chewing at all. Hard lumps of food got swallowed down, unmolested by teeth or saliva. Back home Virgil was known as a man with a taste for excess. He could put away several times more than his fair share, but he had nothing on these guys. He might have been impressed. In the event he was revolted.

It appeared, from looking round the table, that the other diners must have started their meals at different times and were therefore eating different courses. Waiters delivered starters, main courses, desserts, fish courses, savouries, to different parts of the table. But Virgil saw, and soon discovered at first hand, there was no order or logic to these deliveries. A man might finish some sort of chocolate pudding and then be presented with a plate of smoked fish. Hors d'oeuvres followed sweets, soups followed cheese selections. Nobody seemed to object. They all kept stuffing it down. And in fact, the more Virgil looked at the food being served the less sure he became of what anybody was actually eating. Food was piled into unlikely shapes, covered in strange-coloured sauces, or mashed into bright marbled purées that disguised its true nature. Nothing being eaten at the table was unmistakably identifiable as a simple piece of flesh, fowl or vegetable. Virgil felt this was going to be a wild eating experience. He was ready for it. Maybe the Everlasting Club wasn't so bad after all.

His first course arrived. He wasn't sure if he was fortunate or not to be presented with something as unchallenging as a bowl of soup. He tried a spoonful. There was plenty of challenge in the flavour. It etched furrows across his tongue, activating small, clashing areas of taste; sweetness, salt, vinegar, nuts, cherries, a hint of liver. It was a weird brew, not exactly a success in Virgil's opinion, but perfectly edible. Leo, Virgil's chef in his restaurant in L.A., would enjoy hearing about this. Virgil determined to remember as much as he could and report it all back as a traveller's tale. He put his spoon below the surface of the soup again and dredged up some solids from the bottom of the bowl. He found juniper berries, some strands of saffron, an unfamiliar frond-like vegetable, possibly a seaweed, and slices of dried fig. Virgil took a big mouthful of wine to help it down. The flavours loitered around his mouth like a bum in a shop doorway. It took several swigs of wine before the aftertaste of the soup had been rinsed away, leaving only the aftertaste of elderflower.

Kingsley's first course was different from Virgil's. He was served a pale cerise jelly which he'd eaten without comment. For the next course, however, they were given a mixed grill to share. Kingsley smiled radiantly.

'You'll like this,' he said and he opened another bottle of wine, a Zambian Muscadet.

Virgil took a small, dark chop. It tasted good, rich, gamey, earthy.

'Let me tell you what we have here,' said Kingsley. He pointed delicately around the plate as he spoke. 'Peacock, magpie, swan, and those things there are sausages of course.'

'Swan?' said Virgil.

Kingsley tapped his nose meaningfully. 'Royal connections,' he said.

The peacock, magpie, swan, and sausages went down without much difficulty, though Virgil might have been hard-pressed to say which was which. Perhaps Kingsley was putting him on. Perhaps he was eating nothing more exotic than goat or camel, or some other creature he'd never tasted before.

Virgil kept looking at the girl in the centre of the table. She was young, pretty, quite plump. Her skin was tanned a biscuit brown, her long hair dyed to blonde candy floss. Her lips were as full and ripe as cherries. All the old clichés. He wondered what her terms of employment were. How long were her shifts? Was there a whole set of girls who took it in turn to adorn the table, like Playboy bunnies? He could think of worse ways of making a living.

There were splashes of sauce and gravy here and there on her body, caused by the vigour and messiness of the other eaters. Virgil himself was responsible for a small blob on her shoulder. He was about to wipe it off with his napkin but Kingsley gave him a look of utter distaste and condemnation and pulled his hand away. That kind of thing was obviously not done. Virgil had been on the point of committing some serious indiscretion, an appalling breakage of the rules. He tried to look suitably chastened but he was aware that he probably wasn't very convincing.

The next course was a chocolate and bacon mousse, then there was a selection of rare buffalo cheeses. After that came a turkey, a rather ordinary looking turkey until the waiter began to carve it. He sliced through it vertically, to reveal contrasting concentric patterns. The turkey had been boned and stuffed with a goose, inside which was a chicken, inside which was a pheasant, inside which was a wood pigeon. And inside that was a stuffing made from whitebait and bananas. Virgil managed to avoid most of the stuffing.

'Okay,' said Virgil, 'so the way I see it, the English class system is all based on food, right?'

'I'm not sure I follow,' said Kingsley, and several sets of ears around the table pricked up.

'Like the big noises in England are called the upper crust, right? And the *crème de la crème*. And people who are really low class, you say they're below the salt, is that right?'

'Well possibly,' said Kingsley.

'And aren't upper-class guys called toffs? Isn't that something to do with toffee?'

'Well,' said Kingsley, 'I don't think toffee has ever been a very aristocratic food.'

'And even sex,' said Virgil. 'You call a good-looking woman a piece of crumpet. What's that all about?'

By now, Radcliffe, the white-haired man from the bar, the author of the club history, had arrived at the table. 'Ah well,' he said, 'if I may interrupt, this is potentially interesting. I believe crumpet is an adaptation from the phrase "buttered bun".'

'Huh?' said Virgil.

'A buttered bun,' said Radcliffe, 'is a slang term for a vagina into which someone has recently ejaculated. It therefore has a wet, creamy, buttered appearance. A crumpet, as I'm sure you know, despite being American, is a kind of muffin, eaten hot and copiously buttered.'

'Oh come on,' said Virgil. 'You trying to tell me an English guy's walking down the street and he sees a woman he likes the look of and he says "there's a nice bit of crumpet", but what he really means is "there's a vagina somebody's just come in". Are you serious? Get real.'

Radcliffe gave a slight bow of the head. He was not going to argue but, his manner said, if he *did* argue, about this or anything else, he would unquestionably win.

'Okay,' said Virgil, 'so tell me what's the deal with the snake?'

'Ouroboros,' said Radcliffe.

'Huh?'

16

'It's a symbol largely associated with the Gnostics, although the Everlasting Club uses it in a secular sense. The snake has its tail in its mouth. The digestive tract of the snake is a one-way system. Peristalsis draws in the prey, forces it down. Those muscular contractions allow no release and no going back. Thus the snake is condemned to eat itself.

'However, there is an obvious paradox here, for an organism cannot truly consume itself. The teeth cannot bite the teeth, the gullet cannot swallow the gullet, the stomach cannot digest the stomach. It is a vicious circle.

'The Ouroboros is a symbol of endlessness, of infinity; a well-chosen motif for the Everlasting Club, I'm sure you'll agree.'

'Sure,' said Virgil.

More food arrived, this time on a lidded salver. A waiter placed it on the table between Kingsley and Virgil and removed the domed cover. The thing revealed on the salver was simultaneously fascinating and disgusting. Virgil couldn't quite believe his eyes. Staring up at him was a lurid, grotesque, mythological beast; a whole creature put together from parts of real animals. It had a shark's head, octopus tentacles, lobster claws, four duck's feet, a goat's tail, a torso made from rolled belly pork, and the whole thing was decorated with plumage, feathers from geese, eagles and emus. Virgil tucked in gamely. He was feeling reckless. He felt he ought to be able to handle anything these Brits could throw at him. He probably felt that way because of the Zambian Muscadet.

Other courses arrived, but by now they were starting to merge together in Virgil's perception. In quick succession all manner of tastes and textures assaulted his increasingly bewildered and un-critical senses. There were foods he had never seen or heard of before, unimaginable combinations, food that had been dyed and disguised, sculpted and camouflaged. He ate cuttlefish ink, stuffed gizzard, kidneys with nasturtium flowers, truffle vinaigrette. A thing that started out looking and tasting like a cheesecake would unloose more complex and threatening sub-tastes of cumin, pear, coffee and capers. Chicken livers appeared, dressed up to look like ice cream. He would cut into a perfectly innocent-looking piece of Stilton to find gooseberry and chilli. He found himself eating the tongues and brains of songbirds. Here was lizard. Here were lamprey intestines. And he was forced to wash it down with all manner of unusual wines; Ugandan *vin du pays*, Cambodian hock, something that called itself avocado champagne.

Kingsley talked throughout the meal, naming things, describing processes and seasonings. He had seen it all before, eaten it all before. He devoured each course with the same omnivorous lust displayed by all the other members of the Everlasting Club.

Virgil's stomach was now full beyond capacity. The strange richnesses were weighing heavily and moving unexpectedly inside him. They seemed even to be filling up parts of his body other than his stomach. His veins and chest, his neck and head all started to feel as though they too were crammed with food. He kept drinking, kept washing it down, kept going. Waiters continued to waft around the table. Some new diners had arrived. Someone else had passed out at the table, falling face down in what looked like a plate of pasta bows with frogs' legs and cockscombs. Someone sprinted from the table, clutching mouth and stomach, breaking for the toilet, or perhaps for an antique chamberpot.

A plate of oysters and raw eggs arrived in front of Virgil. He said to Kingsley, 'When does all this end?'

'It doesn't, of course,' replied Kingsley. 'While ever there are people at the table, the chefs in the kitchen keep cooking and the waiters keep serving. It goes on forever.'

'So it's been going on for centuries, right?'

'That's it,' said Kingsley.

Virgil looked at his food. He really didn't think he could face it. He tried to think about something else, not easy. As the meal wore on, Virgil, because he was that kind of a guy, became increasingly fascinated by the naked girl just a fork's length away from him, the more so since his attempt to wipe her splattered shoulder had caused Kingsley such consternation. Surreptitiously while Kingsley wasn't looking, while he was involved in eating some curious blend of shellfish and veal offal, Virgil slipped a black grape into the girl's mouth. He saw the faintest of smiles crease her lips. She chewed it very, very slowly and then swallowed. A little later he did it again, and this time he was pleased to find that as he popped the grape into her mouth, she pursed her lips and gave his fingers a soft, gentle suck.

It might have been the surreptitious nature of this flirtation, or simply her nakedness, or the drink, but Virgil was now mightily aroused by the situation. The girl kept her eyes more or less fixed on the ceiling, but occasionally she turned half an eye on Virgil, and he was sure there was an invitation there.

The rest of the table became submerged in a conversation about cricket. This demanded everybody's serious attention, everybody except Virgil, and since he had nothing to contribute to the conversation he became even more interested in the girl. He had an urge to tear off his clothes, leap on to the table and crush down on her, spattering grapes, plums and kiwi fruits between their naked bodies as they coupled madly and publicly.

Something told him this might not be acceptable behaviour, which was fine by him, but when he really thought about doing it, he realised he felt too drunk and stuffed to be able to perform. Nevertheless, he felt he ought to do something to confirm his reputation as wildman and hell-raiser. Besides, these guys talking about cricket were pissing him off. So he picked up three oysters from his plate. They slithered smoothly into the palm of his hand and then he slid them into the girl's mouth. As her lips opened to accept them, he leaned over her and French kissed her; lips, tongues and oysters stirring together passionately.

Back home in L.A. that surely wouldn't have created much of a stir, but it was a different matter here at the Everlasting Club. Powerful hands seized him from all directions. Virgil didn't worry too much at first. He assumed they were thrusting him back into his chair. Okay, so there was a no-kissing rule in the dining-room; typical asshole English regulation. But weren't they being a bit rough? Why were they throwing him around with such ferocity?

These same powerful hands were not merely returning Virgil to his seat. They were dragging him away from the girl and away from the table. They were dragging him out of the dining-room into the bar where everyone jeered at him, where a number of drunken slobs took kicks at his backside, and where someone poured a glass of something sticky and perfumed over his head. It seemed to take forever to pass through the bar, to get back to the small entrance hall, then out of the hall, out through the front door so that he felt the coldness of the night for just a moment before he landed heavily, his limbs loose and tangled, on the pavement outside.

The sudden change of air, the violence, the speed at which he'd been propelled, made him feel very ill. He knew he was going to barf. A tide of weird, though not always very wonderful, delicacies drenched in strange alcohol and coated in bile, was fighting its way up through his body. Here it came, hot and acidic, all that flavour and saucing and seasoning, all those garnishes and little touches, all boiling together, reduced to vomit and searing up his throat.

It burst out of his mouth like a vile, liquid firework and there seemed to be no end to it. The magpie and the turkey and the oysters came bursting forth, head over heels, fighting each other, as though his whole body was trying to turn itself inside out. Wave after wave of spasms wrung every last bit of food from him. He stayed down on the pavement, actually lay down, his face finding some comfort in the rough coolness of the paving slabs. Virgil knew he had to die some time. This would be a better time than most.

He heard footsteps close to his head. Cops? Muggers? Junkies? Someone who liked to kick people in the head? He looked up, ready to plead. But it was Butterworth. Virgil thought of butter, cream, fat, grease. He retched some more. Butterworth helped him to his feet and handed him tissues to wipe his mouth.

'Home, sir?' asked Butterworth.

'I do believe so, Butterworth. I do believe so.'

Butterworth helped Virgil into the car and blindfolded him again before driving back to the hotel.

Scenes from a History of the Everlasting Club.
Number One: The Simple Pieman.

The year is 1887. Harold Hardwick is a seventeen-year-old apprentice with the firm of F. Workman and Sons, Bakers, of Halifax. The apprenticeship is long, as are the hours. The work is hard and hot; the weight of the baking-trays, the temperature of the ovens. The days slouch past, a slovenly parade of loaves and pies, breadcakes and teacakes, pikelets, apple Charlottes, jam turnovers, pasties. Harold is as happy as he ever expects to be. He has no illusions. The work is steady and useful and a lot softer than most of the work to be had in the town. But the absence of illusion is not the end of hope. Harold has imagination. He has dreams. These dreams are a little unspecific, a little formless, but he knows there is a better life available, some other way of existing, and although he wants it, he is shrewd enough not to expect it. At the very least, he wants a bit of excitement, a bit of colour. He has thought of joining the army.

Excitement and colour arrive in an unexpected form when it is announced that Workman's have won the contract to bake the Golden Jubilee Denby Dale pie. Mr Workman and a few trusted staff will have to move to Denby Dale for a week or more to get the job done.

The Jubilee referred to is that of Queen Victoria. But this pie is also to celebrate the fact that it is ninety-nine years since the first Denby Dale pie was baked – to celebrate George III's recovery from madness. Well, any excuse. That one was a large game pie, baked and shared by the villagers in 1788, and although it was legendary, it was in reality quite small. In 1815 the Victory Pie was baked to celebrate Waterloo. In 1846 there was another to mark the repeal of the Corn Laws. But this Golden Jubilee pie is going to be something very special indeed, and much larger than anything ever seen in these parts before.

The pie is to be paid for by public subscription, but the Pie Committee sees from the beginning that there is money to be made from this escapade, even if it will have to go to charity. This will be an event. Crowds will come from the surrounding area, especially if excursion trains are laid on from Bradford, Dewsbury and Halifax. They will be charged to look at the pie. A funfair is to be organised, commemorative plates will be manufactured, and caterers will pay for the right to feed the crowd.

The caterers are required because it is not certain there will be enough pie for everyone. Indeed, the pie is intended to be a spectacle as much as to provide a good feed. The pie is intended primarily for the local people of Denby Dale. The crowd will only be fed if there's any left over.

Harold wonders if a holiday crowd will really be prepared to pay sixpence merely to look at a pie and then to watch the inhabitants of Denby Dale eat it. It doesn't sound like entertainment to him. It doesn't sound like good value. But he is shrewd enough to keep his thoughts to himself.

Messrs W. C. Holmes of Huddersfield are employed to rivet together a vast pie dish; eight feet in diameter and two feet in depth. An oven big enough to house the dish is then built; fourteen-feet square on the outside, ten-feet square within, erected behind the White Hart Inn in Denby Dale.

Mr Workman is overjoyed to be baking the Jubilee pie. He thinks of himself as a master craftsman. Nevertheless, he has never been involved with a project as big as this. But then who has? And he feels sure that his confidence, experience and expertise will get him through; that and a lot of hard work. Lots of hands will be needed, including Harold's. Harold is one of the trusted staff who will be in Denby Dale for a week or two. Harold is as overjoyed as his boss.

Harold is amazed by the quantities of ingredients required just for the crust. Sixty stone of flour are to be used, the weight of four or five men; over a hundred pounds of lard, fifty pounds of butter, several stone of suet and dripping. Elsewhere, Mr Workman has been ordering the filling; sides of beef, whole pigs and sheep, scores of rabbits, ducks, grouse, pigeons, hare. They are assembled and displayed for a week in a local butcher's.

It is a hot August and Harold wonders if this is in keeping with the best culinary practice, but again he keeps mum. The meat sweats behind the shop window, flies circle, land and sun themselves, colonising the display. But it is certainly all good publicity and the excitement which Harold feels is spreading to lots of other people.

The meat now needs to be cooked. It is boiled in small, separate batches. When each batch is cooked it is tipped from the boiler into the riveted pie dish where it cools. Meanwhile, the next batch is cooked and then joins the first batch in the dish; hot meat and juices mixing with cold.

It is a mammoth job and the dish continues to look ominously empty. More meat is rapidly procured. Much of this is of uncertain provenance; a hundred small birds, some sparrows and thrushes. Someone proffers a fox. Who knows what kinds of meat get included in the *mélange*? In all the haste a good number of birds get into the pie undrawn. Still the dish looks empty. As a last resort forty stone of potatoes are rapidly peeled and put in with the filling.

Harold is present at two minutes to midnight on Thursday when the pie is put into the oven to bake, and he keeps watch over it all night until ten the next morning when it is declared done. The pie is taken to an outhouse to cool. There are still more than twenty-four hours before it is due to make its triumphant public appearance on Saturday.

Mr Workman is delighted with the finished article. The pie looks magnificent. The crust is thick and even, and baked to a beautiful suntanned brown. Harold is delighted to have been a part of it all. As a bonus for all the many extra hours he has had to work, Harold is allowed to stay in Denby Dale for Saturday's celebrations. Mr Workman catches the last train back to Halifax on Friday evening and wishes everyone the best for tomorrow. Harold thinks it's a little strange that his boss won't be there for the cutting of the pie. The committee members put this down to modesty, but Harold already wonders if there might not be some other explanation.

Harold spends Friday night in Denby Dale, wakes early and is delighted to see that the sun is shining and the day is set fair. As he walks through the village he sees visitors already arriving. A Punch and Judy man is unloading his booth. The men who are to set off the fireworks at the evening's display are taking metal trunks from a cart.

Harold is given a programme of the day's events: donkey races, tug-of-war, throwing the cricket ball. The pie is to be on view in Norman Park from one o'clock to three thirty, then serving will begin, first to subscribers, locals, the very young and the very old. And at five ten the general public will be served, if any pie remains.

The plan is for the pie, decorated with flowers and herbs, to be brought through the town on a cart, in procession. It is to be taken to the park where it will be housed in a marquee. The marquee itself is within a fenced-off enclosure. The enclosure will house those entitled to a slice of the pie, and those who have paid to view it. Those who are not entitled to a slice and have not paid will be kept at bay outside the enclosure behind barriers.

The pie passes through the streets without mishap and is safely lodged in the marquee. But a good two hours before it is due to be cut, crowds have started to mass behind the barriers. The crowd looks fearsome to Harold; unwashed, unpredictable and mostly drunk. They are gawpers all right, and they're eager to see the pie, but they don't look the type of crowd to pay good money for an experience that's merely visual.

The crowd swells throughout the early afternoon. People are twenty or thirty deep around the barriers, most of them having little or no view of the proceedings, and they press forward in the mistaken belief that this might somehow help them to see better. Access to the central enclosure becomes very difficult. The Denby Dale Brass Band loses its rhythm trying to push through the throng. Those inhabitants of Denby Dale who are entitled to be in the enclosure are having trouble getting in.

The big moment eventually arrives. At three thirty prompt, the pie is wheeled into position to be cut up. White-aproned men stand by to do the carving. Mr John Brierley, guest of honour, will make the first cut. He takes up a ceremonial knife which he wields like a priest of some ancient sect. 'Ladies and gentlemen,' he says, 'we hail you with right good cheer on this occasion . . .'

Suddenly there is shouting and screaming, a frantic jostling, and the great weight of people erupts through the barriers. The crowd is no longer held back. A dirty sea of people gushes into the enclosure and washes around the pie like a tide of thick gravy. Hands grab at the crust, try to snatch lumps of the pie. One or two policemen are to be seen attempting to give orders to the multitude, a committee member lashes about him with a cane, but it is hopeless.

The carvers, seeing that it is too late to stand on ceremony, think it best to begin cutting the pie. They slice into the crust. As the pastry is pierced the odour of its contents gushes out; gamey, meaty, rich. But there are other odours too; sourness, bad meat, dead animals. The smell spreads like an evil cloud. A stink hits the nose and the back of the throat. The contents of the pie are rotten. A dense, putrid stench wells from the filling. Villagers hold rags to their noses, some start to retch. The crowd that was so eager to press forward is so disgusted by the smell they turn and try to run from the pie. Soon the pie stands alone at the centre of a circle some fifty feet in diameter, the public held at bay by the stink. A weird, uneasy truce holds for a while. All attempts to serve the pie are abandoned.

Perhaps the smell disperses a little, perhaps the crowd becomes braver, but gradually people return to grab morsels of the pie. Men fight each other to see who gets the biggest piece. Some of them try to eat what they have grabbed, and while much of it is rank and inedible, parts of it, they say, are more or less palatable. It is something of a curate's egg. But most people just want some crust or a few bones to keep as a souvenir. Lads grab whole chickens from the pie and hurl them at one another, or use them as footballs.

Harold watches with sadness and horror. This is not what he imagined when he thought of excitement and colour. He had a belief, he now realises, that good food and a holiday atmosphere might have a nurturing, softening, civilising effect on people. This now seems an utterly foolish belief.

Harold is still there the next day when the remains of the pie are taken to Toby Wood for burial. The contents of the dish are tipped into a deep pit and covered with quicklime. There is much mock pomp and in the end it is quite a festive occasion. A funeral card is printed. It reads, 'In affectionate remembrance of the Denby Dale pie which died August 27th 1887 aged three days'.

Harold wonders if the bakery trade, if any trade concerned with satisfying the appetites of others, is really for him. His employer, Mr F. Workman, is never seen again within many miles of Denby Dale. Yet he need not regard the episode as a complete disaster. He has, after all, been paid, and a few weeks later, after news of the event has spread as far as London, he receives an invitation bearing a snake with a tail in its mouth, an invitation to have dinner at the Everlasting Club.

TWO

The trademark of the American 'Golden Boy' chain of family restaurants is a plump giant cherub wearing a diaper and chewing on a chicken leg. Ten-foot-high, three-dimensional effigies of this cherub are to be found sitting on the red tiled roof of every Golden Boy outlet in the state of California. They are made of light but strong weather-proof, matt gold plastic. At night they are illuminated. There are powerful fluorescent tubes inside the cherubs that make them glow with an eerie, internal light.

Let's say you're on the freeway heading maybe for Oildale or Shafter or Cucamonga, and you've been to see the wife's family, and you've had a long and tiring drive, and the kids are jumping around in the rear of the car, complaining they're hungry and car sick and needing to pee, and you'd be more than willing to stop but you want something a little better than the usual fast food junk. Then suddenly you see a golden cherub glowing in the sky up ahead of you, and you know right away that civilisation (in the form of wholesome family eating at affordable prices at a Golden Boy) is close at hand. You pull off the exit ramp, into the big car park and there you are. It feels like coming home.

A Golden Boy restaurant is a place without dark, romantic secluded corners. The light is kept bright and even, cheerful and homely. Nobody ever got their head turned or got seduced at a Golden Boy. Nobody ever really got a great meal there either, but then again, they never got a really lousy one, and that's something these days. You know what to expect from a Golden Boy. The menu is short and simple; soups, steaks, pork chops, salads, pieces of pie and ice cream; nothing fancy and nothing too expensive. Beer and wine are served but no liquor. The waitresses are all aged over forty. They look as though they've had some personal tragedy in their lives, but they're holding up bravely and you'll be glad to know they don't want to talk about it. They're friendly, concerned for your welfare, and apparently chosen for their lack of overt sexuality. They are indulgent but they stand for no nonsense. They aren't sassy but you get uppity with them and they'll put you right back in your place. They don't expect good wages or big tips, which is just as well.

The golden boy, the cherub, pops out at you from every angle: on the menus, on the napkins, on the coasters, on the walls. His big smug face is seen descending around that chicken leg in a kind of ecstasy. But diners at the Golden Boy have seldom been known to experience that, or any other, kind of ecstasy.

There are forty restaurants in the Golden Boy chain; all in Californian locations chosen for their lack of glamour. They are to be found within one long geographical strip, nothing north of San Francisco or south of Los Angeles, and nothing east of Barstow. There is one restaurant in Frisco, near Candlestick Park, and one in West Hollywood, but by design, Golden Boys are not to be found in the big urban centres. They belong out there in the sticks; uncomplicated, unfashionable, and unfailingly profitable.

This is not a franchise operation, you understand. The Golden Boy's only begetter is one Frank Marcel, and he is comfortably, if not seriously, rich on the begetting. Today, still married to his first wife Mary, he is fifty-four years old; a short, solid, healthy-looking man, with a generally benevolent manner but with a certain cold meanness around the eyes. In 1964 his father died, died comparatively young, and left Frank everything he had: a not very successful diner on the edge of San Berdoo. Frank took over the business. He was kind of grateful to have something serious and substantial in his life. He'd been drifting along not knowing what he ought to be doing, thinking about trying to get into real estate or pool cleaning or working in radio. Frank was twenty-eight years old. He had a wife and an eighteen-month-old son called Virgil. It seemed like being left the diner was his big chance. But shit, he soon found it was hard work keeping that place running. He was busting his ass, working every hour God sent, just to stay in the same place, to keep from slipping back and going broke and wasting what his Pop had left him. There had to be some trick, some way of mastering this restaurant business that made life easier, but Frank sure hadn't been able to figure out what it was.

Then, one hot, blustering day in early June, eighteen-month-old Virgil crawled his way around the diner when nobody was looking. Frank had enough to do without keeping his eye on the goddam kid all the time. Little Virgil crawled along the tiled floor behind the counter, reached up to its top and somehow, they could never quite figure out how, managed to bring a plate of food (chicken drumsticks, French fries and coleslaw) showering down on his head. Frank was too busy at the griddle even to notice the crash, and in any case he'd have assumed it was just one of the dumb waitresses dropping something again. But Mary, his wife, his English wife at that, with whom he wasn't getting along particularly well at the time, looked down to see her baby covered in coleslaw, and saw that he was not tearful or unhappy, but instead was sucking on a chicken leg and appearing to have the time of his short life. She had an idea. She went for her Kodak and flashed a couple of snapshots of her offspring. She did it for no particular reason. It was no big deal. Virgil just happened to look cute sitting there and Virgil didn't look cute very often. It was worth a picture.

She had the film processed and was well-pleased with the results. Even Frank, who was not predisposed to be pleased with anything Mary was pleased with, thought the photographs had a certain something. They had a big blow-up made of the best shot, framed it and had it up on the wall by the milkshake machine. It caused a lot of comment. It was a couple of months before Frank had his big idea.

It took a while to find anyone willing and able to make a ten-foot-high sculpture of tiny Virgil sucking the chicken leg, as shown in the photograph. Besides, he didn't want anything too literal. He didn't want anything too artistic. It had to be cute, cartoon-like, a caricature. At last he found a couple of talented, though not *too* talented, girls who were home from college for the summer and were prepared to take a crack at the job. He fed them a little money and all the hamburgers, Cokes, French fries and shakes they could eat; a surprisingly vast amount. They made a papier-mâché cherub in Virgil's image. The face wasn't much like Virgil's, and the arms looked a little out of proportion (later models would smooth out these imperfections and get the trademark just so), but it was a good piece of work for a first attempt and Frank was thrilled. He loaded it into the back of his pick-up and took it down to the local paint shop where he had it sprayed gold. A week later Frank held a grand renaming and 'reopening' ceremony (though the diner had never been closed) at which the golden boy was winched up on to the roof and bolted in place.

From such modest ideas and such tame beginnings are wild successes made. Word got around about this thing, this weird eyesore on the roof of Frank's diner. People began to travel considerable distances to get a look at the golden boy. Some found it funny and some found it plain ugly, and some said it wasn't worth the trip, but they kept coming, and once they'd arrived Frank made sure they stayed a while and spent some money. Nobody left without buying at least a burger and a Coke, and before long they could also buy home-made Golden Boy fudge to take away with them, or a souvenir Golden Boy sundae glass with the cherub painted on it. Turnover shot up. Frank became a success and something of a local celebrity. He got invited out by local businessmen. They thought he was a little eccentric but he obviously had a good head for business. He was making money and that made eccentricity forgivable. Suppliers lined up to do deals with him, giving big discounts in order to be associated with the Golden Boy. The bank was falling over itself to lend him money. So he began to expand his operation. Another Golden Boy opened in Palmdale, one in Victorville, one in Norco. By now the cherubs were made of fibreglass and were a lot more streamlined and seamless than the papier-mâché original.

Frank had to think seriously about quality control in his restaurants, about standardisation of portions and procedures. He had to choose colour schemes for internal and external décor. He chose mostly golden yellow, of course, but with certain features picked out in burgundy and Prussian blue. He had to oversee menu design, and he devised a uniform for the waitresses that he thought was pretty snappy. He became concerned with recruiting and training, and he wrote a staff manual bursting with good sense, written in a breezy, unsolemn style. He became adept at spotting new sites. He avoided prime locations and developed an unfailing expertise at finding exactly the right kind of less-than-first-rate location where his style of operation could thrive. Frank became a master of his trade.

Golden Boys settled on southern California like a visitation of incubi, making a small but highly profitable splash wherever they landed. Frank didn't try to compete with the giant chains and franchises. He didn't attempt too much too soon. He kept his standards up, his head down, and the bucks kept rolling in.

Frank never underestimated how much of a debt he owed to his infant son. If Virgil hadn't crawled into the diner that day and tipped up that chicken platter, Frank's life would have been completely different and infinitely worse. Probably he would still have been sweating behind that counter in San Berdoo. Frank also surely owed something to Mary for having taken the photograph and crystallised the image of the Golden Boy, but this was a debt he *did* underestimate. So Virgil grew up revered, spoiled and overfed.

As Frank's success and fortune grew he found Mary a whole lot easier to live with. They had separate rooms. He was away from home a lot, and even if Mary had known about his little flings on the road, and he was sure she didn't, she'd have put up with them. She knew which side her bread was buttered. And Frank didn't have enough imagination to think that she might be flinging in his absence. It never occurred to him that what was sauce for the goose might also be sauce for the gander. Life looked pretty good to Frank; materially, domestically, even spiritually.

He only had two regrets.

As he got older and wealthier and a little more worldly, he began to develop the tastes that go with a certain kind of age, wealth and worldliness. He became stylish. He wore expensive suits. He travelled in luxury. He stayed in the best hotels. Not least, he began to develop sophisticated eating habits. His palate cried out for mousses, purées, Châteaubriand, for French sauces, hollandaise, béchamel, Béarnaise, for the finest wines and the very best brandies. He soon got to the point where he would not have been seen dead eating anywhere so bargain basement as a Golden Boy.

And a part of him wanted to make this his profession. He wanted to own and run the kind of restaurant he liked to eat in; something very classy and expensive and European. He thought long and hard about it, getting more and more excited at the prospect. But he talked to his financial advisors, and some of the guys in the firm whom he particularly trusted (not that there was anybody in the firm whom he actively *dis*trusted) and they all told him it was a very bad idea. Ritzy French restaurants were all very well, but they were a pretty good way of losing a lot of money unless you knew exactly what you were doing and unless you had a truckload of luck. Frank, they said, had no expertise in that direction. He should stick to what he knew and what he did best. Frank listened to his advisors. He believed them. He thought they were probably right. Years went by and he never did open the restaurant he wanted to. He knew he'd done the right thing, taken the right business decision, but that didn't entirely still the urge. The ambition still burned in him, burning all the hotter for being untested. This was his first regret. His second regret was Virgil.

In the very early years of Frank's restaurant career people had come to the Golden Boy just to get a look at Virgil and compare the human original with the papier-mâché model on the roof. As Virgil grew up there was still a certain amount of entertainment to be had in seeing how the big, sturdy three, five, nine-year-old *diverged* from the model. 'My, how he's grown.' 'I'll betcha he could eat a whole plate of chicken legs now.' 'You're not a baby any more, Virgil.'

Diverge he certainly did. Always spoiled, always kowtowed to, he grew into a thin, gawky, surly, bad-assed kid. His father still loved him and his mother too, no doubt, but precious few others. He simply wasn't lovable. At school he was smart but lazy, and he had the vicious capacity to lead others astray without straying himself. This took different forms depending on his age and on circumstances. He might persuade small children to eat worms, or get little girls to take off their underpants, or get teenage boys to put sugar in their fathers' gas tanks. He never did the dirty deed himself and so was never caught and punished, but any time there was trouble in the school or neighbourhood everybody always knew that Virgil was behind it. That suited Virgil just fine.

By the time Virgil was able to drive, Frank was starting to worry that his son might be homosexual. He didn't know quite why he thought that, it wasn't as if he knew anything about homosexuality, but there was definitely something strange and not right about his son. So he pressed money on Virgil, bought him a car and told him to take out girls. He made sure Virgil had enough dough to take them out in some style, to rock concerts or whatever, and enough to buy something good to eat on the way home, and maybe (he wasn't too old to know what kids were like) enough to buy some beer or sweet wine.

Virgil took the money and the car, and he never had much trouble getting dates, but he didn't seem very grateful to his father. Despite his lack of physical charm and a complete absence of likeable personality he even managed to get the girls to 'do stuff' with him, to him. Admittedly these girls might not be exactly the type Frank would have chosen as companions for his son, but Virgil knew he couldn't afford to be too discriminating. But he didn't really enjoy all this dating routine because he didn't really have anything in common with the girls. Even then, his idea of a great evening out would be to find some little, out of the way seafood restaurant and work his way through clam chowder, oysters and lobster. The girls never liked fish. They didn't like dry white wine. They were always on diets. Virgil found them tiresome and dull. But that didn't mean he was a homosexual.

He was seventeen years old and a nerdy misfit; an arrogant, antisocial pain in the ass right through his teens, right until he left home to go to college, or rather, colleges. He passed through a number of well-meaning Californian liberal arts establishments, taking a litter of unrelated courses that didn't amount to much: the novel, the Renaissance, hand-weaving, photography, typing. He never showed much interest in any of them, but he was always able to pass, though always with lousy grades. The life seemed to suit him; a life without responsibilities, with occasional, mild intellectual stimulation, with enough money from home to make it comfortable, and to enable him to hone his tastes in food and wine.

However, something strange was happening to his hormones in all this. He stopped looking like a nerd. He stopped being gawky. He began to develop muscle and to carry himself with a certain amount of poise. Suddenly, almost overnight, he became a good-looking rich boy with money, with good taste in food and drink, with a Ford Thunderbird, with an enormous capacity for having a good time. His dates became classier and better looking. He became the object of more female attention than his father could ever have dreamed of. He still had a highly unattractive personality, but that really didn't seem to hold him back.

The girls, though plentiful, still weren't quite right. They still weren't exactly what he was looking for. But they were getting closer. Occasionally he'd meet one who enjoyed a good bottle of Rioja, or one he could persuade to try sautéed sweetbreads, and back in her room she'd let him smooth her clitoris with Chivas Regal and let it burn gently for a while before licking it off. But he was still a long way from finding the real thing.

All this made Virgil's life pretty tolerable but Frank still worried about him. And then one day Frank stopped listening to his financial advisors and started listening to his heart. He was over fifty years old now, financially secure. All his ambitions, with one exception, had been fulfilled. He decided he could afford to take a gamble, and if the gamble failed he could stand the losses without facing financial ruin. He decided to open a restaurant in Los Angeles; not a Golden Boy, a *real* restaurant. He hoped a *great* restaurant.

Ideally it might have been situated on North La Cienaga, or on Melrose or Wilshire, but he settled for premises downtown, premises close to South Olive Street, not exactly a fashionable location, a little off the beaten track, but not so far off that people who wanted the finest eating experience in all of L.A. wouldn't be able to find their way there.

He tried to do everything right, as right as he knew how. He called the restaurant Trimalchio's. No expense was spared on the décor; acres of burgundy carpet, huge, gold-framed mirrors, chandeliers, real oil paintings, china and cutlery and cut glass imported from England. He hired the best waiting staff that money could buy, and chose to pay them more than the going rate to be sure of keeping them. In the kitchen he installed a boy genius chef called Leo who had trained at the Ritz-Escoffier School in Paris and at the Dorchester in London. Probably he was older than he looked, Frank thought he had to be, but he'd been hailed and raved about by every gourmet in L.A. (a growing breed); and his way with duck terrine, veal loin and *crème plombières au chocolat* left Frank breathless and had him offering an insanely high salary to secure his services. Frank thought he'd done okay with Trimalchio's. He'd given it his best shot. He'd spent a bundle, an absolute bundle on advertising for the launch, he'd done everything with infinite care and attention, even with love, and of course the restaurant was a flop.

It wasn't a resounding, spectacular, epic flop; more a gentle deflation, a slow implosion. At first people came to Trimalchio's, quite a lot of people it seemed, including the important restaurant critics. There were no doubts about the quality of the food, and the customers all appeared to have a good time and to go home satisfied. The reviews, when they appeared, weren't bad either. None of them damned the food (how could they?), the service or the atmosphere, but neither could they bring themselves to be anything other than lukewarm in their approval. And people kept mentioning the Golden Boy. Somehow people resented paying luxury prices to eat in a restaurant owned by Frank Marcel, the family restaurant mini-mogul. As they ate their breast of mallard with green and black peppercorns they kept thinking of big golden cherubs. The plastic, illuminated golden boys cast long shadows over their pleasure. Business soon dropped away.

Frank wasn't a man to be completely and utterly destroyed by one failure. At least he'd tried. He'd put a lot of himself into it, and the failure hurt, hurt like hell, but he wasn't about to jump off a bridge because of it. Neither was he going to pour good money after bad. He was too much of a businessman to keep the restaurant running indefinitely at a loss, but he still had plenty of pride. He decided to run the restaurant for six months. That was enough to keep his self-respect and not to incur too vast a loss. Then he'd close up, pay the bills and put it all down to experience. He was wounded and disappointed, but he wasn't despairing.

He was far more likely to despair about his son. Virgil was now out of college and untrammelled either by a degree or a career. He had good looks, if you valued that sort of thing, an L.A. apartment, a string of cars and girlfriends, an allowance from Frank that Frank regarded as ludicrously generous (but he did owe that boy); and Virgil had never done a day's work in his life.

Frank didn't know where the allowance went, but go it certainly did, and before the end of each month Virgil would be back asking for more. He asked more or less politely and Frank never denied him, but the boy was getting through more money than seemed decently possible. And what did he have to show for it? A couple of closets full of clothes that were out of fashion and therefore unwearable the month after they were bought, state of the art stereos and videos that had to be regularly replaced as the state of the art changed; and a lot of credit card bills for meals that were no doubt exquisite at the time, but could hardly be regarded as an investment for the future. Virgil led a full and colourful social life. He mingled with minor Hollywood celebrities. He went to the right discos and night-clubs, parties and openings. Frank hoped he wasn't involved with heavy drugs.

Frank didn't entirely disapprove of Virgil's appetite for good living since to a large extent he shared it. Frank was prepared to be an indulgent parent, it was just a question of degree. He didn't want to come the heavy father. He didn't want to change his son's lifestyle completely, he just wanted him to live it a little more cheaply.

He met Virgil for lunch in a very reasonable Thai bistro he knew. Frank felt the time was right to take some sort of stand; as much for his own self-respect as for anything else. He knew Virgil needed talking to. He knew that a good father would do the talking. Frank knew he had to try.

Over the Thai fishcakes he said, 'I worry about you, Virgil. Seriously, I do.'

'You don't need to worry about me, Dad.'

'But I do. I wonder where and how you're going to end up. I wonder what you're going to do with your life.'

'Is this a serious question?' Virgil asked, bored.

'Yes.'

'You're asking me how I'm going to end up?'

'Yes.'

'Well obviously, Dad, I'm going to end up dead, just like everybody else. The trick is to have as good a time as possible before that happens.'

'And are you having a good time at present?'

'Well sure,' said Virgil. 'Can't you tell?'

'At my expense.'

'Well, that's one way of looking at it.'

'As far as I can see, that's the *only* way of looking at it. I give you money and you spend it. Maybe you can make me see it another way.'

'Sure,' said Virgil. 'The way I see it you're going to be dead sooner or later, Dad, just like everybody else. And in your will you're going to leave me everything, right?'

Frank nodded reluctantly.

'So the money you're giving me now is money that would be mine in the end anyway, right? And I think we'd both agree it's better for me to have the money while I'm still young enough to enjoy it. So, you know, I'm grateful and all but really you're just giving me what's mine.'

'But what if I didn't have any money to give you?'

Virgil looked blank. He didn't understand the question. 'Is that a possibility?' he asked.

'We're just talking here, Virgil, that's all. I'm asking you to imagine what your life would be like if you didn't have my money keeping you afloat.'

'Hey, I know you're losing money on Trimalchio's but we're not going broke, are we?'

'No. We're just talking. So what I'm doing is asking you to imagine what you'd do with yourself if you were poor like ninety-nine per cent of the rest of the poor bastards in the world.'

'Well, I guess I wouldn't eat so well. Look, hey, it's an impossible question. It's like saying what would I do if I was black or blind or a starving peasant. How can you know? But I like to think the same ground rules would apply. I'd try to have as good a time as possible on the limited resources at my disposal. Maybe I'd get a job.'

'A job?' Frank sneered. 'What kind of job? What kind of work could you possibly do?'

'You know, whatever jobs poor people get: garbage man, filing clerk, working in a gas station.'

'This is what is really worrying me, Virgil, and I'm no longer just talking now, this isn't just hypothetical. I'm saying that as your father

I think it might be a good idea if you were able to do some kind of job, if you had some sort of profession.'

'You want me to become a lawyer?'

'All I'm saying, and you know me well enough to know I'm no Puritan, I'm saying that your life is going nowhere and I think a job might do you some good.'

This was not precisely what Frank had intended to say. He was bluffing slightly. He knew there were fathers in the world who would say to their sons, and probably with good reason, 'Either you get a job or you're out on your ass.' Frank almost wished he was that kind of father, but he knew he wasn't and that was the end of it. He wasn't going to cut off Virgil without a dime but he hoped that if he could somehow make Virgil aware of the importance of being able to fend for himself in this world, well, it was hardly likely to turn him into a diligent, thrifty, model citizen, but it might make him realise the value of a dollar. It might make him tighten his belt a little. It might make him try to live within his monthly allowance.

'I look at you, Virgil,' said Frank, 'and I see a decent boy. You're not dumb, you're not useless, but I just don't see that you have any skills or talents. I don't know how you'd survive in this world if it wasn't for the money I give you. If it wasn't for me you'd be eating out of garbage cans.'

'Is that what you want? You want me to start eating out of garbage cans?'

'No, but I don't think it would do any harm if you worked up a little more of an appetite between meals.'

'You want me to get a job?'

Frank wondered if he did. It seemed such an unlikely eventuality he'd never seriously considered it.

'I don't want you to have to become a garbage man,' said Frank.

'But if I don't have any skills or talents, who'd ever give me a job?'

'A lot of people would. I know a lot of guys in business.'

'Would *you* give me a job?'

'Of course I would. You're my son. If you wanted to be a part of the business you'd make me the happiest father on earth.'

'Look, Dad, I don't want anything to do with the Golden Boy, okay? Let's get that clear. That little golden bastard has haunted me all my life. I'd like to see him melted down and turned into Tupperware. But I'll make you a proposition. Let me run Trimalchio's for you.'

'But it's closing down in six weeks' time.'

'That's right. So what have you got to lose? Gimme those six weeks. If I haven't turned it around and made it a success in six weeks you'll close it anyway. So you've nothing to lose. It sounds like good business to me.'

It didn't sound like such bad business to Frank either. Things weren't going to get much worse at Trimalchio's whatever Virgil did, nor, Frank thought, much better. Virgil would see what a hard and difficult job running a restaurant was, and he'd probably despise it, but if by some chance he enjoyed it or even (it seemed impossibly optimistic even to contemplate) proved to be good at it, then he might have found something to do with his life, which was precisely what Frank wanted. At the very least it would keep the boy off the streets, and Frank imagined that Virgil must surely spend less money while working than he did while on a permanent vacation.

Frank gave Virgil the job. On the day he took over Trimalchio's he fired the entire serving staff. Gone were the good manners, the politeness, the decorum and skill, the knowledge of food and wine, to be replaced by a bunch of big-eyed, sulky, teenage, speed-freak waitresses. They were as thin as filo pasty, dressed in thrift-shop rags held together by studded leather belts and thongs. They weren't so good at remembering orders but, boy, could they move fast.

He ripped out all the fancy décor, all the chandeliers and wall lights, the chintz and the curtains and the mirrors, the burgundy carpets, the velvet banquettes, the oil paintings. And he didn't replace them. The floor remained bare. A start was made to strip the ersatz William Morris paper from the walls, but it turned out to be a job that required a certain persistence, so the wallpaper remained here and there in misshapen squares or long, thin, tattered strips. Light, where there *was* light, came from bare bulbs, car inspection lamps and strings of Christmas tree lights. Elsewhere, nooks and crannies remained in deep, dangerous darkness.

He did replace the tables and chairs, and got in substitutes which resembled unfinished metal sculpture. Irregularly shaped table-tops rusted interestingly. The chairs were as uncomfortable and as unwelcoming as those to be found in any fast food outlet, but these were guaranteed to leave an abstract pattern of bolts and rivets imprinted in your ass. There were no table-cloths, no napkins, no flower arrangements. He got rid of the fine china and went for thick, unbreakable plasticware in nursery colours.

Virgil assembled the loudest lowest-fi sound system he could, and put together background tapes of Bartók and Varèse intermingled with Ethel Merman, Doris Day and the MC5. The noise distorted so much as it slammed through the speakers and smashed around the bare surfaces of the restaurant, that it didn't matter too much what the music actually was. It was soon converted to abrasive, ugly noise.

Virgil went through the whole establishment changing things, messing things up, throwing things away, wrecking organisation, destroying systems. He changed the prices; everything on the menu went up by thirty percent. But he didn't change the chef. Amid all the mayhem, little Leo, the boy genius whom Frank had employed, continued to do his stuff. The décor and noise said 'end of the world', but the food was still saying delicacy, discrimination, civilisation. The food was, as the second wave of restaurant critics would soon be saying, redefining the new American cuisine.

On opening night Virgil assembled a Felliniesque crew of diners. Trimalchio's was awash with movie and TV people, food writers, rock stars, gallery owners, interior designers, and they mingled, or at least collided, with teenage hookers of both sexes, Chicano gang members, female body-builders and an over-sixties gourmet society from Pasadena. When one of the Chicanos pulled a knife on one of the gallery owners and was disarmed by one of the female body-builders, who broke his hand in the process, Trimalchio's success was more or less assured.

Every night the place was packed. And if the crowd was never again quite as colourful as on that first night, there was still the right mix of names and extravagant nonentities to make it a gawper's paradise. Bookings were solid for weeks ahead. Every night there was overcrowding, noise and chaos, and a vast amount of money spent. There was no way Frank was going to close it down. Virgil presided over it all in his good-looking, bad-assed way, and became one of its attractions. To be insulted by Virgil made a trip to Trimalchio's complete.

Whereas a fancy restaurant owned by Frank Marcel was seen as laughably *démodé*, a restaurant owned by his arrogant wastrel son, the Golden Boy run to seed, seemed to be just what the market required. It was wild, new, dangerous. It was the hottest ticket in town.

Frank had various feelings about the new-style Trimalchio's. They included horror, disgust, disbelief, morbid fascination, grudging admiration, awe, delight. Frank had never understood or followed fashion, but he had seen enough to know that fashions didn't last. Like the hula-hoop, raccoon coats and goldfish swallowing, Trimalchio's, he feared, might all too soon become last year's thing. And this was where Virgil won his father's ultimate approval.

Virgil didn't need to be told that fashion moved on. He saw as clearly as Frank did that Trimalchio's would have a very limited life if it wasn't able to change. But whereas some people might have tried to make Trimalchio's more extreme, weirder, wilder and more of the same, Virgil did the opposite. He gradually toned it down. He turned down the noise, softened the lighting and the décor, adopted chairs that you could sit in comfortably. He reintroduced staff who knew what they were doing. He added a few old-fashioned touches, like flowers on the tables and soap in the rest-rooms. And he did it without losing either his image or his clientele. Trimalchio's remained an ultra-hip restaurant. And the food remained as exquisite as ever. Before long it had turned into more or less the kind of restaurant Frank had always wanted to own. Frank's golden boy had given him everything he'd ever wanted; twice.

Virgil still hung out at Trimalchio's once in a while, put in an appearance, chatted to staff and casually abused customers, but his real work was over. The restaurant ran itself. Slowly Virgil returned to his old, idle ways. He was happy and successful and in a very limited way, famous. Then he got an invitation from the Everlasting Club, and his life was never the same again.

Scenes from a History of the Everlasting Club.
Number Two: The Mother Tongue.

Dartford, 1949. Mary remembers the war; just. She remembers the German bombers returning from their missions over London and discharging their surplus bombs over her head. Birds' droppings; pellets of death without her name on them. Bomb alley. Well, at least she wasn't evacuated. Evacuation; a thing to be done with your children or your bowels. She is eleven years old now and already she knows she will be leaving this place, though she doesn't know how, nor what her destination will be. She knows that her real life will take place elsewhere. In America, why not? Or Japan. Or Yorkshire, or even Germany, or anywhere but here.

She is good at school, bright, but not so bright as to scare off the boys. They are usually a little older than she is, boys with lean faces and torn trousers and stolen Woodbines; tough guys, but not as tough as they'd like to think, and certainly no tougher than her, and definitely not as bright. She already knows that none of these boys will be her ticket to a better place, though they are good enough for now, and she's prepared to kiss one or two of them, and she sees how the activity *might* be enjoyable, but with these boys who taste of dripping and cigarettes it leaves a lot to be desired.

The war took her father away and brought her a new one, a stepfather, a fake. There is a photograph of her proper father that sits on top of the piano. It shows a very young man in a sailor's uniform. He isn't as good-looking as her new one. His face is heavy, his eyes look a little dead. Her mother says she's lucky to have this new father but she doesn't feel lucky. She doesn't hate her stepfather, but she would prefer it if he were not in her house, in her real father's house.

Obviously he isn't as brave or courageous as her real father or else he would be dead. That's what being brave and courageous means. But she can see he's trying hard to be nice to her. He talks to her a lot, asks her about school, is more polite and concerned than he would need to be if he genuinely liked her. Still, she appreciates the effort. Sometimes she feels sorry for him. He is having to work as a hod-carrier now and he comes home every night with his hands all dry and cut. But he knows someone on the building site who has access to an endless supply of jelly babies and he comes home every Friday with a big bag of them, and he says they're just for her and she doesn't have to share them with anyone. She know she's being bought, and she doesn't like jelly babies all that much, but she knows it's the thought that counts.

In her mother's bedroom (she still thinks of it as her mother's bedroom even though it is shared by the new stepfather) she makes up her face. She plays with the powder compact and the lipstick. She has an idea in her head of how her face ought to look, how a real woman's face might be made to emerge from her little girl features; but she can't get that face to come out. She feels clumsy, childish, hopeless. Surely it isn't so hard. Enough women manage to do it, women who, she is sure, are not nearly as clever or as artful as she is. One day she will get it right. So she tries on her mother's nylons and she thinks they look all right, though she wishes her legs weren't so thin. She wishes she could grow up faster.

Beside the bed, at her stepfather's side, there is a trunk of his. It is tan in colour, has long straps with buckles, and his initials are stencilled on it in several places. In it are all sorts of treasures, some of which she suspects she is not supposed to know about. Certainly nobody knows that she goes through the contents when she's alone in the house. Most of it is actually quite boring. There are playing cards, photographs of soldiers sitting around tables that are jammed with empty beer bottles, foreign coins collected on his war travels, some cricket scorecards, and what interest her most: some dirty postcards. She can look at them for hours. They fascinate her, though that fascination is inseparable from a certain dread. The postcards have a creamy, matt finish and the photographic dyes are a yellowish brown. It seems to her that they have a faint bad smell to them, a smell of cooked sprouts and burning rubber and ammonia. Something strange and scary is depicted in those images but she hasn't yet worked out exactly what it is.

She knows about periods and penises, and her mother has told her where babies come from, and she knows all that must have something to do with what's going on in those pictures, but she still can't get it clear. The women aren't pretty. They're old and rather fat. They're foreign, swarthy, and they kneel on fringed benches and stretch out on ornately furnished beds of a kind she has never seen in real life.

Their faces are masks of make-up, but they hardly seem any better at applying it than she is. They have thick, smeared lips and ugly black eyebrows. She sees they have dirty feet. But what she really doesn't understand is that thing they're doing with their mouths. It looks as though they're trying to swallow the men's penises. It doesn't look very comfortable. The women don't seem to like it. They look as though they're not enjoying the taste. And Mary has never seen penises like the ones in the postcards. They're so angry and livid, like big, taut sausages. She imagines smearing one with Colman's English mustard. Yet it is the postcards' very strangeness, their capacity to frighten her, that somehow suggests to her that these images are messages from, windows looking into, some other country, some better place she knows she is destined to inhabit.

At first she had taken the contents out of the trunk with infinite care and returned them to their original places so her stepfather would have no idea she'd touched anything. Over the months, however, she has become more careless in her packing and unpacking, and she thinks that perhaps he knows how she goes through the trunk from time to time. If so, he has said nothing and she feels this gives her some undefined power over him.

He tries harder than ever to ingratiate himself. He spends one weekend hammering and sawing in the garden shed and when she looks in on Sunday afternoon she sees he has built a small, wooden cage, and when he returns from work on Monday he is carrying two small, frightened baby hamsters. They are hers, he explains. She has to look after them. She has responsibilities now.

She would never have asked for these responsibilities and she has never had the usual child's desire to keep pets, but nevertheless, she is happy to feel some obligations towards these two little creatures. They are warm and silky, and although they sometimes try to bite her, their teeth aren't sharp enough to break her skin. She feeds them and changes the straw and sawdust in their cage, and sometimes she plays with them. She tries to work out if they are male or female. She pulls back the brown and white swirls of fur to peer at their genitals, but it is all too confusing down there for her to see properly.

As they get bigger they seem to become more vicious. Their bites start to hurt. A girl at school tells her gravely that they have to be separated or else they'll fight and kill each other, but Mary doesn't believe this any more than she believes a lot of the things she is told by the girls at school. Then, sure enough, she gets home from school one day, goes out to the shed and finds one of the hamsters lying dead amid the wood shavings at the centre of the cage. She can't tell if it's dead because it's been attacked or if it died of natural causes, whatever natural causes might be in a hamster.

She has a feeling that girls are supposed to be very upset when their pets die, that it has something to do with responsibility and love. But she doesn't see how you could love a hamster, or be upset at its death, so she doesn't tell her mother or stepfather. She takes the little corpse into the garden and puts it in the compost heap, hiding it under grass clippings and some rhubarb leaves. And she decides that if anyone asks her where it has gone she'll say it escaped.

She peers at the remaining hamster, the survivor, and it does look a big, tough thing now. It looks arrogant, fat, dominant, and yet somehow still soft and fluffy. And that is when she realises that the surviving hamster is pregnant. She sees little lumps and ripples of movement inside its belly and she knows the hamster is going to produce a litter.

She tells nobody about it. This is special to her. She keeps a close eye on events in the cage but she misses seeing the birth itself. She simply looks in one morning and can see that the mother is thinner, and then she sees four tiny, blind, naked, infinitely vulnerable baby hamsters curled up together in the nest. She isn't sure what she is supposed to do now. She assumes nature will take its course. She hopes so.

She sees the mother go over to the nest and drag one of the litter out into a corner of the cage. Mary thinks she may be going to feed it or wash it or do something else motherly, though the dragging looks too rough and erratic for that. Mary stands motionless and watches in fascinated silence as the mother sinks her teeth into the flesh of her offspring. Slowly, with some deliberateness, with apparent enjoyment, she begins to eat the baby alive.

Mary can do nothing at first, only watch in horror, then she slowly raises her skirt, slips her hand inside her blue school knickers and brings herself rapidly to her first orgasm.

From such simple beginnings . . . Mary will go on to become one of the very few female members of the Everlasting Club.

THREE

Virgil woke early next morning, feeling better than he had any right to. There was a thick dullness about his head and his stomach felt unstable, but this was not a serious hangover. He knew what serious hangovers were like and this was definitely not one of them. No doubt last night's vomiting had helped.

The hotel room looked unfamiliar. He saw the dinner jacket he'd worn last night, his own suit thrown over a chair, and he felt very adrift and very far away from everything he knew. He wondered if he would be sent a bill for what he'd eaten and drunk last night.

He wanted breakfast. He didn't want it in the hotel room. He wanted entertainment, something to watch, people to look at. He didn't want to be alone. But he went down to the hotel dining-room and it was hot and dark and full of little knots of businessmen, of all ages and several nationalities, wearing ties but no jackets, hunched over the breakfast tables comparing computer print-outs. It was not for him. He walked through the hotel lobby, out through the revolving doors, out into the fresh air. He stood at the top of the hotel steps and looked up and down the street. He half expected to see Butterworth still waiting. At least Butterworth might have been able to tell him where to get a good breakfast.

The street, he didn't know its name, was wide, and the buildings were tall, grey and sculpted. Overhead, the sky was the same colour as the grey stone of the buildings. The air was cool and still, with only a trace of exhaust fumes. Virgil realised this was an English summer's day. Everything was alien, the humped, black taxicabs, the double-decker buses, the names on the billboards, the way the people dressed.

Virgil knew that breakfast in England might be a special problem, even within the generalised set of problems that English food represented. Nobody would know what he wanted if he asked for eggs over easy, or even sunny side up. He would be unlikely to get pancakes and maple syrup. Hominy grits would be unheard of, not that he wanted hominy grits, but it would have been reassuring to know they were available if he did.

He was in a part of town that seemed to specialise in little cafés and sandwich bars. Some of them had signs in their windows offering 'Full English Breakfast', others listed endless combinations of eggs, bacon, baked beans, mushrooms, toast *et al*, each with a price. He saw a McDonald's in the distance and was tempted for a moment by its glib charm but then he was ashamed of himself. He was in England. He had to do this right. Finally he found a cafeteria. It wasn't crowded. It looked clean and neutral and not too English. It would do. He picked up a tray and a plate and moved down the line collecting bacon and scrambled egg and some things he wasn't too sure about, like potato cakes, and fried bread and plum tomatoes. By the time he got to the till his plate was overloaded and the food was heaped into a many-textured mound, so that the cashier had some trouble identifying its component parts. Virgil took on board orange juice, bottled spring water and, just to get the local flavour, a pot of tea.

Virgil was the kind of guy who normally liked to make his presence felt in the places he ate. He liked to joke with or insult the waiters and counter assistants, even the other diners. He liked to talk about food, and what was good today and what little extra ingredients or cooking methods gave the food its special taste. He would do this even at breakfast. But today, away from home, sufficiently if not seriously hungover, he felt an unaccustomed desire to keep himself to himself.

He paid the cashier and selected a window table. The seat was a thick, padded bench that sank irregularly under him. The table wasn't big, and by the time he'd unloaded his tray it was full. He surveyed the spread with some pleasure. One or two items might have been a little unfamiliar, but after last night's excursions into culinary wild places it felt safe and ordinary, like coming home. And it didn't taste half bad. The bacon wasn't like the bacon he knew back home. The orange juice was scarcely orange juice at all so far as he was concerned, but it was still a good breakfast. He ate slowly, taking his time, and he kept looking out the window, watching the street, the traffic, watching the girls go by. *They* weren't so alien. Sure, you could tell they weren't California girls, but they looked like they had plenty to offer. He liked their briskness, their look of efficiency, the way they planted their high heels firmly one in front of the other.

These were English women with destinies, with places they had to get to. Maybe Virgil could persuade one of them to go to bed with him.

Then he saw her in the street. He didn't recognise her at first because she was clothed. She was wearing a thin, flowered dress that didn't look warm enough for the weather, and she was carrying a large shoulder-bag. Her legs were bare. Her hair was tied back. And she was vertical rather than horizontal, and, of course, she was a lot more mobile than she had been as a centrepiece of the refectory table at the Everlasting Club. But she was every bit as plump and pretty, blonde and tanned, as she had been last night.

He was about to abandon his breakfast and run after her, but that would have been a terrible waste of food. He was torn. He seemed to remember they didn't have doggy bags in England. But his dilemma was solved when she entered the cafeteria. She picked up a tray and put her breakfast together. He watched her pay. Then she looked around for an empty table. There was no shortage. Virgil waved at her. She didn't see him, or didn't want to. So he decided to call out. He would have liked to have been able to call her by name but, not knowing her name, he shouted, 'Hey, over here babe!' Perhaps this happened to her all the time. She seemed to ignore him even more pointedly.

Well, Virgil thought, maybe it wasn't such a great idea. Maybe it wasn't meant to be. You meet a woman; you're drunk, she's naked, and you happen to share a French kiss stuffed with oysters. Okay, maybe that wasn't much to base a relationship on. So he ate some more breakfast. Then he realised that most of his relationships had been based on far less and he decided once more to give it a try, but he was going to play it cool this time. He finished his breakfast, keeping half an eye on her to make sure she didn't finish quickly and dash out. But it was all right. She ate very slowly and she was reading a newspaper. Virgil poured himself another cup of tea. He picked up the cup and crossed the cafeteria and sat down at her table. She moved her newspaper to make room for him but she didn't look up. Virgil settled across from her. He watched her eating. She chewed carefully. She cut each sausage and rasher of bacon into small, regular pieces and chewed each one thoroughly and swallowed it before moving on to the next piece. She seemed unaware that he was watching her. He stared harder.

'That looks like a great breakfast you've got there,' he said.

'Yes,' she said without looking up.

'Nice enough to eat. Just like you.'

Then she did look up. At first she didn't appear to recognise him. He was just someone bothering her, just a pest. Then her eyes showed something, some memory, some flicker of recognition, though still faint and distant. And then it clicked and she smiled, apparently amused by the memory of last night, perhaps a little embarrassed. Virgil thought this might be something of an act, and maybe she'd recognised him from the beginning.

'You think I'm nice enough to eat?' she said.

'Sure.'

'Where would you start eating?'

'Wherever you wanted me to.'

'Would you go for the best bits first or would you save those for last?'

'I guess I'd start by having a little taste of everything and then I'd decide which the best parts were.'

She had almost cleared her plate, but there was one thick sausage remaining. She had been saving it. Now she picked it up. Her fingers were long but well-fleshed, her nails sleek and painted cherry red. She offered the sausage to Virgil. He bit it in half with his big, white, all-American teeth. She ate the rest herself.

'I could keep on nibbling for a very long time,' said Virgil. She still didn't reply. So Virgil added, 'Do you work?'

'Yes.'

'What at?'

'This and that.'

'Like last night.'

'That's one of the things I work at, yes.'

'Are you on your way to work now?'

'That was the idea.'

'Could you be late?'

'I suppose I could.'

'Could you not go to work at all?'

'And do what instead?'

'I dunno. I guess I had eating you in mind. I mean sex. I guess I had food in mind. I could take you out to brunch maybe, if you're still hungry after your breakfast. I could put my head between your legs and chew on your pussy from now until lunch-time.'

'Your tongue would get tired.'
'Then we could have lunch.'

They got into a taxi. Virgil gave the name of his hotel. He asked his companion's name. It was Rose. He couldn't really have picked up an English rose, could he? Then he wondered if she was a professional, a prostitute. There she'd been last night, naked on the table, and today she'd put up with his dirty talk in a way he imagined most English girls wouldn't have, but then again, what did he know about English girls? What did he know about paying for sex? It wasn't a thing he'd ever done but he thought it wasn't so bad, as long as you knew all along that was what you were doing. It was bound to be a bummer if you thought your style and charm had seduced some girl and then you found out she was only seduced by the prospect of being paid.

Rose said, 'You're not the usual type they get at those dinners.'
'No?'
'No. You're younger. You're better looking. You're more interesting.'
'Aw, shucks.'

She started licking his ear. Then she sucked his fingers. Her saliva coated these extremities. She held herself close to him. He smelled her hair and skin. It was all clean and wholesome and freshly baked.

As the cab pulled up outside the hotel, Virgil saw the black Mercedes parked a little way up the street, with Butterworth standing stiffly beside it. Virgil paid his driver and Butterworth approached. He looked disapprovingly at Rose, then not much more approvingly at Virgil.

'Good morning, Mr Marcel,' said Butterworth.
'Hi, Butterworth. How's it hangin'?'
'I'm very well,' said Butterworth.

He continued to stand stiffly, as though wanting something from Virgil, but not prepared to say what.

'What's on your mind, Butterworth old man?' Virgil asked.
'I'm here to take you to the Everlasting Club, sir.'
'I only recently got back, and besides, they kicked me out, and in any case,' he said, looking at Rose and smirking, 'I've made other plans.'

Butterworth looked uncomfortable.

'Well, sir,' he said, 'obviously it isn't my place to take you anywhere you don't want to go . . .'
'Too damn right.'

'So I'll just wait for you, and let me say, sir, you're *expected* at the club.'

'Hey, what are you, Butterworth? My Jewish mother? Gimme some room will you?'

He shrugged Butterworth away, and he and Rose went up to his hotel room.

'This is nice,' she said. 'And expensive.'

'It's okay,' said Virgil. 'Especially if I'm not paying for it. I'm not sure if I'm paying or not.'

'No such thing as a free lunch, huh?'

He undressed her and she undressed him. He began to kiss and stroke and lick her body. Slowly he explored her textures and flavours, the smoothness and softness. He tasted her sweat. His tongue and hands went everywhere. He tasted everything. And she did the same for him. It took a long time. They made a meal of it.

Afterwards they lay on the bed together. They held each other, but not too tightly. They were close but not too close.

'So how did you get the job at the club?' he asked.

'Well, I'm an artist.'

'Yeah? That's interesting.'

'It's not all *that* interesting. Everybody's an artist. You're an artist too, I'm sure. But I happen to paint and draw, that's all. Anyway, you know, three years at art school, all wild untrammelled creativity. Then the real world, making ends meet, waitressing, working as a life model. So one thing led to another. So lying naked in the middle of a dining-table wasn't exactly a major career change.'

'They pay well?'

'It's okay.'

'Long hours?'

'Yes. Hey, if you're looking for a job, it's no good. They only use women.'

'Is it hard work?'

'You saw me working.'

'It didn't look so hard.'

'Except when someone tries to kiss you.'

'Yeah well,' said Virgil, 'I guess that wasn't the smartest thing I ever did. That happen often?'

'You're my first.'

He phoned room service. A waiter brought champagne and smoked salmon with lemon slices and black pepper. She fondled his penis, pumped it up tenderly, making it fully erect. Then she

49

reached for the smoked salmon, took the pale, pink, translucent strips and wrapped them round his penis like a second skin. She anointed it with lemon juice and black pepper, then closed her mouth around it and began to eat. She sucked and licked and chewed at the smoked salmon until she'd devoured it and Virgil's flesh was left behind, vulnerable, raw and naked.

They talked about their favourite foods. He said oysters, without much hesitation. She said black pudding, which was a thing he'd never heard of. Her description of it didn't make it sound all that appealing. She said all the best foods were phallic, especially sausages. She said most people knew nothing about good sausage, especially not the Americans. Virgil said he knew enough. They were full of ground-up lips and eyebrows and asshole, and she said what was wrong with that so long as it tasted good? And if you added herbs and spices and wine or port or brandy, 'Mmmm,' she said, 'ecstasy.' And even as she described it she did indeed seem to be experiencing a mild form of ecstasy.

They discussed what were the best and worst meals they'd ever eaten. Virgil was fairly sure that last night's extravaganza at the Everlasting Club had been one or the other, but he wasn't sure which.

He called room service again and ordered fruit and cream and tapenade. He poured the cream over her plump, pink toes and sucked it off, his tongue pressing into the gaps and crevices, licking over the smooth varnished nails, cherry red like her fingernails, glimpsed through the film of cream.

He took the fruit; grapes, bananas, oranges. He crushed the grapes over her breasts and licked them clean of pips, juice and grape skin. He halved the oranges and squeezed them, dousing her body in more juice and licking that off too. He crushed bananas into her navel and thighs, and wherever there was flesh or juice his tongue would be exploring, his mouth devouring. He painted her neck and nipples with the rich blackness of the tapenade.

Hours passed, absorbed in sex and conversation, eating, drinking and dozing. They lost track of time. The day passed. It was starting to get dark outside.

More food was ordered, for the purpose of eating this time; bread and cheese and pâté; but even here they passed food from mouth to mouth and she licked the crumbs from his belly.

She turned on the bedside lamp, got out of bed and reached into her shoulder-bag for a sketch-book. She did fast, jagged drawings of the hotel room, of the view through the window, of Virgil. Then she drew the clutter of plates and left-over food. She sketched the knives and forks resting at wasted angles, the orange peel, the spent lemon slices, crusts, wine glasses marked by fingers and lips.

He said, 'Is this what you draw?'

'I suppose so,' she said. 'I do a lot of still-lifes.'

She put down her sketch-pad and crawled back into bed. They slept an exhausted, satiated sleep. In the middle of the night the telephone rang for a very long time but Virgil didn't answer it. When they woke it was light again, but Virgil was unsure if it was morning or afternoon. They made love again. He was still hungry for her. He looked at her drawings. He had no idea whether or not they were any good but he said he kind of liked them.

'Jesus,' he said, 'this is a little different from my last trip to England.'

Rose said, 'You mean you didn't get laid last time?'

'I didn't get laid and I didn't get fed. This time I get sensory overload. First at the Everlasting Club, now with you. Food makes a great sex aid.'

'None of this is really very authentic,' she said, pointing at the remains of the food. 'None of this is what English food is really all about.'

'What is it all about?'

'Real English food is Blue Cheshire and Nottingham roast goose and Bakewell pudding and clotted Devon cream, oatcakes and Lancashire hotpot and Richmond maids of honour.'

'I've never heard of any of that stuff.'

'Well of course you haven't. You're American.'

The telephone rang again but Virgil ignored it. Then, a couple of minutes later, there was a heavy pounding on the door of the room. Virgil ignored this too, but when it was repeated and when its urgency suggested it wasn't going to go away, Virgil realised he was going to have to answer the door.

Virgil opened up and saw Butterworth, his shiny suit, his brown shoes, his big face. He looked like a man who had spent the night sleeping in a car. What Butterworth saw was more spectacular. Virgil was naked, unshaven, his hair matted, his body splattered and discoloured with food stains, dried cream and orange juice all over his face, tapenade in his pubic hair.

'You'd better come in,' said Virgil. 'Want a snack?'

Rose stretched a sheet over herself. Virgil put on his trousers. He offered Butterworth a seat, but Butterworth preferred to stand, taking up a place by the window. In fact he opened the window. A gust of cold air billowed in, dispersing the ripe muskiness of the room.

'This isn't easy for me,' said Butterworth. 'I don't usually care too much what people get up to. I know it's none of my business. But I've got a job to do. It may not look like much of a job but it's all I've got and I'd rather not lose it.'

'What are you talking about, Butterworth?'

'You and the young lady have had twenty-four hours together. That's enough for anybody, surely.'

'Speak for yourself, Butterworth. But what the hell, you're here now, why don't you tell me what you want?'

'Only what I wanted before, sir. They want to see you, quite urgently, I think. I've got to take you to them. That's my job. It would save me a lot of trouble if you'd just come along.'

'What do they want from me?'

'I wouldn't know, would I?'

'They give me a free flight, a hotel room, a few drinks, a meal; what do they think that buys them?'

'I really don't know.'

'And how do I get them off my back?'

Butterworth said nothing, but Rose said, 'Maybe by seeing them.'

Virgil reluctantly nodded. He knew she had a point.

'Please, sir,' said Butterworth.

It sounded like the plaintive cry of a man who only wanted a quiet life. Virgil thought Butterworth was maybe in the wrong job, or at least working for the wrong organisation. The Everlasting Club did not seem to foster quiet lives. By the time he had showered and dressed, Rose had done a sketch of Butterworth, much to Butterworth's embarrassment. As they left the hotel room Rose was phoning room service and asking them to send up a plate of Cumberland sausage.

There were more foolish high jinks, as Virgil saw it, with a blindfold. He was loaded into the car and driven to another unknown destination. The journey was longer this time and there was no conversation from Butterworth. That might have been because he was tired after a night sleeping in the car, but Virgil thought it was done deliberately to give weight, dignity and an air of foreboding to this trip. Unlike his previous outing, this was not going to be a social event. This time, Butterworth seemed to imply, they were not playing. This time the Everlasting Club meant business. Virgil refused to take it seriously.

The ride was soon over. The car slowed down, pulled off the road, and negotiated several tight bends and sudden steep drops as they descended into an underground car park. Butterworth removed Virgil's blindfold. He looked around. Even for an underground car park this place was dark. There weren't many cars around, and one stood out. It was a Bentley Continental, one of those mid-fifties models with the smooth, streamlined fastback.

'You're required over there,' said Butterworth, pointing at the Bentley.

Virgil got out, crossed the oil-stained floor of the car park and approached the Bentley. The passenger door was pushed open from within and Virgil saw that Kingsley was sitting in the driver's seat. He was as smooth and plump and pink and English as ever, and now he was wearing a pin-striped suit. He was drinking from a brandy snifter. Virgil slid into the passenger seat beside him.

'Yo, dude,' said Virgil.

Kingsley feigned tolerant amusement, but it was obvious he was not going to chat with Virgil. He had a script in his head and he was not going to stray from it. This was his show, his set piece.

'How did you enjoy your introduction to the Everlasting Club?' he asked.

'Not a whole lot,' Virgil admitted.

'You certainly seemed to be enjoying it at the time.'

'Yeah? I was probably faking.'

'Are you suffering from morning-after remorse? Surely not. The morning after was a good twenty-four hours ago.'

'I didn't enjoy it a whole lot when you bastards tossed me out.'

'Oh, come, come,' Kingsley scolded. 'You must realise you overstepped the mark.'

'I didn't know where the mark was.'

'But now you do.'

Virgil shrugged. 'I've been thrown out of better places.'

'Would you like a brandy?' Kingsley asked pleasantly.

'Sure,' said Virgil.

Kingsley, smiling, poured brandy from a small decanter that lodged under the dashboard. It was a generous measure. Virgil sniffed it. It wasn't bad.

'You have to say thank you,' said Kingsley.

'Do I?'

Kingsley looked saddened.

'Why this lack of manners, Virgil?' he asked. 'Why this hostility? I'm not very well versed in etymology but according to our Mr Radcliffe it appears there are certain historical, linguistic connections between hostility and hospitality. A stranger approaches. We feel hostility towards anything strange. We feel threatened. But we offer hospitality in order to appease the stranger.'

Virgil looked out of the car window, bored, dismissive.

'What does this have to do with me?' he asked.

'It's only a theory,' said Kingsley.

'I don't know how grateful you want me to be for all your wonderful hospitality. I don't know how you want me to show my gratitude.'

'You could begin by saying thank you.'

He said it threateningly. There was a sense of 'or else'. He looked at Virgil with the mean, stupid eyes of a school bully. Virgil thought you should stand up to bullies.

'Lemme tell you why I'm not grateful,' he said. 'I'm not grateful because you serve lousy food, because the guys at the club are a bunch of upper-class slimeballs, and because the whole idea of the club is so fucking juvenile. I'd join a bowling club if I wanted that kind of crap. Blindfolds, rules about what you're allowed to drink, naked girls on the table; you people never grew up. Which English public school did you go to, Kingsley? Don't you wish you were still there?'

Kingsley threw his drink in Virgil's face. It was a waste of good brandy. Virgil didn't flinch. The act seemed petulant, almost girlish, much what Virgil might have expected. They sat for a while in silence. Virgil smirked annoyingly. Kingsley was duly annoyed.

'Nobody likes to have their hospitality spurned,' said Kingsley. It was part explanation, part apology.

'Okay,' said Virgil. 'Send me the bill. I'll pay for everything; the air fare, the hotel, Butterworth's wages, all the food and drink, everything. I'll pay for *your* meal too, and for the brandy you just tossed in my face. That way I'm clear, right?'

'Offering money is the worst insult of all,' said Kingsley.

'Gee, I'd forgotten how sensitive you Brits are.'

Kingsley, with great effort, forced himself to relax, to change tactics. He began to play a new scene.

'This is silly,' he said. 'What's the point of sitting here hurling insults at each other?'

'I don't know,' said Virgil. 'You tell me.'

Kingsley continued, 'Your first night at the Everlasting Club may have been less than a complete success, for either side, but for our part we're more than happy to forgive and forget.'

'Big of you. I kissed some girl. I got a little drunk. What do you want to do? Crucify me?'

'That isn't our intention.'

'So don't invite me again.'

'That certainly isn't our intention either.'

'So what is?'

'Quite simply, we want you to become a member of the Everlasting Club. We want you to become one of us.'

Virgil laughed. 'Why?'

'Why not,' said Kingsley. 'We found you amusing company. We recognised you as a kindred spirit. The club always needs new blood. We want you to join us.'

Virgil was finding this alternately absurd and infuriating. He had expected to be yelled at and sent a bill, but suddenly he was a kindred spirit. Kingsley handed him a clean, folded handkerchief with which to wipe his brandied face. Virgil accepted it gracelessly, wiped himself off, and tossed it back.

'What do you say, Virgil? Are you batting for us?'

Even Virgil had no absolute objection to being wanted, even if it was by a group of people he didn't rate very highly. Yet the idea of spending any more nights in that club, with those strange guys, eating that weird, weird food . . .

'No, I don't think I'm batting for you,' he said. He almost said 'sorry' but managed to stop himself.

'Let me put it this way,' said Kingsley calmly and with finality, 'if we want you to become a member then you become a member. Nobody turns us down. That is not an option. We always get our man.'

'You serious? Who the fuck do you think you are? The Mounties?'

Kingsley ignored this. He said, 'I have your membership card already written out.'

He handed Virgil a card, white with bevelled edges, again showing a snake eating its tail, and Virgil's name and a membership number had been written on it in an elegant italic hand.

'You know where you can stick it,' said Virgil.

'I won't have you talking to the Chief Carver like that.'

Even Kingsley must have been aware of how absurd this sounded.

'I'm out of here,' said Virgil.

He started to get out of the car but Kingsley grabbed his arm and shoulder to force him to stay. Despite a reputation as a hell-raiser, Virgil had never belonged to the brawling fist-fighting school of hell-raising. Nevertheless, he was sick of Kingsley and wanted to make the little bastard let go of him. He waved his fist in Kingsley's face. It was not meant to be a killer punch, but perhaps he waved it harder than he intended, or perhaps Kingsley just bled easily. Kingsley barked with pain, and a torrent of thick blood gushed from his small, pink nose. His grip on Virgil loosened. Virgil shook himself free and got out of the Bentley. But Kingsley was right behind, clutching his handkerchief to his nose to stop the bleeding, and breathing in brandy fumes. He tried to kick Virgil in the backside. He missed. Virgil stopped and turned. He was more irritated than angry. Kingsley was an irritating little squirt. This time Virgil gave him a shove in the chest. It was a strong shove, but not meant to be particularly vicious or dangerous. Kingsley, however, toppled over backwards and his head made an ugly snapping sound as it hit the concrete floor. He curled himself up in a ball and moaned.

Butterworth came trotting over from the Mercedes.

'Have you killed him, sir?' he asked.

'Well, of course I haven't killed him. Don't be dumb. He just fell over. He's fine.'

Butterworth wasn't convinced by this and, in truth, neither was Virgil. The moans from Kingsley were getting quieter. He was lying ominously still.

'We ought to get him to a hospital,' said Butterworth.

Virgil had heard about English hospitals. He had no intention of visiting one, especially not when he had an English rose waiting for him in his hotel room. Having come to blows with the big cheese of the Everlasting Club and having done him some injury it might have been prudent to run away, but at the very least he wanted to get back to the hotel and pick up Rose.

'*You* take him to the hospital,' Virgil said to Butterworth. 'I'll, I'll walk back to the hotel.'

'But you don't know the way, sir.'

'So I'll get a taxi.'

'No sir, I don't think that would . . .'

'Look Butterworth, don't tell me what to do. Your boss is lying there bleeding and unconscious. Do you want to end up the same way?'

Butterworth looked shocked.

'Please,' he said. 'I don't think this is necessary.'

Neither did Virgil. He didn't know what had come over him. He had only been in London a couple of days and already he was acting like a psychopath. Was it him or the city? Wasn't this supposed to be the cradle of civilisation? Or was that Barcelona?

'Okay, you're right,' said Virgil. 'I'm sorry. Now how do I get out of this mess?'

'Very well,' said Butterworth, and he was suddenly extremely cool and authoritative, 'I'll take Mr Kingsley to the hospital. We'll go in his Bentley. You take the other car.'

'I don't know,' said Virgil.

'Here are the keys. Take the Merc, get out of town for a while. Keep cool. Lay low. Take your girlfriend with you if you like.'

Butterworth pressed the car keys into Virgil's hand. His advice sounded okay, and it was the only advice on offer. Virgil didn't want to have to think too much. He just wanted to obey orders. He accepted the keys and took possession of the car.

He drove for what felt like hours. Butterworth had given him directions to the hotel, but he was soon lost. Driving in London was a nightmare. It made driving in L.A. seem sane and well-regulated. He couldn't work out these things called bus lanes or the traffic lights or the roundabouts. He wasn't at home with the stick-shift, nor with being on the wrong side of the road and the wrong side of the car.

But somehow he eventually made it back to the hotel. This was achieved only by stopping at each road junction and asking directions. It was tough when all he knew was the name of his hotel. But with the help of half a dozen pedestrians and several taxi drivers he managed to get back to Rose.

She was waiting for him in the lobby. She was showered and dressed and she was sketching on her pad. She had packed Virgil's things and put them in his suitcase, which now stood beside her.

'Good journey?' she asked.

'Fair,' said Virgil. 'I thought you might have gone.'

'I'm very loyal,' she said.

'Look, I need to get away from here for a while. I've got a car outside. Wanna go driving?'

She did, of course.

Scenes from a History of the Everlasting Club.
Number Three: A Choice of Filling.

It seems to us that the sandwich is not a form that required very much inventing. While ever people have baked bread, they must surely have cut it into slices and put other, usually more expensive, foodstuffs, between them. It seems absurd that we had to wait until the eighteenth century, until precisely 1762 according to some authorities, and the intervention of John Montague, Fourth Earl of Sandwich, twice First Lord of the Admiralty, before this utterly simple concept was realised. And even if, as you might suppose, people had been eating 'sandwiches' for centuries and the good Earl merely gave his name to them, it still seems inexplicable that the form had remained nameless for so long.

The Scandinavians, of course, lovers of openness in all things, still don't seem quite to have got the hang of it. The open sandwich may look pretty, is no doubt intended to, but things slide off an open sandwich. It gets your hands messy. The filling falls down the front of your shirt or into your cleavage. It is too delicate and too fussy for the English sensibility. Can you imagine an open bacon sandwich or an open chip butty, for example?

It is 1780 and John Montague, Fourth Earl of Sandwich, sits at his desk in the Admiralty. He makes a great show of being busy, as well he might. This second spell as First Lord would have to be reckoned a limited success. He only took the job as a way of exerting influence, promoting his friends, and making a little money by accepting a gratuity here and there. But now he finds himself in charge of a less than adequate navy, fighting a colonial war against America, and he is being pilloried for 'corrupt practices' and 'failures of administration', as though it was all *his* fault. The only consolation in all this, and it is a small one, is that the explorer James Cook has discovered some islands out in the Pacific and named them the Sandwich Islands in his honour. It is pleasant indeed to have things named after you.

London in the summer of 1780 is as foul as any city he knows.

The filth and stench and the gross, unsensual bodies disgust him. He has a hangover of a solid and immobile complexion, brought on by last night's rigours, rigours which he does not entirely remember, and perhaps is happier to forget. He dozes in his chair. To sustain himself he calls a clerk and demands food. The clerk in turn sends a lesser minion out for slices of beef arranged between slices of bread. When it comes, the Earl is able to keep up the show of working, clutching the bread and beef in one hand, and quill in the other, and he can give the unfailing impression that he works even as he eats. This looks like efficiency and dedication to the public purpose, as though he is too busy with the affairs of state to leave his desk for something as trivial as food. The beef is good, rare and moist, the bread as thick as a ledger.

This way of eating was indeed devised during a twenty-four hour gambling session; the candles burning low, whores seen in the flickering yellow light, the table decked with cards and decanters, money flowing, bids and counterbids crossing and recrossing the table.

He finishes the 'sandwich'. He brushes crumbs from some naval documents and sees that one or two spots of grease have created embellishment in certain areas of the page. He is inclined to think this will not matter so very much.

Then he begins to think about sex, a perennial subject, something base and gross and not entirely pleasant or healthy, but an urge he finds it wiser not to deny. Lubricious scenes enact themselves before his mind's eye, like living, moving engravings. He sees monstrous, overripe harlots, low, brimstone viragos smelling of camphor and sweat and semen. Something stirs. It is not the fetid, dead air of his chambers. There is nothing else to be done. He must visit his mistress. Fortunately she is close at hand. Again, thinking only of economy and his country, he has installed her in rooms only a short walk from the Admiralty. This way, whenever the urge seizes him, he can visit her, assuage his lust, and be back at his desk with the minimum of fuss and the least expense of time. The same principle as the sandwich.

He waddles from the Admiralty, with the gait of a man 'walking down both sides of the street at the same time'. As always his mistress is ready for him. She is ever willing and unquestionably able. Undressing is not required by either party. Nakedness would be time-consuming. The act is short, intense and perfectly satisfactory for both of them. He has been milked and can return to work. She is satisfied that not too much time or effort was demanded of her. It is an economical arrangement.

Back at his desk he eats again. He moves papers back and forth across his desk, consults charts and budgets, looks something up in a volume of law. The working day is finally disposed of. New pleasures and appetites await him with the night.

Tonight there will be nothing so insubstantial as filled bread on the menu. Tonight he has been invited by Sir Francis Dashwood to another meeting of the Hell Fire Club. As a matter of fact the Earl finds certain aspects of these gatherings less than wholly agreeable. The early part of the evening is always most satisfactory. Good food and wine are consumed in generous, copious quantities. Later, at the very end of the evening, in the Roman Room, a goodly number of whores are drafted in from St James's and they are had serially or simultaneously as the mood takes him. This too is fine. But he is not entirely enamoured of what takes place between the feasting and the whoring.

First there is the dressing up in monkish habits, followed by the tedious rituals of the Black Mass. These seem to him to be every bit as tedious as the most uninspired Low Church sermon. It is only the thought of the coming sexual debauchery that enables him to put up with these weary blasphemies. There is much nonsense with blood and animals, with crucifixes and wafers, with semen and bodily orifices. He is glad when it's all over.

Now it is midnight. The Black Mass is finished. He finds himself happily in the Roman Room. The whore he favours most at present is a young, raven-haired wench, spectacularly fleshed with big soft breasts, belly and buttocks. He loves her cunt; all soft and pink and infinitely elastic.

Alas, tonight he finds that particular entrance rather fully occupied by the phallus of a Justice of the Peace from Somerset. She sits astride and atop the West Countryman, riding him jauntily. Sandwich watches for a while and feels a strong urge to participate, but at first he is not sure how. Then it comes to him. He pushes the whore's body forwards, down towards the JP's chest. Her buttocks rise a little. He kneads them, parts them with both hands. He finds her anus, purple and puckered and slick. He inserts a finger. It is gripped snugly but he knows from experience that there is room for a much thicker digit. His penis is wet and hard and more than ready. He eases it into her. It is an effort but it is worth it. Things are wonderfully snug in there. The three bodies ripple in loosely co-ordinated pleasure. Again he can see this as a form of sexual efficiency; three appetites satisfied at once. He can feel the other man's presence through the wall that separates the whore's two orifices; another kind of sandwich.

Of course, the Earl of Sandwich was a member of all the famous and infamous clubs of his day. He used to say that after the exhausting debaucheries of the Hell Fire Club there was nothing he liked better than a few hours of the continuing, civilised excesses of the Everlasting Club.

FOUR

Frank Marcel put on a disguise; false beard, blond wig, a Guns N Roses T-shirt, jeans, cowboy boots and sunglasses. He looked weird, but it was a successful disguise in that the props, though absurd, were impenetrable. You might have guessed that here was a man in disguise but it would have been hard to say which man. You wouldn't have guessed it was Frank Marcel. To complete the effect he had a hire car, not the sort he usually drove, a nice little unnoticeable compact. This was to make the job of tailing somebody that much easier.

He started to tail his wife. Mary had been acting differently of late, not acting 'strangely' exactly, there was no particular behaviour he could categorise as out of the ordinary, but a husband knows these things, or at least likes to think he does. A lover, of course, seemed like the obvious explanation, a little too obvious for Frank's tastes, a little too banal. Frank knew that after twenty-eight years of marriage, Mary's pulse did not quicken at his touch. Indeed, to persuade Mary to let him touch her at all required a round of negotiations that made Middle East peace talks look feebly unchallenging. But Frank had persuaded himself that Mary's coldness was because of a distaste for sex *per se*, not a specific distaste for sex with him. That's why he wasn't entirely sold on the lover theory. However . . .

His suspicions were aroused because there were an increasing number of hours in his wife's day that she couldn't (or at least *didn't*) account for satisfactorily. She claimed to go for pre-breakfast jogs. She wouldn't be home if he phoned her in the middle of the afternoon. She said she went swimming, or playing tennis, or having lunch with her female friends most days of the week. All this sounded like standard wifely behaviour, but Frank wasn't convinced. She never looked as though she'd been jogging or swimming or playing tennis. She didn't even look as though she'd had lunch. It was a subtle business but Frank knew all about subtlety. That's why he put on his snappy disguise, hired a car and started tailing her.

It was harder work than he'd imagined. He had to go to work

in his own car, park, leave the office on foot, find somewhere to put on the disguise, pick up the hire car, then drive home and find somewhere inconspicuous to stake out his own house so he could see Mary's exit. Frank, naturally, lived in the kind of neighbourhood that discouraged people who hang around in parked cars staking out the houses. Several times as he waited, passing locals slowed their cars and stared at him, checking him out, giving themselves time to take the car's number. Maybe he should have employed a private detective, but no, he wanted this masochistic pleasure all for himself. And sure enough the pleasure came.

It was three in the afternoon. Mary came out of the house, got into her car and took off. Frank began to follow. It was easy at first, along wide, empty, local roads. He was able to stay several hundred yards behind her and still keep her easily in view. But then she took to the freeway and it got harder. She kept sweeping from lane to lane, in a hurry, driving fast, eager to get somewhere. Frank's own small-engined car had trouble keeping up. He wondered where she was heading; south, certainly. Long Beach? Malibu? That would really be a pisser. What if she was on her way to meet some surf stud or some leathery-skinned movie star? Jesus! Frank started to sweat. Then he lost her, lost the car. Traffic clustered together in front of him and suddenly his wife's car was no longer there. He found himself on the Santa Monica freeway not quite sure where he was or where he was going. He took the next exit and turned back.

Next day he rented a different car from a different company, something bigger and more powerful. She wasn't going to get away this time. He kept the same disguise however. He'd asked the rental company if they could give him a car with smoked glass, which would have enabled him to abandon the disguise completely, but it would have taken a couple of days to get such a car, and they obviously thought he was pretty whacko for wanting it.

This time he was too embarrassed to park in his own neighbourhood and be stared at by passing neighbours, so he cruised the streets, never straying too far from his own house. At three, just like the previous day, Mary left the house. Frank was immediately on the trail. He drove closer behind her than complete discretion would have demanded, but he was feeling angry and reckless. She came off the freeway at an exit for Redondo Beach and he followed her past the new and used car lots and the fast food outlets until she pulled into, Frank couldn't fucking believe it, the car park of a Golden Boy family restaurant.

Profoundly mixed feelings bubbled up in Frank. If she was running around having afternoon assignations, was it better that she do it in one of his own restaurants or not? Would he have been more hurt had it been taking place in a Denny's or a Taco Bell? Was she doing it just to rub salt in the wound? But could she really be having an assignation in a Golden Boy? It sure as hell wasn't the most obvious place for erotic dalliance.

Frank drove past the entrance to the restaurant and parked a couple of streets away, then walked back. Mary had entered the restaurant. The car park was nearly empty but there was a beaten-up old Porsche that looked somehow familiar. Frank walked to the door of the restaurant and hung around as though reading the menu; the menu he'd designed and knew by heart. He looked in through the big plate-glass windows, into the cheery, brightly lit burgundy, Prussian blue and gold interior. He could see a couple of motherly waitresses scooting around, and he could see Mary sitting at a corner table with a man.

Then he knew why he'd recognised the beaten-up old Porsche. It belonged to Leo, little Leo, the chef from Trimalchio's, his chef, the man on whom the success of Trimalchio's and of Frank Marcel was based. Frank wanted to throw up. This was betrayal on the grand scale all right. He watched as Mary and Leo chatted with the waitress, chatted for a long time, laughing and joking, coming on like a couple out enjoying themselves. They ordered. The waitresses left but Mary and Leo carried on laughing. Their heads came close together, conspiratorially. And what were their hands doing below the table where he couldn't see? When the food arrived – spare ribs and a pepper steak with Golden Boy super salads – Mary playfully fed Leo a lettuce leaf. Frank wanted to kill something.

He returned to his car. There was a gas station a couple of blocks away and three young black kids were hanging around the air hose, squirting air in each other's faces and down the necks of their T-shirts and up each other's ass. Frank had an idea. He stopped his car next to the kids, stuck his head out the window and said, 'Hey, any of you fellers want to earn a few bucks?' Frank believed that black kids were vicious, craven and gullible, and would do almost anything for a few bucks. But these kids looked at the creep in the fake beard and sunglasses, and Frank could tell that maybe they weren't as craven or as gullible as he'd been hoping.

'Doing what?' asked one of the kids.

'You see that car over there . . .'

The kids looked in the general direction of the Golden Boy but Mary's car wasn't visible from this far away.

'What if we do?' said the kid.

'Well,' said Frank, 'that's my car, my other car, my wife's car, and you know, my wife and I we're wild people, a little crazy maybe . . . and I want to play a little trick on her. See, I have this paper bag here,' and he showed them a brown paper bag, it was the one he'd been carrying his disguise in, 'and what say each of you boys takes a good shit into this bag and I'll give you five dollars each.'

The kids sneered and walked off. They showed a dignified hauteur that Frank had often seen on black people but he had never been so directly on the receiving end of it before. So Frank had to go into the rest-room of the gas station and shit in the bag himself. He was a little disappointed at how neat and regular and wholesome his turds looked. He'd been hoping for something rank and wet and lurid, but nature would not provide.

He drove back to the Golden Boy and got out of his car carrying the bag of shit. He looked into the restaurant to see that Mary and Leo were still wrapped up in each other. He walked over to Mary's car, opened the door, and began to smear the shit all over the driver's seat and the steering wheel. It didn't create nearly as much of a mess as he would have liked, but the point was made. Then a voice behind him said, 'Can I help you, sir?'

Frank looked round and was confronted by a man in a Golden Boy assistant manager's uniform, but not so much a man as a boy, a great hulking boy, but Frank didn't feel immediately threatened. He was experienced at dealing with Golden Boy employees.

'No, you can't help me, son.'

But it wasn't help that the boy was really offering.

'Just what exactly are you up to here, feller?' he asked, a good helping of aggression in his voice.

'I'm minding my own business,' said Frank. 'Why don't you do the same?'

'What have you wiped all over that seat?'

'What's it to you?'

'Christ, it's . . .'

'Yeah, yeah, so what?'

The boy grabbed Frank in an arm-lock. It hurt like hell.

The boy said, 'This car belongs to a customer of the Golden Boy, and I think I have a duty . . .'

'No you don't,' said Frank though his pain. 'The training manual says quite clearly that customers' cars are parked at their own risk.'

That threw the boy. He softened his grip on Frank, but only slightly.

'And as a matter of fact,' Frank continued, 'this is my car anyway.'

'Oh sure.'

'Yes it is, you asshole. It's mine. I paid for it. And if I want to coat my own car in my own shit I'm free to do it. This isn't Iran, you know.'

'How can this be your car? I don't . . .'

'Look, I don't need to prove anything to you, but it so happens I can.'

Frank moved his hand towards his pants pocket to extract his wallet. By some weird stroke of luck his wallet happened to contain a photograph of Mary, Frank and Virgil leaning up against this very car. The boy twisted Frank's arm to excruciating intensity.

'No tricks, feller,' he yelled.

'I'm getting my wallet.'

'Make sure that's all you're getting. I'd just love you to pull a knife on me.'

Frank prised out his wallet and with some difficulty, using only one hand, took out the photograph.

'See!' Frank said.

The boy looked at the photograph, but although he could see that the car might well be the same, and indeed that the woman in the photograph was the woman now eating inside the restaurant, the man in the photograph, having no false beard, blond wig or sunglasses, bore no relation to the one he'd apprehended.

'I don't know about this,' the boy said.

'It's me in the photograph,' Frank shouted. 'Of course it's me.'

He yanked the wig off and tugged at the beard which only came away reluctantly, leaving his face smarting and blotched with glue.

'Hey,' said the boy slowly, 'don't I know you?'

Frank said nothing.

'I've seen your picture in the papers or something.'

Then the boy suddenly recognised Frank and released his arm as though it was red hot.

'Jesus,' he said. 'Mr Marcel. Of course. I mean, your picture's in the staff newspaper every month. Hey, I'm pleased to meet you, I guess. Sorry about your arm.'

Frank saw he had gained an advantage and he intended to press it home.

'It's okay,' Frank said. 'I suppose you thought you were doing your job. You were being a little damned officious for my liking, but we'll let that pass.'

He pulled fifty dollars from his wallet.

'Have this,' he said. 'You haven't seen me. None of this happened. Tell the lady that three black kids did it.'

'Sorry for the misunderstanding, sir, I thought I was doing the right thing. Hey, sir, maybe I could talk to you about promotion . . .'

But Frank was already in his rented car and in the process of driving away. The boy tucked the money in his pocket. There was a wig and a false beard lying on the ground. He picked them up and used them to start wiping the shit off the seat of Mary's car.

Frank returned to work. When he got home that evening, Mary's car was parked outside the house. The interior was spotlessly clean. Frank guessed she must have had it valeted. He asked her what kind of day she'd had and she said it had been quiet; she'd done a little shopping and a little jogging and been out for lunch.

She was such a lousy liar! Obscene images danced in front of Frank's overheated imagination. Getting the car cleaned must have slowed them down a little, but there would still have been plenty of time for them to visit some neutral, air-conditioned motel room with a big bed and an in-house porno channel. He saw Leo's short pudgy hands and big pink lips marauding over Mary's body. And he saw Mary, his own wife, his formerly virtuous, faithful wife whom he'd loved and worshipped all these long years, he saw her sucking on Leo's fat little cock. Or maybe it wasn't so little, maybe it was vastly, grotesquely oversized, wholly out of proportion to the rest of his small body; and there was Mary sucking on it, barely able to get her mouth around it, licking and gnawing it as though it was some grotesque pink sausage. Frank took several strong drinks that night and didn't say much to Mary.

Next day he followed her again. He still used a rented car but he abandoned any attempt at disguise. Mary was such a lousy driver, he told himself, she never noticed what was going on around her. She didn't look in her rear-view mirror much and even if she did, she'd never look closely enough to see that it was Frank in the car behind.

This time she drove north, away from the coast and got off the freeway at an exit for San Bernardino. This time he could see where she was going, to the original San Berdoo Golden Boy, his Dad's restaurant, now much modified and refurbished. And he was right. The Porsche was already in the car park. Leo was visible at a window table, looking out on to the street. He waved to Mary. She waved back. She skipped from her car. She looked excited and girlish, in a way Frank hadn't seen for years. It made him feel sick and angry.

Frank watched them order. There was lots more chat and cheeriness with the waitress. The food arrived quickly. Mary and Leo sat close together at the table. Frank got out of his car and headed into the restaurant.

'Table for one?' the waitress asked, and then she recognised him. It was well known that Frank Marcel might drop in at random at any Golden Boy restaurant to see that standards were being maintained.

'Hello there,' he said to the waitress. 'How's business?'

'We've been real busy, Mr Marcel.'

'Not *too* busy, I hope.'

'There's no such thing as too busy, Mr Marcel.'

She was making a direct quotation from Frank's training manual.

'Good, good,' he said distractedly, and then, as if surprised, 'well, what do you know? Excuse me, there's a couple of friends of mine sitting over there. I think I'll join them.'

The waitress gave a kind of curtsy and Frank went over to the table by the window where Mary and Leo were involved in some intense and, he had no doubt, sick, filthy, innuendo-laden conversation. But Frank was trying to keep his disgust in check.

'Hey guys,' he said, slipping into a seat opposite them. 'Is it a small world or is it a small world?'

Leo and Mary looked somewhat surprised to see Frank, somewhat puzzled and awkward, yet they didn't react with the shock you'd expect from two lovers caught in the act by the wronged husband.

'Are you here making one of your spot checks?' Mary asked.

'That's one way of describing it.'

'The food's pretty good here, Mr Marcel,' said Leo. 'And the service is great.'

God, that little weasel could certainly play the innocent, thought Frank.

'This is tough for me,' he said. 'Maybe I'm old-fashioned or something but when I find my wife running around with my best chef, I feel, well I don't know exactly what I feel, betrayed certainly, but a whole lot more than that. It's like my professional life and my personal life are conspiring against me. And I don't mind admitting that hurts, that really fucking hurts.'

Mary and Leo looked at each other then turned their gaze towards Frank. The gaze was sympathetic, gentle, resigned.

'I guess we'll have to tell him,' said Mary.

'I guess so,' said Leo.

'Too damn right you will,' said Frank.

'This is a hard town to keep secrets in,' said Mary. 'It was meant to come as a surprise.'

'It does, Mary. It certainly does.'

'Oh well, it's perfectly simple. We were organising a giant surprise party for you. We've been visiting all the various Golden Boy restaurants, getting signatures, talking to loyal employees. We've collected some heart-warming stories about you, Frank. I was going to retell them at the party. And Leo was going to cook something really special for you. You've ruined everything now, Frank. But then, you usually do.'

Frank felt bad. He felt let down. He had been all pumped up with adrenalin, ready for a fight, then the ground had been pulled away from under him and he had been made to look petty, suspicious and absurd. He felt he had cast doubts on the honesty of his wholly trustworthy wife and employee. Or was that merely what they wanted him to feel? They were a sly pair, and maybe they were able to think fast too. Coming up with the surprise party explanation was pretty clever and not implausible. But did that mean it was true?

Frank didn't know one way or the other when it came right down to it, and that made him feel worse than ever. He was helpless. He didn't know what was going on. He decided he was out of his depth. It was time to turn to a professional. He decided to have Leo tailed.

He looked in Yellow Pages and found a detective whose ad looked appropriately professional and impressive. Frank was surprised to find that the whole transaction could be done by phone. He told the detective, a man called Miller who had a very rich, deep voice, about Leo. He described him, said he was the chef at Trimalchio's (Miller said he'd heard of it and Frank felt very gratified) and he gave Leo's home address and said he wanted him followed.

'And why will I be following this man?' Miller asked.

'To see what he gets up to.'

'What do you think he gets up to?'

'Well, I'm not sure,' said Frank.

'Is this a matrimonial case?'

Frank seemed to recall from fictional sources that some detectives considered it beneath their dignity to handle matrimonial cases, and certainly Miller's telephone manner suggested he was loaded down with dignity.

'Not necessarily,' said Frank.

'You think he might be stealing from the restaurant?'

'Yes,' said Frank eagerly, glad of this plausible motivation. 'Yes, I think he could be.'

'It's not that you think he's banging your wife or something?'

'Well, I mean, for all I know, well, you're the detective.'

'Okay,' said Miller. 'I'll get back to you within a week.'

There had been no interview in a seedy office, no bottle of Scotch hidden in a desk drawer, no need to go into lengthy explanations about adultery and betrayal. Frank was relieved but again felt a little let down.

It was a tough week for Frank. He tried to imagine Miller out there somewhere, hiding in doorways, driving a big, anonymous, blue car, his hat pulled down, chain-smoking, following Leo from home to work and then home again or, more likely, to that same sleazy motel of the imagination where Mary would be waiting, naked, maybe a little drunk, and ready to do all those things with her lovable Leo that she had never been prepared to do with Frank. In reality, Frank hadn't wanted her to do much with him for some years now, but the thought that she might be doing them with somebody else stirred him profoundly.

Then he got the call from Miller.

'Mr Marcel, I have some news for you.'

'Really?' said Frank, a burn starting in his stomach, prickles racing up his back.

'Yes. I've discovered what our little friend Leo gets up to.'

'Great,' said Frank, and then, 'oh, my God.'

'It's not very pretty,' said Miller, 'but I think you ought to see for yourself.'

Frank assumed he would be shown a pile of eight by ten glossies revealing Leo and Mary in a variety of sexual positions, like illustrations for some sex manual.

'When can I see?' he asked.

'Well, one night seems to be as good as any other. Let's say tonight around two thirty a.m.'

'You mean two thirty tomorrow morning?'

'Yes,' said Miller. 'Be at my office about then and we'll go together.'

'Go where?' asked Frank, realising he couldn't be talking about eight by ten glossies.

'You'll see. We're going to catch the little bastard in the act.'

Frank agreed to be at Miller's office at two thirty, but he was confused. Whatever it was Leo was going to be doing at that time in the morning he surely wasn't going to be doing it with Mary. Mary would be at home with Frank at that hour. Okay, so they had separate rooms but he knew she didn't go wandering off in the night. Then again, if, as he would have to, he concocted some excuse for being away from home for the night in order to meet Miller, that would give Mary the opportunity to meet up with Leo. Frank recognised there was something circular and illogical in that line of thought but he assumed Miller knew what he was doing.

He arrived early at the detective's office at about two. He was in a frenzy of nerves and anticipation. He had a few drinks inside him to help him relax but he remained taut and sober. He had gone to a movie to try to make the evening pass more quickly. He wasn't even sure what the film was; a comedy, he thought, but he lost track of the plot and just sat there for an hour or more watching these fake people getting in and out of bed, in and out of cars, saying fake, humourless things to each other. He left long before the end.

Miller did not look nearly so dignified as he sounded. He was a short, narrow, dishonest-looking man. His hair was thick and blue-black with long sideburns. He looked dated. His image was that of an early-seventies executive trying to be hip.

'I'll drive,' said Miller, and sure enough, he did drive a big, blue, anonymous car. He drove it with one hand, either very competently or very carelessly, Frank wasn't sure which.

'Let me say, Mr Marcel, that in my line of business I can't afford to eat in joints like Trimalchio's. But when I'm on a case I often stop in at a Golden Boy. They never let me down.'

He said this as though he was expecting to be quoted in an advertisement for the chain. Then he said, 'How is that son of yours?'

Frank hadn't thought much about Virgil recently. He knew he'd gone to England on some half-assed invitation. But wherever Virgil was, Frank felt sure he'd be enjoying himself and spending too much money.

'He's fine, I guess,' said Frank.

Miller parked about half a block from Trimalchio's. Frank didn't know what was going on. He'd been assuming they were either going to Leo's house, which he knew was some miles away, or to some isolated motel. But maybe Leo rented a love-nest near to the restaurant so that he could stroll over there in quiet moments, get rid of his odious lust and return quickly to work. But it became apparent they weren't going to any love-nest. They were going to Trimalchio's. Frank thought this was pretty strange.

The building was closed and deserted. It was after two thirty now and all the staff and diners were long gone. There was a dim light visible inside but that could have been a single bulb that somebody had forgotten to switch off. Miller produced a set of skeleton keys. Frank was impressed by this kind of professionalism. Miller said, 'Now we need to be very quiet.'

He opened the door of Trimalchio's and stepped inside in perfect silence. Frank followed as quietly as he could but he had no gift for it. The light they had seen from outside was coming from the kitchen, and Frank could hear the rattle of bowls and utensils. They peeped through the windows in the swing-doors and Frank experienced yet another disappointment. There was nothing vile or orgiastic going on in there. All there was, was Leo working long into the night, apparently trying out new recipes, experimenting with seasonings, making batches of sauces and mayonnaise. Miller saw the disappointment on Frank's face and lifted his hand in a gesture of, 'Wait, you'll see.' And Frank surely did.

He watched as Leo put down the spatula he was using, unzipped his jeans and pulled out his penis. Frank's fears about Leo's sexual adornment had been unnecessary. Leo began to masturbate. It was a smooth and caressing act, nothing rough or gross about it at all. Very quickly he came, and here Frank did have some cause for astonishment and envy. There seemed to be gallons of the damned stuff. It burst forth in repeated, generous servings, and as it hit the air Leo directed it into the bowls and pans of sauce that were set around the kitchen on the surfaces and worktops. And when he had shaken every last drop from his penis into the vessels, and after he'd tucked away his genitals, he stirred the contents of each bowl and pan, then tasted them. He seemed well satisfied with the flavours.

A trembling, gagging, horrified Frank Marcel detonated through the kitchen doors, and before Miller could stop him he had Leo by the throat and was trying to strangle him. Wiser counsels prevailed only when Miller clubbed Frank around the skull with a blackjack and Frank released his grip on Leo only as he fell to the floor unconscious.

Ten minutes later Frank had come to and calmed down a little. He had sat Leo on a chair at a table in the main body of the restaurant. A single spotlight was trained on him. It was not an entirely convincing interrogation scene since the spotlight threw a rather warm, softly focused beam of light, and Frank had opened a goodish bottle of Colombier-Monpelou and given a glass to both Miller and Leo. But it would have to do. Certainly Leo looked appropriately terrified and Miller was a dark, threatening, authoritatively-voiced presence just outside the beam of light.

'First things first,' Frank said to Leo. 'Are you fucking my wife?'

'No sir. No way,' said Leo, sounding astonished.

'Okay,' said Frank, 'I believe you. Secondly, why were you jerking off into the food?'

Leo said nothing, but it didn't seem as though he had no answer, rather that his answer was too complex and weighty to be easily expressed, and that it might be wasted on his current audience.

Frank, in any case, didn't wait for an answer. 'Are you trying to ruin me, Leo?' he blurted. 'Is that it? Are you trying to bring shame and dishonour on Trimalchio's?'

'No sir.'

'I could understand it if maybe you hated me, loathed my restaurant, were unhappy about the pay, despised the work, if this was some act of revenge . . .'

'No, Mr Marcel, I'm not unhappy.'

'So is it that you hate the world? Are you saying to the world, or at least to my customers, "Eat shit!"? Although I know shit isn't the right word.'

'No, Mr Marcel, I'm not saying that at all. I love my work. I love my customers. I did what I did for love.'

Frank's eyes got bigger with anger and disbelief.

'I'm finding this tough to understand, Leo,' he said. 'You see, call me a boring old Republican, but personally I don't want to ejaculate

into the food of people I love, and just as important, I don't want
people I love ejaculating into my food. And in any case, I don't love
you Leo, and even if I did . . .'

He knew he was rambling. Leo nodded. Frank had made his
point.

'Was there something sexual about all this?' Frank asked. 'Was that
it? Is this some new perversion I haven't heard about? Did you get
off on the idea?'

'No I didn't,' said Leo. 'It was about love, not sex.'

Frank didn't understand that remark but thought it best to press
on. Leo's terror was receding and was being replaced by a glassy-
eyed calmness, the calmness of the true fanatic. Frank didn't like
it one bit.

'And how long has this been going on?' he asked.

'Right from the beginning, sir. Right from day one.'

Frank wondered how many meals Leo had adulterated. He wondered how many of those meals he, Frank, had eaten.

'It was just an experiment at first,' said Leo. 'You see, I knew my
cooking was good, but I knew it lacked a certain something, that
little bit extra that would make me a star. I tried exotic herbs and
spices. I tried just about everything. Semen was kind of a last-ditch
attempt. And you can't deny it worked, Mr Marcel. Nobody ever
complained. People lapped it up. The proof of the pudding is in the
eating, as the British say, and the eating around here has always been
pretty good.'

This was not what Frank wanted to hear. He'd have preferred
it if Leo had done the deed as some act of mania, if it had been
something beyond his rational control. He didn't want Leo to have
an explanation, for God's sake. The last thing he wanted was for Leo
to sound reasonable about it. Frank stood up. He fiddled with a place
setting on an adjacent table. He drained his glass of wine.

'Are you following all this, Miller?' he asked. 'What do you
make of it?'

Miller made a suitably ambiguous moue.

'Okay, I'll try to explain,' Leo pleaded. 'It won't be easy but
I'll try.'

'I'm not sure I want to hear this,' Frank said, 'but you might as
well give it a whirl.'

'Thank you, sir. You see, in my job, well, I guess in most jobs,
people want to give of themselves. People talk about giving their
blood, sweat and tears . . .'

'Don't tell me you bled into the food as well!'

'No sir, I'm talking figuratively. But a time came when I didn't want things just to be figurative. I don't know if you're at all religious, Mr Marcel . . .'

Frank thought he was going to scream. You catch an employee doing unspeakable things in your kitchen and he wants to quiz you about your religious beliefs.

'I don't know that I want to discuss my religious convictions with you, Leo. Not right now.'

'I understand that, Mr Marcel, but it really is very relevant. You see Jesus said, "This is my body, this is my blood." He wanted to give of himself in a big way. And so do I.'

'If it were up to me,' said Frank, 'you'd be chopped into small pieces and given to the sharks.'

'That's what they try to do to a lot of visionaries,' said Leo.

'Are you out of your mind?' Frank bawled. 'Visionaries do not jack off into the mayonnaise.'

'This one does,' Leo protested.

Frank actually did scream then. It seemed an appropriate response. So now the little bastard thought he was a visionary. Well that explained everything. Clearly there was no arguing with a visionary. Visionaries marched to the beat of a different drum. They could do what they liked with their jism and nobody had any right to complain! Frank thought he must be going mad. In a way he hoped so. He would feel a lot happier if this episode was an hallucination brought on by overwork, too many late nights and too close an acquaintance with the bottle. No such luck. Frank walked over to the bar, poured himself a slug of Jim Beam and balanced on a bar stool. Miller came over to him.

'What do I do about all this?' Frank asked, though he was asking it of the cosmos in general as much as of Miller.

Miller was not a man given to hasty, unequivocal statements. He said, 'You think about it.'

Frank said, 'I'm thinking about it.'

'Yes, but are you thinking clearly?'

'No,' Frank admitted. 'It could just possibly be that I'm not.'

'Then let me do some of your thinking for you. First thing you do is get the guy to take a blood test. From what I hear, swallowing semen is a comparatively low-risk activity so far as AIDS is concerned. And Leo doesn't look to me like a drug user or a fruit.'

'I guess not,' said Frank.

'Leo strikes me as an okay guy.'

'An okay guy!?' Frank raged.

He thought of screaming again but what good would it do? There seemed a great many opinions you might hold about Leo, but the idea that he was an 'okay guy' was not one he'd considered. Still, he was paying this bastard Miller good money, he might as well listen to what the asshole had to say.

Miller said, 'We live in a secular age.'

'I know! I know!!' said Frank beginning to shake. So here was another jerk who wanted to discuss religion. 'So what? So fucking what?'

'Please be calm,' Miller said, and for a moment Frank glimpsed something in his dignified manner that was genuinely calming. 'So. We live in a secular age. Spirituality is in short supply. Leo here is not your typical, indifferent, clock-watching employee. He wants to give. He wants to give of his body and spirit. I think we ought to respect that.'

'He wants to give of his sperm as well as his body and spirit,' said Frank.

'Sperm can be regarded as a very spiritual substance,' Miller continued, 'depending on your beliefs. And Leo has been generous enough with his. I don't have to talk to you about the Eucharist, do I, Mr Marcel? I don't have to lecture you about transubstantiation, surely.'

'No you don't,' said Frank, but that was because he didn't want to be lectured, not because he knew much about transubstantiation.

'Leo may not be Jesus Christ,' said Miller, 'but he's doing his best.'

Frank found his glass empty. He poured himself another Jim Beam. He didn't offer Miller one. He was coming to the conclusion that Miller was as crazy as Leo.

'I don't know,' said Frank.

'That's right,' said Miller, 'you don't. So after the blood test you consult a tame lawyer. I guess you have plenty of those in the Golden Boy organisation. Find out exactly what the legal position is on this.'

'You think jerking off into other people's food may be legal?'

'Well I don't think it's likely to be a capital offence. It mightn't be more than a misdemeanour. Just so long as our boy isn't diseased.'

'I'm not diseased!' Leo called out across the restaurant.

'The other thing to consider is whether it's wise to change a winning formula.'

'Huh?' said Frank.

'Leo's recipes work. People like the food at this restaurant. You didn't get complaints, did you? Nobody ever said, "Hey this food tastes of sperm, take it away," did they?'

'That's not the point,' said Frank.

'It's precisely the point,' said Miller. 'So the food contains a mystery ingredient. Lose the mystery ingredient and maybe you lose your customers. Remember what happened when they changed the recipe for Coke.'

'Oh Jesus,' said Frank.

It was a heartfelt blasphemy. It was a cry that any of us might make if we found ourselves stuck in a restaurant in the early hours of the morning in the presence of madmen. Frank's anguish was compounded by the fact that he was beginning to think Miller might just be talking sense.

'I need to talk to my son about this,' he said.

Scenes from a History of the Everlasting Club.
Number Four: The Miracle.

At night in the wrecked fuselage of the Fairchild F 227 the sixteen Uruguayan boys described to each other magnificent meals they had eaten or one day planned to eat. They described meals their mothers had cooked, meals eaten in expensive restaurants, their favourite desserts, their favourite foreign dishes. They tried to remember all the restaurants they had visited in Montevideo and came up with nearly a hundred. They devised exotic menus, invented new recipes, imagined colossal feasts and banquets. They recalled the most exotic and unusual food they had ever eaten, but here there would have been little room for debate. These survivors of the air crash were sustaining themselves by eating the flesh of their fellow travellers who had died in the air crash or the subsequent avalanche.

Before very long they decided that thinking and talking about food was nothing more than an exquisite form of torture, whetting appetites they could not hope to satisfy, stirring up saliva and gastric juices that could only go to waste. So they turned to other matters. They discussed theology instead. After all, the rugby team to which the boys belonged was called the Old Christians XV.

Their theology was not very sound. They compared themselves with Christ and the disciples at the Last Supper. Each mouthful of flesh they ate was a kind of communion. The bodies of the dead were giving them physical life in much the same way that the body of Christ gave them spiritual life.

Of course, in reality this was not so much theology as self-justification. Clearly they did not eat human flesh for the sheer hell of it. They ate it because they had to if they were going to survive. But they also needed to believe that their survival was sanctioned by God.

They had salvaged only modest rations from the aircraft wreckage; eight bars of chocolate, five bars of nougat, a packet of biscuits, three jars of jam, two tins of mussels, a few caramels, some dates and dried plums, and a tin of salted almonds. To drink they had eight bottles of wine, a bottle of crème de menthe, a bottle of cherry brandy, and a bottle and a hip flask of whisky.

Clearly this was never going to be able to sustain the twenty-eight original survivors for very long. It seemed that if they were not rescued within a day or two they would surely starve to death. But days passed, rescue did not come, and the flesh of the dead, conveniently preserved in the mountain's snow and ice, became increasingly appetising.

In the beginning there were aesthetic considerations. At first they had only eaten strips of flesh cut off the dead bodies with razor blades, then dried in the sun so they resembled nothing human. This delicacy did not last. By the end they were eating livers and lungs, gnawing on the bones of arms and fingers, even sampling testicles and penises. They made a sort of stew from intestines, fat and brains, and they ate it out of bowls made from human skulls.

Not least of the boys' problems was constipation. Human flesh is in no sense a balanced diet. In turn they would squat over a large hole they had dug at the front of the aircraft, and try very hard to shit into it. They had little or no success. They began to bet on who would be the last to go. The 'winner' finally excreted a small, black, dry turd after thirty-four days.

Nor were the boys very neat in their eating habits. When the helicopters finally came to rescue them, there were bits of human body scattered wildly all round the aircraft. They not only had no qualms about their cannibalism, they had no table manners either.

Once saved however, they became consumed by two things: the need to confess and the need to be understood. Priests told them there was nothing to confess, that they had committed no sin. They had broken a taboo but nothing more. The 'theology' here was simple. The bodies were nothing more than meat. The person who lived in that body was dead; his spirit had gone. There was therefore no moral objection whatsoever to eating this flesh. Whether they were understood is a different question. There are those who might insist they would rather die than eat human flesh, but the story of these boys' survival in the Andes suggests that we might all do what they did given the same circumstances.

At home the boys' families had been praying for their safe delivery. Only the prayers of sixteen families were answered, and one would have to ask whether these sixteen survivors were the most righteous, the most favoured by God, and whether their families were the most devout; and if not, why not. Twenty-nine people had not returned, at least not alive. One might argue, and some did, that the act of eating the dead was an act of incorporation. Their flesh had become the flesh of the survivors.

It was said that only a miracle could allow *any* of the people on that flight to survive, and to have a son return after ten weeks lost in the Andes must have seemed miraculous indeed. There were even those who suggested that their sons had received manna from heaven in much the same way that the Jews had received it in the wilderness, that 'manna' was some coded reference to, some euphemism for, human flesh.

It is said that the experience on that mountain had a profound but deleterious effect on the lives of the survivors. Some felt they had been through a mystical experience and had a duty to convey that experience to others. Surely, they thought, there must be some reason for their being spared. It seems to us that a person might become confused and tortured indeed trying to fathom that 'reason'.

Certainly the rest of those boys' lives would inevitably seem a little tame, a little undramatic after all they had been through. One wonders if, in some curious way, they might have begun to feel nostalgia for the shared suffering they went through. One wonders if, having forced themselves to acquire a taste for human flesh, they might not every now and then hunger for it once more.

None of the sixteen Uruguayan survivors of the crash has ever expressed any desire to become part of the Everlasting Club, but if they did, their applications would certainly be looked at most sympathetically.

FIVE

After a couple of hundred miles Virgil felt quite at home behind the wheel of the Mercedes. It wasn't really his kind of car. It was too adult and sober, too Germanic. In a big city it was reasonably anonymous but out in the sticks it was recklessly conspicuous. But what the hell, Virgil had never been a fugitive before. He was finding it kind of fun.

'Where shall we go?' he had asked Rose.

'Leave this to me,' she replied. 'I'm going to show you England. You're going to taste it. I'm going to put some English flesh on those ribs.'

'Sounds good.'

So began Virgil's gastronomic tour of mainland Britain, with Rose as his guide. This was the kind of adventure Virgil liked; driving off who knew where, with a new girl, with the promise of lots of food, drink and sex. A strange country and a purloined car added savour. It was apparently an unorganised tour, with many crossings and recrossings, some dead-ends and some doublings back. It appeared eccentric, without logic, based only on Rose's idiosyncrasies and strange tastes.

As they drove, Rose insisted on singing. She didn't sing very well but Virgil might not have minded that if the songs had been different. As it was, they all centred around food. Rose sang, 'Food Glorious Food', 'The Roast Beef of Old England', 'I've got a Lovely Bunch of Coconuts'. Sometimes he would try to break in and sing a few songs of his own. He felt no real urge to sing but he wanted a break from Rose's voice. He tried a few Elvis Costello songs, something by Tom Waits, but it didn't bring much relief. Rose was soon back in full voice.

There were songs about boiled beef and carrots, about winkles, and one in which Rose insisted she'd never seen a straight banana. There was a song about the varying pronunciations of 'tomato'. There was a song with political overtones that said a hungry man was an

81

angry man. There was one that told him wild strawberries were only seven francs a kilo, but he wasn't sure if that was a good price or not. She sang about brown sugar and her boy lollipop and her little stick of Blackpool rock.

Virgil thought he had an obsessive on his hands. He started to wonder exactly what sort of trip this was going to be.

Kingsley and Butterworth were much on his mind at first. He wondered whether Kingsley was seriously hurt, whether Butterworth had told the police, whether every squad car in England was on the lookout for him. But it didn't cause him much grief. If the police picked him up he'd say it was all a simple misunderstanding. He would deny completely that he'd hit Kingsley, and he would explain the taking of the car by saying he'd assumed the Mercedes had been put at his disposal for the duration of his stay. He'd overestimated the Everlasting Club's hospitality, that's all. And Kingsley was the kind of drunk who could fall over and hit his head on the ground without any help from Virgil.

The English fuzz surely wouldn't want to jail the son of the owner of one of America's finest family restaurant chains, not when he'd been invited to the country by a bunch of hardcore Establishment swells. At the very worst, if they caught him, surely all they'd do would be kick him out of the country with 'undesirable alien' stamped on his passport. He thought deportation might have a certain cachet among his L.A. set. So Virgil didn't worry. He wasn't the worrying kind.

Rose and Virgil spent nights at small bed and breakfast places. The idea was Rose's rather than Virgil's. His tastes ran to sleazy motels or international hotels, and in the absence of these he'd have gone for English country houses straight out of the tour brochures; black and white Shakespearean arrangements, with peacocks on the lawn and roast beef and game pie on the menu. But Rose assured him that all that stuff was hopelessly ersatz and that by doing things her way he would see and taste the real England.

So he woke each morning in a small, square room, the walls of which were papered with flowers and foliage. There was always a carpet and a counterpane that almost matched. There was an improbably small sink in the corner of the room, and a shower and bath (which were only to be found some distance away down a dim corridor) had to be shared with some pasty-faced English holidaymakers, or, worse still, some of Virgil's own countrymen.

Then there were the breakfasts. Virgil preferred the beds, narrow and undulating though they were, to the English breakfasts. He and Rose sat in small dining-rooms that had circular tables positioned too close together, and they were served slowly and ineptly. Virgil found he had too much choice. He didn't know if he wanted tomato or grapefruit or orange juice. He knew he didn't want muesli or Weetabix or Shredded Wheat, but it took him a day or two to learn that he didn't want porridge either. Eggs were always a danger area, in any form. The soft-boiled eggs were always hard. The scrambled eggs could be grainy or foamy or slimy or completely solid. Fried eggs were always greasy and usually burned and crinkly at the edges. There were tomatoes that had been casually mutilated by frying or grilling. Kippers were a new, unsuspected horror, and smoked haddock was a lurid, leaking yellow thing, sometimes made worse by being adorned with a wet poached egg. The bacon and mushrooms he could usually deal with and he developed an unexpected taste for fried white bread.

But breakfast was not the only meal of the day, by no means. In Harrogate they found a restaurant for lunch that offered a 'taste of Yorkshire'. This turned out to be Yorkshire pudding presented in a number of more or less unusual ways. It came harmlessly enough as a starter with gravy and onions. It came as a main course, a pudding eight or ten inches in diameter and filled with stew or chicken supreme or, as Virgil was unfortunate enough to order, with seafood. Then it came as a dessert, filled with lemon curd or home-made raspberry vinegar.

They reeled out of that restaurant and had to spend a couple of hours immobile in the public gardens before they were ready to face Betty's Famous Tea-rooms. They ate Yorkshire curd tart, which seemed authentic enough, but there were a number of Frenchified pastries to be had, including a *citron bâteau*, which Rose very firmly prevented Virgil from ordering.

Each morning they would drive to the nearest town and Rose would buy some local specialities. These might be Eccles cakes or Bath buns or Kentish huffkins, depending on how far their tour had got.

In Ilkley, Virgil parked and Rose took him, and a pack of sandwiches, up on the moor. He had thought moors were more rugged and wild than this, and freer of other people having picnics, but he went along with it. This was England after all; quaint, old-fashioned, overpopulated, utterly incomprehensible. Rose sang to him again, this time 'On Ilkla' Moor Baht 'At', which she also translated for him. It seemed like the old story; love, death and cannibalism, how a king might pass through the guts of a beggar. Virgil felt they didn't write them like that any more, and he was glad.

In Blackpool they went to a Yates Wine Lodge and drank draught champagne. Afterwards they had oysters in a little oyster bar on the seafront; Virgil's favourite food. There was no lemon juice or Tabasco sauce, so they made do with salt and vinegar. They ate whelks and cockles and crab sticks from a stall. Virgil had his first taste of jellied eels, unwarned by Rose about the presence of bones. He thought he might have been able to handle the bones *or* the jelly, but both together had him gagging. Rose had promised him candy floss at the Pleasure Beach but today for some reason there was none to be had. So they tried their luck with a pineapple ring coated in chocolate, dipped in hundreds and thousands and mounted on a stick.

They rounded off their day in Blackpool with fish and chips, bread and butter and a pot of tea. Again there was no lemon, but there was plenty of vinegar and salad cream. The place they ate in was sad, not very clean. The waitress was as sullen as everybody else in Blackpool. The fish and chips, however, were pretty good. Virgil thought he might be developing a taste for batter.

Dealing with waiters and waitresses was sometimes a problem. Rose was the uncomplaining sort. Back home Virgil was known for being expansively, back-slappingly friendly with waiters, then turning viciously and irrationally angry if the slightest thing didn't suit him. In England his friendliness was spurned. The waiters weren't to be deceived. The waitresses thought he was trying to pick them up. Oddly this wasn't the case. And when food arrived Virgil could never be sure if he had grounds for complaint or not. Those fish heads staring up at him out of a star-gazey pie must surely have been put there deliberately, but that didn't necessarily stop him wanting to complain.

'Is this for real?' he would say very loudly, addressing Rose, the serving staff, the other customers, the walls of the restaurant. Their lack of response assured him that it was, so he would shut up and eat it.

He had thought toad-in-the-hole might be some not too distant relation of frogs' legs, and he expressed his surprise and alarm in a kind of hysterical, derisive laughter when the thing itself was served. By contrast, he thought the term 'pig's trotters' must be some kind of folk term for pork casserole and was left speechless when served with actual pig's trotters.

Some traditional dishes sounded fine and proved to be so. Norfolk turkey and leg of lamb with mint sauce, Dover sole and saddle of venison all lived up to their reputations and to Virgil's expectations.

They went to Wales and experienced cawl, laverbread and Anglesey eggs. In Scotland he had no trouble eating haggis, stovies or Cullen skink. He still had trouble with porridge, however, and when it crept up on him disguised under the name of Highland Brose and containing cream, honey and whisky, it was transformed into a powerful emetic.

He sometimes felt the need for an emetic, to empty his stomach, to make room for more food. Even by Virgil's standards (though not, he suspected, by those of the Everlasting Club) the consumption on this jaunt was a little excessive. Virgil spent most of his days feeling bloated, dyspeptic and crapulous. He was even putting on weight.

He was also becoming confused. Every day he would be confronted by half a dozen food items he really liked, and by half a dozen he detested. But he could never tell in advance which was going to be which. When a Bakewell pudding was set before him he didn't know whether it was going to be delicious or loathsome. He didn't know if it was going to be sweet or savoury, fish or fowl. Would there be something vile and acrid lurking in the middle of a Derbyshire fidget? Was there a mysterious and stomach-turning ingredient waiting to hijack his tongue as he bit into a Wiltshire lardy cake?

He was becoming geographically disorientated, too. The topography of England had always been a mystery to him, but driving around it with Rose wasn't making it any clearer. She navigated and he drove anywhere she told him to go, pushing on into a landscape of narrow country roads and jammed motorways. Names meant nothing to him, except when Rose pointed out their connections with food. 'Pontefract, that's where the cakes come from.' 'Colchester, famous for its oysters.' 'Dunmow, that's where they have the flitch.' He found the Dunmow flitch particularly perplexing. He became lost and adrift. If he was eating a pasty this must be Cornwall.

There was drink, too. My God, there was drink. The beers, which he gradually found more drinkable, all had whacko names: Stag, Old Peculiar, Wee Heavy. There were English wines which were as weird as anything he'd drunk at the Everlasting Club. The Scotch whiskys were fine. Many of them he'd heard of and some of them were even available in the States. The cider was okay as well. But he really didn't know about mild ale, nor about lager and lime, and what, for the love of God, was this stuff they called mead?

Often Virgil was a little drunk as he drove. He didn't mind that. He was used to it. The drink gave him confidence and he needed confidence to take on the English traffic. All the roads seemed too narrow for the size of the cars. Other people's driving was neurotic and unpredictable. A little alcohol in the bloodstream enabled him to float above the neurosis until it was time for more food and drink.

Before long, the sheer Britishness of all he consumed began to weigh heavily on Virgil. He had never been much of an anglophile, certainly not where food was concerned, but Rose was determined he wouldn't eat anything that didn't have a British pedigree. What was this all about, he asked. Diet as a form of racial purity? Sometimes he wished his next meal might be Italian or Greek or Mexican and that he might be drinking grappa or ouzo or tequila. Not that he really had any wishes about food and drink any more. He was increasingly passive. The food was delivered and he ate it. Sometimes it seemed that he was delivered to the food.

The only distraction Rose allowed was sex. Virgil had always known that sex was not a reliable indicator of anything. Good sex could happen between people who didn't like each other. Bad sex could happen between the best of friends. He wasn't the best of friends with Rose. In fact, he was beginning to think he didn't even like her. He thought they maybe had enough in common to sustain a fling for a week or so, but he was getting bored. This was nothing unusual. Virgil soon got bored with girls, with girls he'd seen much less of than he had of Rose. They had been travelling for two weeks now, two weeks shut up in a car, or a bed and breakfast joint, or a restaurant, doing nothing more than eat, drink, drive and fuck.

Not that there was anything boring about the sex. No way. Rose had a sexual repertoire and imagination that was still giving Virgil plenty of surprises. Somewhere in the Lake District (of all places) she managed to find a shop selling chocolate penises. She bought several, in different flavours, plain and milk and white chocolate, one flavoured bitter orange, and one with a white fondant centre that oozed all over her lips as she bit its head off.

Then, when they were in Northumberland, she visited a high-class butcher, that's what Virgil read on the window, and came out with a batch of extravagantly shaped and textured sausages. They took them back to their room and Rose spread them out on the bed, like a sniper setting out his armoury. They were mottled and tawny, or black and creased, or smooth and taut.

'The saveloy is the English version of cervelat, or brain sausage, though today it may well contain lights, rind and pig cheek, flavoured with white pepper and young sage leaves. The red tinge is caused by saltpetre,' she said, sounding like a textbook.

And she lifted up her skirt, no knickers, and pushed it into herself. Virgil didn't know what textbook this was out of. She dealt similarly with a straight black pudding and a gerty meat pudding, but the pride of the collection was a huge Aberdeen sausage. 'Twelve solid inches of minced mutton, bacon fat and oatmeal,' she said to Virgil. She had a little trouble accommodating this one, but her face suggested that the trouble was worthwhile.

Boring it wasn't, but at moments like these Virgil did wonder what precisely he was doing in this strange country, far from home, watching some strange woman impaling herself on a sausage. There was a bit of a thrill to it all, a welcome feeling of being outside regular parameters, of doing things that would scandalise the average client of the Golden Boy. That was okay, and yet a doubt lingered. Was this healthy? Was this sane? Would it all lead him into places and spaces darker and more dangerous than he would wish to visit? Had his sense of adventure been so rapidly exhausted? Was he maybe feeling homesick?

Rose continued to make sketches as they travelled. She would draw the drab little rooms in which they stayed, the view through the window, the street, the scenery, Virgil. And she set up still-lifes of the food she bought for them to eat, and sketched it all meticulously.

Virgil thought things might have gone too far when Rose went to a small local supermarket and came back with chocolate spread, peanut butter, Rice Krispies, raisins and food colouring and mixed them all together to form a thick, stiff, faecal product. She then took lumps of the mixture and rolled them out between her fingers to form thick cylinders which she carefully moulded so they resembled (there was no doubting the intention or the effect) turds. Of course, the smell was perfectly wholesome and no doubt they wouldn't have tasted at all like shit, not that Virgil knew what shit tasted like, but the visual effect was enough for him to decline fiercely when Rose tried to feed him one of these delicacies. She seemed surprised. She ate one herself to show how easily it might be done, but Virgil's lips were sealed.

Later that same day, having overeaten on a rather good lemon sole served with buttered hops, they returned to their room with a bottle of port and some Stilton.

'I've had enough,' said Virgil.

'Oh well, wait a while. Have some Stilton later.'

'I'm not only talking about port and Stilton,' said Virgil. 'I've had enough, period.'

'Enough food and drink?'

'Enough food and drink, enough driving round the country going nowhere special. Enough of you and me.'

Rose looked disappointed, not with the disappointment of a rejected lover, but rather with the disappointment of someone whose plans had gone wrong.

'Why exactly?' she asked.

'Who knows? Who cares? Look kid, it's been great but hey, you can have too much of a good thing. I feel like I need a long session in a health farm.'

'And you're bored with me.'

'Not exactly,' he said.

He was being unusually gentle. His customary technique was to tell girls to get the fuck out of his life.

'I mean, I don't even know you,' he said, 'and yet here we are shut up together every hour of the day and night for two weeks . . .'

'You need space.'

'Some cliché like that.'

Rose didn't say anything but she was obviously thinking hard. Virgil couldn't figure what about. Was she going to scream at him for being a user and a slimeball? He could handle that. He'd handled that before. Or was she going to beg and plead and do the weeping woman act on him? That was tougher to deal with but Virgil had been there too. Or maybe she was going to try something else, like pregnancy, although surely there hadn't been time, or a suicide threat, or like gently letting him know that her brother was a member of a death squad.

Instead she said, 'No, Virgil, I can't let you go.'

This was a vocabulary he didn't understand.

'Come on, babe,' he said, 'I can't go on, it's that simple. I'm sick to my stomach of too much food. I have a permanent hangover. I throw up twice a day. I have diarrhoea. I have heartburn. My cock's sore from all the sex. I'm getting fat. Give me a break.'

'I still can't let you go.'

'What are you talking about?'

'I'm not allowed to let you go. I can't let you out of my sight. I'm your guardian angel. I've got to stay with you for two more weeks. It's my job.'

'What fucking job? What are you talking about?'

'I'm being paid to stick with you for a month.'

So one of his premonitions had been right. She *was* a professional, though he still didn't know a professional what.

'Who's paying you?'

'The Everlasting Club, of course.'

'The Everlasting Club are paying you to stick with me?'

'That's right.'

'What? I don't believe this. But hey, it's okay, I don't need to believe it and I sure as hell don't need anybody sticking with me. Okay? Fuck this.'

'Sorry, Virgil, you have no choice.'

'What do you mean, no choice? I'm walking out of here right now. That's it.'

'No, Virgil, that isn't one of the options.'

'Options? What language are we speaking here? What is this? Am I supposed to be a hostage, or what?'

'Nothing like that, Virgil. You're on the end of some enforced hospitality, that's all. It's my job to be your guide and hostess for four weeks, to take you round Britain, fill you full of good British food, maybe fatten you up a little. Every day I phone the club, speak to Mr Kingsley, tell him where we are. It's a living. But there's still two weeks to go.'

'Why?' Virgil asked. 'In God's name why?'

'I don't know. I only work here.'

'And if I run away?'

'Then I understand it gets tricky. I think then they tell the police that you beat up Kingsley and stole the car, and I'm supposed to say that you abducted me and made me do disgusting things with sausages. It won't look good.'

'I though I was dealing with a gentleman's club. You make 'em sound like the PLO.'

Rose smiled sweetly. 'It will only be for two more weeks.'

'And at the end of those two weeks?' Virgil demanded. 'What happens then?'

'Look, Virgil, I don't really know anything about all this, but I think that at the end of the month you're a fully paid-up member of the club, that's all.'

'Fucking great. Just what I always wanted.'

'I think this is like an initiation. But I could be wrong. Nobody tells me much.'

'I don't want to be initiated. I don't want anything to do with those mothers.'

'They obviously want to have something to do with you. And so do I.'

Rose smiled again. It was meant to be persuasive. It was meant to say she wanted him, maybe even loved him a little, but Virgil was having none of it. He didn't know who was paying for the smile.

'They've paid me quite a lot of money,' Rose said, 'and I really need that money and I'm going to be in all sorts of trouble if I fail. You don't want me to get into trouble, do you?'

'I really don't give a shit what you get into.'

Virgil paced around the small, square bedroom. Now he did want some of that port. He took a big swig from the bottle. All sorts of questions about his situation started to trouble him.

'Hold on a minute, this doesn't work. You're being paid to stick with me, but it was me who picked you up.'

'It was meant to seem like that. You came over to my table in the cafeteria, but if you hadn't then I'd have come over to yours. I wasn't in that place just by chance.'

'What if I hadn't wanted to get picked up?'

'They told me you weren't very discriminating.'

'Jesus, it was all a set-up, wasn't it? And having me hit Kingsley, and Butterworth giving me the keys to the car, that must all have been a set-up too, so they had something on me, so that I'd start running.'

'I suppose so,' said Rose. 'I hadn't really thought it through.'

'Well think it through, babe, think it through. Very slick. Jesus.'

He took several more gulps of port then slammed the bottle down.

'This is bullshit. I'm calling their bluff. I don't believe you're going to call the police and tell them I abducted you. I don't believe in any of this stuff. I'm out of here. I'm gone.'

'Where are you going, Virgil?'

'I'm going to the nearest airport, get the first plane out of here.'

'You don't have a passport.'

'Of course I have a fucking passport. It's in my bag.'

'I packed your bag, Virgil. I took your passport. I posted it to the Everlasting Club.'

His other premonition, that he was being kidnapped, was starting to look true as well.

'Fuck this!' he yelled.

'I'm sorry, Virgil. I wouldn't be doing this if I wasn't so poor. We're both victims really.'

Virgil wanted to smash something. He wasn't going to smash Rose because he didn't smash women. It was a kind of principle with him. But he'd gladly have smashed Kingsley. He wished he'd hit him harder when he had the chance. And he would have been happy to smash Butterworth, except that Butterworth looked as though he could probably take care of himself. If he'd been in a soulless modern hotel he'd have been happy to smash the room, but there wouldn't have been much satisfaction in smashing this low-budget bed and breakfast dump he found himself in at the moment.

'Face it, Virgil, you're stuck with me for another two weeks. That's not so terrible, is it?'

Virgil was too furious to reply.

'Here,' said Rose, 'here's something you may not have tried before.'

Rose opened her shirt and pulled out one of her breasts. Virgil pretended not to be interested. She began to play with the nipple, giving it a sort of caress, a sort of massage, a sort of tweak. Virgil didn't know what the hell was going on. Slowly, little white globes of milk appeared through the pores and stood out against the pinkness of the nipple. Now he watched with fascination. He'd never seen anything like this before. Rose took Virgil's head and pressed his mouth to her breast. His rough, tired, jaded tongue licked at the milk.

'There, Virgil,' she said. 'You see. It's not going to be so terrible after all.'

Scenes from a History of the Everlasting Club. Number Five: The Milkmaid Cometh.

Dr John Caius, the co-founder of Gonville and Caius College, Cambridge (a college which has provided the Everlasting Club with some of its most enthusiastic members) lies in his narrow bed in his sealed, airless room, an icy sun seeping in through pale, narrow windows. A warmthless fire consumes itself in the grate. The blankets on the bed seem to crush him and yet let his body's heat slip away. Medical texts line the room. A deformed skull, a meticulous drawing of a human hand, foetuses in bottles, serve as decoration.

The good doctor's stomach aches with hunger and emptiness, a hunger he dare not satisfy, an emptiness it will pain him to fill. He cannot quite remember when he last ate solid food, yet the memory of the agony that accompanied his body's attempts to digest it remains vivid. So he is reduced to taking a liquid diet, specifically milk.

Cow's milk, he knows, is very sorry stuff for a sick man. Ass's milk would be better, but he has realised that his illness is too serious and too advanced to be treated with any but the most powerful remedies. Dr Caius is to be fed only on human milk. He has hired a wet-nurse.

A woman's milk, taken directly from the breast without being allowed to cool or become adulterated, should be speeding the return of his powers, and yet this is not the case. He still feels utterly sick and peevish. The nurse is due to come and suckle him within the hour, but he does not view the prospect with pleasure or hope.

She arrives on time, though not a moment early, and bustles into the room undoing her clothing, ladling out her breasts as she comes. One might think she appeared enthusiastic, keen to help an ailing man, but the doctor knows her keenness is only a keenness to be finished. He observes her pockmarks, her pallor, her reddened hands with their split, dirty nails. He sees her face set in a caricature of sullen bad temper. No doubt she has a hard, poor, wretched life, but the doctor does not see why she should revenge her disadvantages upon him. Small wonder that her administrations make him feel no better. It is as though her bad humour, spleen and meanness transmit themselves through her milk and into him. Her spirit is not life-giving, and her breasts do not offer health or cheer.

She heaves her right breast towards the doctor's lips, without generosity. The thickness of a dark burgundy nipple touches his lips. He thinks he can smell mutton and onion sweating out through the woman's rough, white skin. He recalls happier days, days of greater appetite, college feasts of venison and ripe partridge, sturgeon, capon pasties, parsnips roasted in goose fat; and today's offering seems like very sorry, insipid fare.

'Take that thing away from me,' he snaps.

She says nothing. She takes her breast back. She is annoyed. She knows she is only a servant, but she thinks a doctor might have better manners than to call her breast a 'thing', and anyway, it's not as if she wants him to have it. She is perfectly content not to have his thin, papery old lips on her. She refastens her clothing and stares insolently at John Caius, awaiting instructions, ready to give as good as she gets if he says so much as a word to her.

'Thank you for your good offices,' he says. 'But I shall henceforth be dispensing with them.'

She sneers a little, considers how much umbrage she ought to take. She snorts contemptuously, turns and leaves without a word. The doctor starts to feel better already.

It takes a few days to find and employ a new wet-nurse, days when he has to content himself with ass's milk. But at last she is found and hired. She is very young. It saddens the doctor to think how early in life her girlish body must have been subjected to the strains of fornication and childbirth. Her hair is thick and clean. She smells of fresh bread and herbs. She is kind and patient. She holds his head gently and sympathetically as she feeds him. She gives of herself. She seems to fill the room with warmth. Dr Caius feels the generous heat of her flesh against his face. His lips partake eagerly of her goodness and sweet disposition. He can almost believe that his health and youth are flooding back.

The doctor is a sick old man, without much time to live, but this afternoon in his room, his mind full of soothing thoughts and with a pretty young woman suckling him, he feels as content and as alive as most of us will ever feel. And perhaps it is precisely this feeling of being intensely alive while still confronting and living with the knowledge of extinction that is at the very heart of what the Everlasting Club is and does.

It is worth noting too, that the coat of arms of Gonville and Caius College today bears two snakes, symbols of medicine; though they show no signs of eating themselves or each other.

SIX

'So it all worked pretty well,' said Mary.

Leo was lying beside her in Mary's bed. There was a red velour headboard with recessed lights and a built-in radio and CD player. The food of love flooded from the widely-spaced speakers.

'Frank finally picked up on the many hints we dropped,' she said, 'had you followed and saw what you were doing in the kitchen. Perfect.'

'If you say so,' said Leo. 'I guess.'

In fact he guessed quite differently. He didn't think the situation was perfect at all. He had done what Mary had told him to do, and as far as he could see he was now in some danger of being, at best, out of a job, or, at worst, in jail.

'And did they buy all the stuff about you giving of yourself, all the religious and artistic bit?'

'I wouldn't say they bought it exactly,' Leo replied. 'They seemed to believe I meant what I was saying, but they also thought I was crazy.'

'That's fine,' said Mary.

'It's fine for you.'

'No, it's fine for you too, Leo. Really.'

'The only good thing about this,' said Leo, 'is that at least your husband doesn't think we're having an affair.'

'That's what I would call a failure of imagination,' said Mary. 'Frank can only take one revelation on board at a time. He knew you were up to something but he didn't know what. The idea that you might be up to two things at the same time didn't occur to him. Poor Frank.'

Leo buried his face in Mary's soft, sun-bedded breasts. They moulded themselves around his cheeks. It felt safe and homely there.

'I'm glad he didn't find out,' said Leo. 'I wouldn't want to have to give this up.'

'We all have to give up everything in the end,' said Mary.

Leo didn't know what she meant. He said, 'The real thing I hate is that everyone assumes I did it because I've got something against Frank. Especially *he* thinks that. Like I was committing an act of revenge.'

'No, Leo, it was *my* act of revenge.'

'I like you, Mrs Marcel. But I like Frank too. I wish I knew why we were doing this. I wish I knew what we were doing.'

Mary said, 'I don't see why anybody would object to eating semen. They're prepared to eat liver and brains and kidneys. All kidneys do is filter piss all day. And what the hell do they think they're getting when they eat a hamburger or a hotdog?'

'They prefer not to think about it,' said Leo.

'Well maybe they should think about it. If they really thought about it I can't see that they'd object to eating your sperm. Fortunately, Frank did object. And now he's gone to England in search of Virgil, which is just what we wanted.'

Leo wondered who the 'we' was. He felt sure it didn't include him. He had this recurring problem with Mary. She was a great looking older woman and he liked her and she appeared to like him, and they were really good in bed together, but he didn't understand half of what she said to him. And he certainly didn't understand why she'd asked him to masturbate into the food at Trimalchio's and make sure that Frank caught him in the act. He knew she had a taste for intrigue but that didn't really explain anything. Nor did he exactly understand why he'd agreed to do it. It was just that when Mary Marcel asked you to do a thing you did it. She was that kind of woman. Leo had always wanted that kind of woman.

'Why do you want revenge on your husband?' he asked. 'Mr Marcel has always seemed okay to me. What's wrong with him?'

'If you want to know what's wrong with Frank take a look at Virgil. He's the son and heir. It wasn't easy to produce a dumb, spoiled, arrogant little shit like Virgil, but Frank managed it. Is it any wonder I hate the bastard?'

Leo wanted to ask which bastard, Virgil or Frank, but thought it wiser not to. Instead he said, 'I don't think you should hate anybody.'

'Okay, maybe I don't exactly hate Frank,' said Mary, 'but you know, when you and I sat in the Golden Boy together, in that little temple built in Frank's image, with an icon of my son on the roof, and knowing that before long we'd be naked together in bed, hot and sweaty and dirty, well, that felt very good, Leo. That felt like a very satisfactory act of defilement.'

Leo looked blank.

Mary continued, 'And I can't stand the way Frank takes credit for the Golden Boy concept. Who produced the kid? Who ran and got the camera? Who took the photograph? You know *I* did. And what's more I don't even think it's that hot a concept. I know I have a lot to answer for.'

'Behind every successful man,' said Leo.

Mary might once have been happy to believe she was the power behind Frank's throne, but she found that a difficult belief to sustain. All she'd really done was take a photograph. She had certainly married him believing that one day he might be successful and rich, but she supposed all wives believed that about their husbands. Primarily she married him because (it sounded ludicrous now) he had seemed exotic, different, American. He was not the sort of man she was used to meeting in Dartford.

It was 1961. She was twenty-three years old, still living at home with her mother and stepfather, working in a dead-end job as a shop assistant in a department store in Oxford Street. She still had boyfriends but she never met anybody she thought was good enough for her, nobody who was offering her enough. Her girlish dreams were starting to look precisely that; girlish. She was saving herself, but as her mother told her, you could value yourself too highly. You could wait too long for somebody who wasn't on his way, who didn't exist. You could end up on the shelf if you priced yourself at more than the going rate.

She met Frank while she was working in the department store. He was a customer, buying presents to take home to America. He wanted a sweater for his Dad who wasn't in very good health, and a silk square for his Mom. He needed advice and Mary was the shopgirl he approached. She thought he was trying to pick her up. She hoped so.

Frank was not the best-looking man she'd ever known, but he dressed well in thin, elegant black suits. He held his cigarette in an authentic movie actor sort of way that she found sexy. But it was probably the voice, the slow, deep, strong American accent, that convinced her she would marry him.

He never pretended to be anything he wasn't. He said he'd been drifting around, doing nothing much, 'looking for something'. It sounded romantic. He'd been to Paris, to Madrid. He'd loved it all, he said, but he loved London best of all, and he was sorry his time had run out and he had to get back to the States. He never pretended to be rich, but she knew that all Americans were rich by her standards. Anybody who could travel round Europe 'looking for something' wasn't exactly penniless, and anyone whose father owned a restaurant surely wasn't poor.

She only had a few days to convince him to marry her and take her back with him to California. She had to persuade him that she was the something he'd been looking for. She couldn't believe how easy he was to persuade. He wanted desperately to be persuaded. It would feel good to arrive home with his new English bride and show her off to his parents and family. His mother wanted him to be settled. This way he could be settled yet still keep a hint of romance in the shape of his foreign wife, his souvenir of England. Frank and Mary revelled briefly in each other's foreignness and imagined exoticism.

If Mary was soon disappointed by Frank and California, she still thought it was a whole lot better than staying in Dartford. She never once thought of going home to mother. Drive-ins and Chevies and barbecues may have been mundane once you got used to them, but they were still preferable to the Odeons, Morris Minors and fry-ups of home. Then Virgil was born.

She had never liked babies much. They were too demanding, too much trouble. She thought it might all be different with her own child but it proved not to be. She loved Virgil, she supposed, and she would do her duty by him, but she couldn't find him so very fascinating or likeable. She didn't see how women could make a whole life out of having babies and being a mother. She made absolutely sure that she never had another child.

Mary survived. She was never going to be exactly thrilled at spending her life as the wife of the son of the guy who owned the local diner. It was not what she had wanted or imagined, but she would stick it out. She was not a quitter.

When Frank's father died it was almost as if the old man was moving on, making room for his son, giving Frank the chance to thrive and show what he could do. She tried to be encouraging without being pushy, but she never thought Frank was going to be much of a success in the world's terms. That was when she had her first affair. It was with the guy who delivered paper napkins and towels to the restaurant. It wasn't that much fun. Frank was too busy and unobservant to notice. She could see herself sinking into an unexceptional though not uncomfortable life in which convenient, passionless little flings were going to be the major source of entertainment. It terrified her.

And then her whole life got turned around because she happened to take a snapshot of her baby son covered in coleslaw and trying to eat a chicken leg. Frank's success with the Golden Boy chain was completely unexpected and yet she saw it as fulfilling some inevitable destiny, but hers not his. It was extraordinary to be married to the man behind the Golden Boy, but then she had always expected to be extraordinary.

Money meant that she didn't have to work so hard at being a wife and mother. Money provided privacy and distance. Frank went away on business trips. Virgil went to camp and to music or riding or karate lessons. They lived in increasingly large houses where she was able to have rooms to herself, houses big enough that sometimes she would not even know where Frank and Virgil were. She had more territory and more time for her extraordinary self. She had known all along that it would be like this, that she would have the time and leisure to be mysterious and special and just a little dangerous. She was ready now.

She saw Virgil growing up, becoming rich and spoiled, becoming a dull womaniser. She refused to feel responsible. She was glad that he made a success of Trimalchio's. She supposed it was a good thing. But she found it hard to feel any motherly pride just because her son had succeeded in satisfying the foody needs of a bunch of talentless fashion victims who hung around the restaurants of L.A. Liking Virgil was still too hard for her.

And Frank? Well, she had to be a little bit grateful to him. It was, after all, his money that was making her life possible. And no, she didn't hate him, but she soon found him little more than comical. There was nothing special or mysterious or dangerous about him; a serious deficiency.

She said now to Leo, 'And now he's gone chasing after Virgil to discuss you and your activities, just like I knew he would. But the guy's so dumb. He doesn't even know whereabouts in England Virgil is, and it's not as if Virgil ever had a worthwhile opinion on anything.'

'Trimalchio's wouldn't be the same without Virgil,' said Leo.

'I don't need you to defend my own flesh and blood to me, Leo.'

Leo had thought that maybe she did. He said, 'I mean, I'm

confused, I'm unhappy. I don't know what's going to happen to me.'

He used a little-boy-lost tone that he should have learned by now would fail to impress Mary.

'I feel so powerless,' he added. 'I don't even know what I can do to help myself.'

'I know that feeling, Leo.'

'One of the things I guess we ought to do,' he said, 'is organise this surprise party, because if we don't then Frank will know what we've really been doing.'

'Don't worry. I've been working on it.'

'Really? Can I be involved?' Leo liked parties.

'You'll be involved all right. I need you, Leo.'

'How do you need me?'

Even as he said that, Leo was aware this was a question likely to provoke one of Mary's more incomprehensible replies. She thought for a long time.

'Oh Jesus, Leo, I'm so hungry. Hungry for kisses, for sensation.'

He wasn't sure if she was serious or not. He kissed her.

'And what kind of sensations are you hungry for?' he asked.

He stroked her cool upper thigh. He did it slowly, effortlessly, and he had Mary trembling.

'Yes,' she said, 'for that kind of thing. The way to a woman's heart, Leo . . . it's a very indirect route . . . not through her stomach, not through her pussy either, though it's definitely worth a try . . . shit.'

Leo started to make love to her. He towered above her like a chef over his chopping board, ingredients spread out before him. He kneaded soft morsels here and there, rolling items into shape, checking consistencies, tasting for flavour and seasoning. Mary felt herself melting, rising, blending.

'That's really nice, Leo. But you know what I really want.'

He did, from sweet experience. He withdrew. He lay down on his back. Mary brought her mouth down over his penis and provided a slow, teasing, expert blow job (not a thing Frank had ever had much of a taste for). But not too slow and not too teasing because Mary wanted her boy's essence and she wanted it pretty damn soon.

Soon enough a glob of sperm hit the back of her throat. She didn't swallow. She wanted to run it round her mouth for a while and taste all those flavours; oysters, rubber, salt, zinc, Leo. But mostly it tasted precisely of sperm. At last she swallowed, knowing that the flavour would be with her for the rest of the day. She felt less hungry than she had for some time.

'You know, Leo,' she said, 'if Frank doesn't appreciate your efforts in the kitchen, I know people who will.'

Scenes from a History of the Everlasting Club.
Number Six: The Less Simple Pieman.

There is a huddled mass in the hall of Hanover railway station tonight, this pale, thin night in the winter of 1919; a displaced, dispossessed, rootless rabble. They are poor and hungry. They ache and cough with undiagnosed diseases. They gather their blankets and children and their few possessions around them. Police wander the hall, demanding to see papers, demonstrating their power, their fickleness, their unpredictability. They allow nobody to feel comfortable. And these police have friends among the crowd, informers who are more dangerous and threatening than the police themselves.

Right now two policemen, both young, lean and roughly handsome, are talking with a large, fat, coarse yet well-dressed man. All three look around the crowd with great interest, pointing out faces, laughing without pleasure. It can be seen that most of their interest is reserved for young boys. The man who is not a policeman, whose name is Fritz Haarmann, detaches himself from the other two and strides to a far corner of the hall where a face has caught his eye. He looks wicked and unstable.

He selects a boy from the throng. His victim looks very young, has a soft face hardened by the war; but ages are hard to determine in these hungry, uncertain times. He has dirty red hair, his face is stained, possibly with tears. He sits on the ground, knees pulled up to his chest, head leaning against a stone pillar, his eyes looking away at nothing.

Haarmann is standing beside him now. He towers over him. He taps his black, polished shoes on the station floor. He says, 'Papers.' He speaks quietly. The boy doesn't answer. His mind is somewhere else, somewhere warmer and more hospitable. Haarmann brings him back by kicking him hard in the flank. The lack of flesh means that the toe of the shoe makes sickening contact with thin, brittle bones. There's no resistance, no solidity. The boy topples over, collapses like a sack of old clothes. Haarmann says, 'Papers,' again and the boy pulls the tattered, begrimed proof of his existence from his coat pocket.

Haarmann learns that he is called Peter, that he is fourteen years old and that he is a long way from his home in Augsburg. The papers are in order.

'Do you have a mother and father, Peter?'

'No.'

'Or friends in Hanover?'

'No.'

'Then why have you come here?'

'I was told things were better here.'

Haarmann puts on a sympathetic face.

'They lied to you, Peter. Possibly they told you there was work and food and shelter. They were wrong. Look around you. Our food shortages are as great as in any town in Germany.'

Peter looks at Haarmann. He is plump and smooth. He has found some way round these shortages.

'When did you last eat, Peter?'

'Two days ago.'

'Probably you ate potatoes or a turnip or stale bread.'

Peter is uncertain whether he should agree, establish his utter wretchedness and try to extract sympathy, or whether he should pretend to be better off than he is, to pretend that he ate fruit and pastry and stews and roasts. He would like to be able to retain his dignity. But he knows the man would not believe him. So he nods.

'There are ways round these shortages,' says Haarmann, 'for those who are clever, for those who are realists. Do you know what a realist is? I haven't gone hungry these years. I'm not hungry now, and I don't intend to go hungry in the future. I'm a pragmatist. Do you know what a pragmatist is?'

Peter does not answer, though of course he doesn't.

'I run a cookshop,' Haarmann continues. 'When other butchers and cookshops are empty I always have a source of supply; the best meat, the finest cuts, the choicest liver and kidneys, the very best sausages and pies full of goodness and flavour, dripping with gravy and juices. What do you say to that, Peter? Am I making your mouth water?'

What can Peter say? Hearing about food is an intense form of torture. He says to Haarmann, 'You're very lucky.'

Haarmann replies, 'We make our own luck. Are you a lucky young man? Do you have a girlfriend?'

Peter thinks he must have missed a step in the conversation. The notion of boyfriend and girlfriend is meaningless to him. There is no love in the streets of Hanover these days. He shakes his head.

Haarmann continues, 'Perhaps you don't like girls. Perhaps you prefer boys.'

Peter says nothing. If the man is a police informer perhaps all he wants is for Peter to confess to some nameless crime, then the police will arrest him and perhaps they will give Haarmann a reward, and perhaps that is how he can afford to keep himself in meat. Perhaps confessing to not having a girlfriend is one such nameless crime.

'Don't look so worried,' says Haarmann. 'You need have no worries in Hanover on that score. We're very understanding here. There are cafés and clubs for men who like other men. There are drag balls for those who crave that sort of thing. Do you know what a drag ball is, Peter?'

'No,' says Peter.

'Your education is lacking. Perhaps I could educate you.'

Peter looks sadly at the ground. He thinks he is beginning to understand.

'Look, Peter,' says Haarmann, 'your story has moved me greatly. I don't like to see a young man down on his luck, out in the street, penniless, starving. I'm a soft-hearted man really. Come back to my shop with me. I have food and a clean bed. Let's get you cleaned and fed, get some meat on your bones.'

Peter gets up. He thinks he knows the nature of the bargain he's made. It doesn't seem so bad. People do worse things when they're hungry, even when they're not. They return to Haarmann's cookshop. Haarmann unlocks a vast, forbidding padlock. Inside there is indeed the smell of cooked meat, warm, highly seasoned and appetising. Probably it is horse or dog, but Peter has no objection to that. In the streets they are eating diseased rats and mice. Haarmann chooses a couple of steaks from the meat locker and says he will prepare them while Peter bathes.

Peter stands wet and naked in the zinc bath as Haarmann brings him extra water. Of course, Haarmann wants to touch. His hands move over Peter's thin, hungry body. His lips kiss the neck and shoulders. Peter is almost numb to it. But it soon stops. A few strokes and kisses is all Haarmann appears to want. Or is he merely whetting his appetite?

Haarmann even provides clothes. They are more Peter's size than Haarmann's and they are very fine; a silk shirt, an embroidered waistcoat. Peter doesn't see how he could walk the streets of Hanover dressed in these, but for now, within these walls, it seems to be part of the game, the right sort of fancy dress, and it gives Haarmann pleasure, and giving Haarmann pleasure is Peter's means to a full stomach.

They eat. The steaks are a little tough and fatty but Peter devours them as though they are the food of the gods. His shrunken stomach doesn't seem to have room for all this meat. It starts to hurt, but this is too good to miss, and he doesn't know when he'll eat again, so he forces it down whatever the discomfort.

And then the other half of the bargain, the bill. Haarmann undresses. He has a loose, white body. He pulls Peter's fine clothes from him. He bends Peter over the table. He fucks him. It doesn't take long, and although it hurts a little, Peter grits his teeth, doesn't cry out, accepts. Then Haarmann starts again, kissing Peter's throat, nibbling it. Peter feels the teeth making lovebites under his chin, chewing his flesh, bruising it. Then Haarmann gets down to business. He tears Peter's throat out with his teeth. The boy is too weak to put up much of a fight. He keels over, blood pulsing from his neck, like a slaughtered beast. Haarmann crouches over the body. He looks like a wolf, a vampire, something only partly human.

In 1924, Fritz Haarmann is found guilty of murdering, of biting to death, at least twenty-seven young men he has picked up on the streets of Hanover. He has converted all their bodies to meat, pies and sausages, and sold them in his cookshop to the grateful citizens of Hanover. Among his papers police are surprised to find an invitation embossed with the design of a snake consuming its tail, an invitation to join the Everlasting Club.

SEVEN

John Kingsley would always say he was not interested in money, in much the same way that he might say he wasn't interested in politics or sex. He didn't think of himself as being materialistic, and he did not for a moment think he was rich. He considered himself, if anything, to be generally a bit strapped for cash. The upkeep of his Mayfair apartment was considerable. The running expenses of the Bentley were colossal yet somehow necessary. His bar bills from the Everlasting Club were heroically ruinous.

His was old money. It came out of the heart of England, originally out of farming and property, and only latterly out of trade. Kingsley could trace his family and their money back to the fifteenth century. Vast acreages of Lincolnshire had brought forth crops and cattle, and been turned into a fortune that had been consolidated and increased through careful husbandry. The family had thrived and aspired and was now well connected with the City, the law, the media, even the army. The Kingsleys' was an unostentatious wealth. It brought with it responsibilities. The Kingsley family was prudent. They loathed show and waste. Kingsley felt the weight of responsibility perhaps a little less than his ancestors. He wasn't intending to fritter his money away, but he wanted to have some fun with it.

From the earliest days he had known he was an outsider. At prep school and public school he had always encountered gangs and cliques from which he was barred. He had been bad at sport, academically uninspired, and had lacked the charm or resilience to make his outsider status work for him.

He became a loner. It was not what he would have chosen and yet it suited him. He would have liked to 'belong' but he knew of no group that would claim him as their own. He would have been dismayed at this time to be told that he was privileged or that he belonged to any manner of ruling class. He was on the receiving end of a certain number of beatings, a certain amount of bullying. He could see that one or two others suffered more than he did, but that was little consolation. He tried to pretend that his misfortunes were happening to someone else. Sometimes he wished he might be invisible. Sometimes he wished he could cease to be.

He had always been fat. He knew there were no advantages in that state. It gave others an easy opportunity for attack. Fatness was a marker of slowness, dimness, and, eventually, of sexual unattractiveness. He had never wanted to be sexually attractive within the school world of pashes and tarts, but a time came when he looked beyond his school and he knew he wanted to be attractive to women. He wanted to be dashing and clean cut and handsome. It was about then, while still a schoolboy, that he began to go bald.

He was eighteen when he hired his first prostitute. He knew he would never lose his virginity by any more 'natural' means. She was not much older than him and her trade name was Gloria. She dressed and spoke rather well. She appeared to have breeding and she was very expensive, though Kingsley was then entirely ignorant of the market rate. Nevertheless, he got what he paid for. She was sympathetic and skilled and unhurried. Kingsley, somewhat to his surprise, found himself perfectly capable in matters of sexual intercourse. His erection was adequate, his staying power good, and his gymnastic ability very impressive for someone of his size and build.

At this time Kingsley's two favourite authors were P. G. Wodehouse and the Marquis de Sade. Between them, it seemed to him, they might have written the story of his life. He saw himself as part Bertie Wooster (though he had no Jeeves) and part the Duc de Blangis, from *One Hundred and Twenty Days of Sodom*. He knew the world saw him as a silly ass, a grinning, harmless, overgrown schoolboy who would have been perfectly at home in a world of country houses, maiden aunts and endless, asexual 'engagements'. But he knew he would have been every bit as at home in the Château of Silling, hiding from the world and its plagues. No, no, he didn't necessarily want to maim, poison and murder, that would have been going a little far, but he wasn't averse to a certain amount of orgiastic, godless sex. The chance would have been a fine thing. He didn't even belong to an equivalent of the Drones, much less to any band of twisted libertines.

From school he went to university and studied law in a half-hearted, inefficient sort of way. He found himself somewhat less of an outsider. Being a poor student put him in company with a lot of good chaps. He joined a couple of dining and debating societies. He enjoyed the dining, though the debating left him cold. He was far less lonely at university, felt himself to be far less of a victim, but he still felt himself barred from the company of women. He knew the problem was within himself. It was because he didn't know how to talk to women. He didn't know what they were really like or what they really wanted to talk about. He took a couple of girls out but he was simultaneously too reserved and too intense to make a success of it. He began to see prostitutes on a regular basis.

He was occasionally ashamed of himself, but not sufficiently ashamed to stop. It made him happy. It took a great weight off his mind. He stopped trying to date girls from the university. It seemed a needlessly complicated transaction compared to the simple certainties of paying for sex. Sex with prostitutes wasn't cheap but he knew he might have spent just as much money taking out girls who would decline to give him what he wanted. He found it therefore best to take food and wine in the good company of men from his college. The arrangement seemed to work.

He left Cambridge with a poor degree but with a number of good male friends, and he went to work for a firm of commodity brokers whose managing director was a friend of the family. The work was menial, undemanding, and very far from the centre of power. Kingsley soon discovered that he could do his work every bit as well with a hangover as without one. It was a discovery that changed his life. His days may have been full of drudgery, but his nights were even fuller of food, drink and sex. He paid the going rate for each. You could not expect to eat without paying for your food, and Kingsley did not expect to have sex without paying for a prostitute.

He told nobody about his sexual adventures. There was nobody he would have wanted to tell. His companions were exclusively male and invariably drunk. They would have been surprised to find that Kingsley had a libido, much less a sex life.

There were, admittedly, times when it seemed to Kingsley that his life was not an entirely proper or admirable one, consisting as it largely did of sloth, gluttony and lust. Yet it was a better life than he'd known until then and he had no intention of changing it. He might have been prepared to admit that something was missing but he would not have admitted that it was a lack of love. Kingsley was absolutely certain that love only happened to other people. He might have confessed to wanting a sense of belonging, a sense of community, although he still had no idea to what form of community he might belong.

For a while he wondered if the world of espionage was one in which he might thrive. He had always kept secrets. He had always kept his own counsel. He had always been adept at knowing, thinking and feeling more than other people gave him credit for. Yet he could still feel no allegiance to any particular side. He didn't want to betray anyone or anything, yet the idea of playing all ends against some 'middle' of his own devising had enormous appeal. He felt he might thrive in an atmosphere of intelligence and counter-intelligence, of double and triple bluff. He could see the attractions of serving some higher, or deeper, power, of putting through an agenda that did not depend only on the obvious and the stated.

All this, however, seemed to be irrelevant in his current situation. His work amid the commodities offered no scope for deception or intrigue. A world in which a man's word was supposedly his bond offered few opportunities; and however much he might have wished it, nobody ever tried to 'recruit' him.

He had been to visit a prostitute in one of the better streets in Islington. He was something of a regular there. She was painfully thin, and bony and very young. He suspected she might be a drug addict and the thought excited him. He was leaving her flat, walking quickly away, head and eyes down, when he heard a brisk step and then a brisk voice behind him. At first Kingsley thought it might be a pimp or a policeman, some force of retribution, but the voice sounded friendly and it was calling him by name. Kingsley turned round to see a man he was certain he'd never met before. He was about sixty, white-haired, raffish, immaculate in blazer and MCC tie.

'John,' the man said. 'You probably don't remember me. Friend of your father's. I was at your christening. Radcliffe's the name.'

They shook hands. Kingsley was still cautious. He still thought this encounter might have something to do with his recent departure from the prostitute's flat. Perhaps he had not left enough money as a tip, or perhaps committed some other unwitting indiscretion. But this man was claiming to be a friend of his father's. That sounded ominous. He certainly didn't want details of his sexual practices getting back to the family in Lincolnshire.

'What do you want?' Kingsley said rather sharply.

'A chat,' said Radcliffe.

'I've just been . . .'

'I know where you've just been.'

'Are you spying on me?' Kingsley said, trying to sound angry and affronted. 'Is it something to do with my father?'

'No, it's nothing to do with your father, and I'd scarcely say we've been spying on you, although we do know quite a lot about you.'

'*What* exactly do you know?'

'It's perfectly all right,' said Radcliffe. 'There's no need to be defensive. We rather like what we know.'

'*What* do you like? Who is this mysterious "we"? What exactly are you playing at?'

'I could explain more easily over a drink.'

Kingsley grudgingly agreed. They went to a small, dark pub that Kingsley had never seen before and Radcliffe told him all about the Everlasting Club, and after a couple of hours Kingsley had been well and truly recruited.

What Radcliffe was offering sounded good, but not too good to be true. Kingsley had always somehow imagined that there might be a place for him in some club or society or cabal. Inevitably it must be secret or else he would have found it sooner. It was a place for people like him, he thought, for people who connected with pleasure and history, people who were special. His own isolation and intermittent misery, he now saw, were necessary emblems of his specialness.

Radcliffe hinted that the Everlasting Club had riper, more oblique objectives than simple hedonism. He spoke of dark forces, of the old gods, of immortality, of portentous indirections, of dark rituals. Kingsley lapped it up.

The rise from ordinary member to Chief Carver was swift yet, in Kingsley's opinion, not so very surprising. At times he felt himself to be a walking embodiment of the Everlasting Club: proudly English, profoundly civilised, yet in touch with deep Dionysian roots; plump and smooth on the surface, yet filled with convoluted desires and tastes. The Everlasting Club became his life. He became his role. He no longer had room or time for other interests and activities. His existence outside the Everlasting Club withered away. He resigned from his job, much to his family's displeasure. But he no longer cared what his family thought. He had all he needed or desired. He had arrived and come home. He felt like some restored monarch who had once again taken up the reins of his kingdom after a long and ignominious exile.

And now he was at Heathrow airport. He was meeting a plane,

meeting someone from the States, someone who did not know he was about to be met: Frank Marcel.

Frank did not discuss the mating habits of the praying mantis with his air hostess. He didn't know what they were. Frank had always made a point of treating well the people who served him, whether they were bringing him drinks on a plane or working for him in one of the Golden Boys. Frank liked to tip well, but not too well. Extravagant tipping was phoney and vulgar. Frank did not want to be thought phoney and vulgar.

He would be landing in London soon. He loved London, his wife's home town, more or less. He loved the culture, the history, the tradition, the accents, the cheery Cockneys, the English gents, the politeness, the good manners. In truth, Frank liked the idea better than the reality. The England he knew was that of Agatha Christie and Charles Dickens, especially as it might appear in a well-made TV adaptation.

Despite this affection, he had only been to England a couple of times before, once when he met Mary and once on an abortive business trip. Some years ago there had been talk of opening one or two Golden Boys in England. He'd flown over to meet with some money men. He'd eaten in some of the fast food outlets that would have been his competitors and he had thought at first there would be no problem. All the chains in England served glop. All the serving staff were sullen louts. A chain that provided wholesome food cheerfully served would surely clean up. But as the trip progressed it became increasingly apparent that nobody in England wanted wholesome food. They wanted glop. And if there was such a thing as a cheerful waiter or waitress anywhere in the whole of England, he or she was doing a fine job of laying low. Frank backed out of the deal, deciding to stick with the country he knew best.

He knew this current trip to England was in some danger of being a wild-goose chase. He knew Virgil was somewhere in England, London he assumed, and that he had an invitation to a party or club or something, but that was all he *did* know. He had no idea which party or club it was. He didn't know which hotel Virgil was staying in. He didn't know what plans Virgil had for after the party. But Frank wasn't too worried. Virgil had a way of making himself conspicuous. Virgil stood out in a crowd, any crowd. Frank had a feeling he'd find his son somehow. And even if he failed to find Virgil it was a whole lot easier to think about the madness of Leo and the polluted food at this distance than it was back home.

A part of him wished Mary had come too. He'd asked her to, but she said she wanted to stay and finalise arrangements for the surprise party. Frank found this pretty silly now that the surprise element had been blown, but he didn't need a fight about it. Given how lousy things were between him and Mary it was touching that she still wanted to give him surprises. At least he could leave her and be confident that she wasn't screwing Leo, and her absence gave him the hope of scoring with a buxom English rose who liked rich, middle-aged Americans.

He carried only one small case of hand luggage so was soon through passports and immigration. He glided through the crowds and made for the car hire desk. There was only one girl working there and several customers waiting so he had to stand in a short line. This was irritating, but none of the other companies' desks looked any easier. He had to wait. Then he felt someone touch him on the arm.

'Mr Marcel. Mr Frank Marcel, isn't it?'

'Why yes.'

'You probably don't remember me. My name's Kingsley.'

Frank smiled pleasantly and shook this guy Kingsley by the hand. It made him feel like a real cosmopolitan. He'd just stepped off the plane in a strange continent, only been on terra firma a few minutes, and here he was running into somebody he knew; except that he didn't have a clue who Kingsley was, and was pretty certain he'd never set eyes on him before.

'I ate at your restaurant once,' said Kingsley.

'A Golden Boy?' Frank asked, feeling considerably less cosmopolitan.

'No, no. At Trimalchio's.'

'Ah.' Frank beamed with pleasure. 'I hope you enjoyed it.'

'I certainly did,' said Kingsley. 'I most certainly did. It's good to see you again. Small world.'

Frank still didn't think he'd ever seen Kingsley before, but there were many nights when he hung out at Trimalchio's and fell into conversation with whoever was there. It was easy to forget a face. Besides, he couldn't imagine that anyone would have a reason for pretending to know him if they didn't.

'Are you in England for long?' Kingsley enquired.

'Just a few days, I expect.'

'Business or pleasure?'

'Oh, a little of each I hope.'

'Well, nice to have run into you. Enjoy your stay. Probably see you again in some other airport. Bye now.'

Kingsley turned to leave but then casually, too casually if Frank had but known, had a better idea.

'I say,' said Kingsley, 'if you're in need of transport into town my chauffeur's waiting outside. If you'd do me the honour I could drop you at your hotel.'

The girl at the car hire desk still looked busy, and a telephone beside her had started to ring. A ride into town sounded like a good idea, then he could hire a car at the hotel. He thanked Kingsley and accepted. He was delighted. This was the life.

Butterworth was waiting with the Bentley (the Mercedes being otherwise employed) and he drove Frank and Kingsley into London. Their conversation was friendly and uncomplicated. They talked about food. Kingsley said there were lots of really fine new restaurants opening up all the time all over London if you only knew where to look. They discussed developments in the California wine trade, what Robert Mondavi was up to these days, and how much scope for development there was in South American vineyards. Kingsley decried the number of fake American restaurants in London; bad English food dressed up as bad American food. Frank nodded his head in sad agreement.

He said nothing about his real reason for visiting England. He said nothing about Virgil and certainly nothing about Leo's activities in the kitchen at Trimalchio's. This was not something you discussed with a stranger, especially not with one who said how much he'd enjoyed eating at your restaurant.

Frank found Kingsley to be a proper English gentleman. He seemed to have good breeding. He seemed like Frank's idea of an aristocrat. And if Kingsley could give him the names of the interesting new restaurants in town, that might be as good a place as any to start looking for Virgil. Kingsley was happy to do so. He said Frank must join him one night as his guest. Frank said, fine. It came as no surprise therefore, that when they arrived in central London Kingsley suggested they have a 'quick one'.

'I love a good English pub,' Frank said.

'I'm not much of a pub man myself,' said Kingsley, 'but we could always try my club.'

'My club'; it had such a ring to it, so English and reassuring and traditional. Frank was thrilled. He was a little concerned when Kingsley told him that black tie was required, but cheered up again when he was assured they'd have a spare suit in his size at the club. He found it very strange that he had to be blindfolded before he could be driven there, but he decided to roll with it as a piece of old-fashioned English quaintness, and he joked happily as Kingsley tied a black silk scarf over his eyes.

A little later, in the bar of the Everlasting Club, in his borrowed togs, Frank was in seventh heaven; all those jolly English chaps, those fine, ringing, English voices, all that décor. He loved the panelling, the hunting prints, the stone fireplace, and the thick, atmospheric smog. It was like having walked into a modern dress Shakespeare play, almost. Where was Falstaff? Where was Sir Toby Belch? There were voices raised loud in laughter and debate, there were logs blazing, and there was a whole bunch of drinks he'd never tried before; pale ale, scrumpy, Drambuie. All this was fine by him.

Frank talked to one or two Pickwickian types whose accents were as rich as Stilton soaked in port. He couldn't catch everything they said, but he smiled and nodded and tried to give the impression that he was having a good time, which he was. One remark he did catch was, 'You should have been here earlier, the Earl of Sandwich was in,' and everyone around him had juddered with laughter. He juddered too and although he didn't see the joke he wouldn't have been so dumb as to ask anyone to explain it to him. They did explain certain things, however. Kingsley described the origins and principles of the Everlasting Club, its perpetuation over the centuries, just as he had explained them to Virgil. Frank was impressed beyond belief. It stirred dynastic ambitions in his heart, that the Golden Boy chain might run in perpetuity, year after year, generation after generation, father to son, for ever and ever.

Frank was alarmed when someone standing next to him at the bar finished a pint of beer, then unzipped his flies and pissed into the now empty beer glass. For one vile moment it looked as though he was going to drink that as well, but he placed the full glass of urine on the bar and went into the dining-room. Nobody except Frank batted an eyelid.

Frank soon went into the dining-room too, at Kingsley's insistent invitation. He loved the oak refectory table and the rakish, Hogarthian look of the diners. He was especially taken by the nude girl in the centre of the table. That was a great, sexy idea. He'd suggest that to Virgil, make it an occasional feature at Trimalchio's. He loved the way all the guys at the table carried on eating, completely ignoring the gorgeous female body. The English had such class.

So did their food. There was so much more to English cuisine, he told himself, than roast beef and Yorkshire pudding, and here he was about to explore some of its wilder shores. In a very short time he had eaten otter, goat intestine, some of that soup that tasted of liver, and a mixed grill. Some of it was kind of weird, some a little disgusting, but Frank was too good a guest not to eat it up heartily. And some of it was great. He especially enjoyed the sausages in the mixed grill. The meal was not identical to the one Virgil had eaten but many of the dishes were the same, and the overall effect extremely similar. Just as Virgil had done, Frank thought how fascinated Leo would have been by all this spectacle and flavour, then he remembered he was no longer thinking of Leo with the affection he once had.

Thoughts of Leo threatened to ruin Frank's meal. He tried to clear his mind. He took a big swig of the wine in his glass, a damson and pear spumante. Back home Frank was known as a guy with an iron constitution. He wasn't a hell-raiser, quite the reverse, but he was a guy who could put away more than his share of booze and very often did. But however much he drank, he never got wild or out of control, nor did he ever throw up, and he certainly never passed out. At home, with three-quarters of a bottle of Scotch inside him, he looked and acted more sober than Virgil ever looked or acted. Tonight at the Everlasting Club however, things were to be a little different.

It only happened because he was feeling so good. He was having the time of his life. He was tucking into a plate of sea urchins and bilberries and he was feeling a little light-headed and suddenly he was gripped by an overwhelming sense of belonging.

'Look, fellers,' he said, 'I want *in*.'

There were a dozen or so members eating at the table, including Radcliffe, the white-haired, aristocratic one who had authored the history of the Everlasting Club. He was in a thoughtful, watchful mood tonight and he said little. Mostly he and the others tried to ignore Frank and they were succeeding admirably.

'This is my kind of place,' Frank said more loudly. 'You guys are my kind of guys. All my life I've been looking for a place like this. It feels like coming home.'

Kingsley, seated beside him, leaned over and said very gently in his ear, 'No, Frank, this is not how we do things.'

It did no good.

'Oh come on,' said Frank, 'damn your English reserve. I know that's just a cover anyway. I think people should tell each other when

115

they're feeling good. I'm feeling good. I'm feeling great. I want in. How do I get to be a member of this joint?'

'Not like this, Frank,' said Kingsley. 'Please.'

'No, really, what do I have to do? Get references? I'll get references. Show you my credit rating? My credit rating is good, I mean *good*. You want to see me dance across the room with a bunch of gardenias up my ass? Then pass me the gardenias. Come on, fellers. Loosen up. Give me a break. Make me one of you.'

Frank was aware that he was being a little loud, but he couldn't see that was any big deal. There were plenty of guys in the club being a whole lot louder than he was. He could hear them. But the guys at the table, at least the ones who were still awake and able to focus their eyes, were looking deeply offended, Radcliffe especially.

Had Frank been sober he would surely have realised that increased volume and mounting hysteria were not the way to win over frosty dinner companions. But he got it into his head that he could thaw them with an old party trick he'd perfected on business trips and sales conferences.

'You'll love this, guys,' he insisted.

He asked the waiter to bring him a large glass pitcher, and when it came he toddled into the bar with it, telling the members around the dining-table not to worry, he'd be right back, and they shouldn't go away. He reached the bar and asked a barman to fill the pitcher with twenty-six half measures of twenty-six different drinks, one for each letter of the alphabet. So the barman began with apricot brandy, Benedictine, Campari, Dubonnet, eggnog, *framboise*, and moved alphabetically via mescal, Noilly Prat, ouzo and Pernod, to vodka, whisky, xampan, Yquem and zubrovka. One or two he felt were cheating slightly; the Irish whiskey and the Jamaican rum, but 'i' and 'j' were always tricky. Nor had he ever come across Quinta do Noval or Underberg before, but he was happy to give them a whirl. And at least there were plenty of old favourites like gin, hock, rum, slivovitz and tequila. The set was completed by kümmel, and half a pint of lager.

The cocktail certainly looked convincingly evil as it wallowed there in the pitcher, primarily brown, murky, a head of scum on the top and filaments of liqueur woven through its depths. Still, Frank wasn't worrying. He'd done this before and he knew, he knew with absolute conviction, that this trick couldn't fail to impress.

He returned to the dining-room. He was pleased to see that nobody had left, though one had fallen asleep. He climbed on the table, unsurely, treading on the hand of the naked, female table adornment, and he yelled, 'Check this out, fellers!' and began to down the entire contents of the jug in one slow but relentless act of swallowing.

The other diners did indeed look up at Frank but it was not with approval. Normally when Frank performed this feat there were guys cheering him on, stamping, beating fists and glasses and beer cans on the table. Even as the first few mouthfuls slid down his gullet, Frank knew that something was wrong, and not only with his audience.

It must have been the flight, he thought rapidly, the change of climate, the unusual English food. As the drink hit his stomach the smoky atmosphere of the room seemed to thicken, to become a good deal smokier. Soon it was turning black. Frank was passing out, and firm hands caught him as he tumbled from the table.

When he awoke many hours later he was in an unfamiliar bed and an unknown hotel room. Nausea, muscular pain, headache and remorse campaigned through his body and soul. It was going to be a long and dirty war. He did not leave his bed, in fact could barely open his eyes, for the next forty-eight hours. Even as he lay there, hoping that merciful oblivion might claim him, it crossed his mind that this was not the most orthodox way for a loving father to seek out his son's business advice.

Scenes from a History of the Everlasting Club.
Number Seven: The Conquest of the Old Hunger.

Imagine you are an explorer of a strange land. Imagine you are Spanish and the year is 1519. You are a conquistador in the retinue of Cortés. You are marching to the Aztec capital of Tenochtitlán, though you do not yet know what that might mean. You know you have God on your side, but there are some evils from which He seems unwilling to protect you. You are here to spread His word and His glory but your head is also filled, how could it not be, with dreams of ease and profit and gold, and these dreams will ultimately be sweeter if they are attained at the cost of some pain and danger.

These mountains, these jungles, contain strange beasts, beast-like men, spectres as dark and dangerous as the human imagination can conceive. There will be strange rituals and devilish practices. There may be pure evil. Ever since Columbus met the Caribs it has been known there is headhunting and cannibalism in these parts; stories told in sign language by native women, a meeting with escaped Indian prisoners who had been castrated so they would fatten up like capons. Rumours run wild. No doubt some of the stories are exaggerated, but *any* story of cannibalism is enough to terrify a good Christian. The Caribs have fortunately been wiped out, but that doesn't mean there aren't others to fear. So you march on, through an alien world, into enemy territory, deeper into this hostile, godless zone.

Yet the land looks like a paradise. There is water, plentiful supplies of fruit, fish and wild game. This habit of eating human flesh cannot be merely the product of desperate, devastating hunger. There must be darker reasons.

You have seen some of the other local habits. You have encountered blood-stained altars, derelict temples scattered with human bones and skulls. Cortés has preached to the natives of each village, telling them to abandon theft, idolatry, human sacrifice and sodomy. You are not convinced that the message has lodged firmly in these

Indians' dark, unknowable hearts. But Cortés believes he has made converts and on you go to the next village, speaking to the elders, more sermonising from Cortés, more crosses erected, and on again, further inland.

In Tlaxcala, a city of Montezuma's enemies, you find bamboo cages and in them are men and women being fattened until they are well-fleshed enough to be eaten. The locks on the cages are smashed open, the victims released. Cortés rails against the city's heathen ways, and after his passionate sermon he receives promises that the inhabitants will desist from such activities. You are aware that these promises may be broken.

The Aztecs live in a permanent state of fear, in thrall to numerous jealous gods. They inhabit a precarious universe always on the edge of collapse, under constant threat of cataclysm. They live in the fifth world, the previous four having been lost in eruptions of cosmically destructive violence. The same will happen to the present world if the gods are not constantly appeased. Above all, the sun needs to be kept in motion, and this is only achieved by constantly offering up fresh heart's blood. Daily bloody sacrifices are needed or else the sun will not rise and the fifth world will end. Each day demands new horrors; burnings, skinnings alive, the drowning of children.

A stock of sacrificial victims is required, so the Aztecs are constantly fighting small, skittish wars with their neighbours, wars just big enough to supply a regular number of prisoners of war who can then be sacrificed. You do not understand why your God has allowed this to continue for so long.

You arrive at Tenochtitlán, Montezuma's citadel, a place of peril and sin, you and four hundred other bedraggled Spanish soldiers. It is (this you do not understand) a city of exquisite beauty with white stone, fountains, formal gardens, lakes. Fine craftsmanship and design are everywhere on display. There are glorious buildings and temples, but dedicated to the glory of who or what? How does this beauty and order co-exist with plain, pagan evil? You are graciously received. Cortés delivers a sermon, and Montezuma is very diplomatic in telling him when he's had enough. All appears, briefly, to be well.

Then you are shown the temple of the war god. More white stone and carvings of dragons, serpents and demons, but this time there is a magnificent altar, wet with fresh blood that runs to earth through an elaborate network of pipes and channels. But not all the blood is fresh. Walls and floors are caked with layers of old, dried blood, wave after wave, sprays and splashes. The oldest blood has turned black. The more recent torrents are the colour of chocolate. Human blood has formed a thick impasto of colours and textures. And everywhere there is this stench, the stench not only of blood and bodies and meat, but of death itself.

When this temple was dedicated, an orgy of human sacrifice began, a festival of slaughter that lasted four days; four days in which twenty thousand people were sacrificed. Montezuma began proceedings by killing the first victim.

The temple's outbuildings resemble an abattoir or perhaps a cookshop, complete with butcher's knives, chopping boards and cooking pots. Steam and smoke billow up from secret places in the earth. A spicy, meaty flavour fills the air, and you might almost find it appetising if you didn't know what it was.

You see more bones, more skulls, arms and legs, pieces of human flesh preserved by smoking, fresh innards, brains. You see that awful horror when the skin has ceased to be a barrier, a screen between inner and outer, when the insides are no longer inside.

It seems to you that you have been granted an unwanted glimpse of Hell. You have seen a sophisticated society, a golden city, with pure, stinking evil at its heart. You know, you absolutely know, long before Cortés issues the order, that this must not be permitted. In the name of everything that's holy all this must be utterly destroyed. You know that a new kind of godly killing is about to begin.

EIGHT

It had all suddenly fallen into place for Butterworth and he was appalled. He was sitting at the wheel of Kingsley's Bentley and suddenly he knew what was going on. It had taken him a long time to work it out, far too long. He had never been encouraged to think of himself as very bright, but even so he believed he should have realised sooner. He'd had to go back a very long way to piece everything together, back to the very beginning, to the first day when he was interviewed for the job as Kingsley's chauffeur.

Butterworth arrived an hour early for the interview. The bus had made good time into London and to the hotel off Baker Street where the interview was to take place. But even if it hadn't made good time he would still have been absurdly early. That's how Butterworth was; prompt, calm, well-prepared, judicious, overcautious; not bad attributes in a chauffeur.

He had thought carefully about whether or not to drive to the interview. In one way it seemed inappropriate for a chauffeur to travel by bus, on the other hand it wasn't as if he was going to take the car into the interview with him, it would have been difficult and/or expensive to find somewhere to park and, most important, his car was not so reliable that he could depend on it to get to the interview at all, certainly not with an hour or more to spare.

This was one of the paradoxes of Butterworth's professional life. He had driven some extremely smart motor cars in his time, Jaguars, Daimlers and now a Bentley, but when his working day was over, he always had to go home in some soulless, distressed old banger that was only ever a couple of months away from being declared unroadworthy.

In some men this might have created resentment, but not in Butterworth. He knew he was destined to work for those who were richer, more successful and less godly than he was. He had driven for chiefs of industry and their wives, for tennis players, for visiting American pop stars, for foreign movie directors, and he had succeeded in not feeling aggrieved about it. He knew he had *cause* to feel aggrieved, and not only about the clients he drove, but he had quite coolly decided *not* to feel aggrieved. A black man had plenty of things to feel bad about in this world if he chose to, but Butterworth had chosen otherwise. He knew that God had helped him a lot in this choice.

He didn't have a very clear idea of who or what God was. He didn't think he was a white man with a white beard, but he found it hard to believe he was a black man either. And Jesus? Well, Jesus wasn't exactly white. He was Jewish, swarthy at the very least, heavily tanned no doubt, but that still left him a whole lot whiter than Butterworth. Not, of course, that skin colour meant anything, at least not in a perfect world, not in God's world, and however white God turned out to be, he would at least be a paragon of anti-racism.

Inevitably, Butterworth would have liked a little more in the way of money and possessions, but he knew all about the dangers of wanting something too badly, of wanting *anything* too badly. He saw black kids who had developed a taste for trash, and he could see plenty of people around (not all of them white) who were all too ready to satisfy and exploit that taste. He wasn't stupid enough to go around badmouthing earthly treasure, he didn't want people to think he was crazy, but in his heart he knew most of it was worthless. Fortunately there was something up ahead that was worth a million times as much.

Life, it seemed to Butterworth, was an obstacle course in which you had to keep your head down, try to stay honest and out of trouble. You were free to enjoy it if you could, but if you couldn't that wasn't too serious, heaven was waiting for you. Life was just the first course. You don't walk out of the restaurant just because the soup course isn't too good. The main course and the dessert could still be pretty enjoyable.

Butterworth's life had never been bad. He had no complaints. He enjoyed rum and cricket and a good smoke and good company. He liked food, but nothing too fancy; just coo-coo or goat curry or ackee salt fish or callaloo soup or Johnny-cakes or chocho cabbage. And if he could find a good Christian woman to cook it for him and share it with him, then so much the better.

Unlike a lot of people he usually had a job he enjoyed. He loved to drive. That was what he'd always done for a living. He enjoyed any kind of driving, but driving a big, black limousine, that was the best.

He had done his share of mini-cab driving, but you needed a four-door saloon for that, reasonably new, and by the time you'd paid for the car and the insurance it was hard to make much money at all. You could do it illegally, but that wasn't his way. He had driven vans and made deliveries, but he was a driver not a labourer, not a humper of boxes, and he was getting older and he wanted to appear dignified and there was no dignity in loading and unloading vans. Driving a bus would have been similarly ignominious. Being a chauffeur suited him just fine. You wore a suit, you stayed clean. That's why he really wanted this job. He didn't know much about it, but what was there to know? He'd been put on to it by the friend of a sister of someone he knew at church. The job, as he understood it, was to be a chauffeur for a gentleman's club. He didn't think he was going to like these gentlemen very much, but there would be no need to hate them either. And he had an interview at eleven o'clock with somebody called Mr Kingsley.

After killing an hour, he announced himself at the hotel desk and the receptionist pointed out Kingsley, who was sitting at a small, circular table in the coffee lounge, flapping a copy of *The Financial Times*. His manner was confident, his manners impeccable, his smile infinitely reassuring.

'Mr Butterworth, how very good of you to come. Please sit down. Would you like some coffee, some tea? A biscuit? Something stronger?'

'No thank you very much, sir.'

There was a flurry of small talk before Kingsley asked Butterworth to tell him about himself. Butterworth did. It seemed to be well received. Kingsley seemed to be genuinely interested in the life and times of a chauffeur. It was a new world to him.

'I've never had a chauffeur before,' said Kingsley, confessionally, boyishly. 'I've never felt the need, but here I am, a big wheel in the Everlasting Club, Chief Carver they call me, and suddenly everybody's saying I ought to have a chauffeur. And it doesn't seem like a bad idea at all.

'Basically, your job would be fairly straightforward. You'd be *my* chauffeur, and your first allegiance would be to me, taking me hither and yon on club business, but if I didn't need you, you'd be sent to collect the odd member and bring him to the club. And on those occasions when members have had a few too many, you'd be required to take them home again.'

It sounded to Butterworth as though he might have to do some clearing up of vomit in this job. He would cope with that if he had to. He wasn't proud; dignified yes, proud no. Pride was a sin. Who sweeps a room as for thy laws . . . No doubt the same could be said for vomit.

'Can't tell you a great deal about the Everlasting Club,' Kingsley continued. 'Two reasons for that. One, we're a bit private. We like to keep ourselves to ourselves. And two, I'm fairly new to it all myself. I only joined a little while ago and more or less immediately got made Chief Carver. Talk about meteoric. And if the powers that be tell me I need a chauffeur, who am I to argue?

'Actually, there's a little book published on the history of the club. I still haven't got round to reading it yet, but if you get the job I'll let you peruse a copy.'

'Thank you.'

'Do you do much reading, Butterworth?'

Butterworth noticed that Kingsley had already stopped calling him 'mister'.

'A little, sir.'

'What kind of thing?'

'The Bible mostly.'

'I've never got round to reading that one either. Is it a good yarn?'

'It certainly is, sir.'

'Everybody lives happily ever after, that sort of thing?'

'Not everybody, sir.'

Kingsley went ominously quiet, as though mention of the Bible didn't suit him. Then suddenly he said, 'I say, Butterworth, how do you feel about the Third World?'

'I feel all right, sir.'

'Good. You see I know as well as you do that an awful lot of people in this world are hungry. Oh yes, I know they've got lots of horrid diseases as well, and they have all kinds of toxic waste dumped all over them – which can't make them very happy either – but essentially their main problem is they're starving.'

'Yes sir,' said Butterworth. He was tempted to say something about 'spiritual hunger' but this didn't seem quite right.

'And most of these hungry people you'd have to admit, Butterworth, most of them aren't white. And you're not white either. So I wondered if that was a problem.'

Butterworth still wanted this job. He wanted to say the right thing. But he wasn't sure whether finding mass hunger a problem was a good thing or a bad thing in Kingsley's eyes.

'Well, it's not a problem for me personally,' he said.

Kingsley looked at him as though he had missed the point.

'Let's take Ethiopia,' he said. 'Or the Sudan, or any of these places where there's mass starvation. You see some programme on TV and it's damned moving. You dig in your pocket, stump up the cash and keep them all alive for a year or two longer. Then what do the buggers do? They start having babies. There's a population explosion and before you know where you are they're all starving again, only now there's twice as many of them. I don't know, Butterworth, all these babies, all this reproduction.'

Butterworth felt that he wanted to deny personal responsibility for the world's population explosion, but he kept silent.

'The fact is, there are only so many babies because there's so much fucking goes on in these countries. They may be starving to death but that doesn't seem to slow them down when it comes to burying the old beef bayonet. Why don't we hear about *that*?'

Butterworth felt that he personally didn't want to hear about starving people having sex, but again he kept his peace.

'But don't think I'm prejudiced against black people,' Kingsley said. 'I don't think you'll find any racists in the Everlasting Club. You won't find any bleeding-heart liberals, and you'll find precious few democrats, but you won't find any racists either. Racism, I fancy, is based on fear. We at the Everlasting Club know we have nothing to fear.'

Butterworth found himself nodding, though he couldn't be sure what he was nodding at.

'Of course you don't hear much about cannibalism in these Third World countries, but you can bet your life it goes on. When people are hungry they'll eat anything, their own shoes, their own shit, anything. I know a lot of them don't have any shoes. Probably they don't have much shit either, but you know what I mean. So I feel fairly certain that some of these starving people must be eating each other. It stands to reason. It's only human nature. You don't see that on TV either. Do you think you'd eat human flesh, Butterworth?'

'Well, I enjoy soul food,' Butterworth said.

Even Butterworth wasn't quite sure what he meant by that but it sounded like a good answer. Kingsley certainly appreciated it. He doubled over with laughter, and guffawed, the sound being quickly absorbed by the plushness of the room. Butterworth smiled sheepishly.

'I think we're going to get on splendidly,' said Kingsley. 'When can you start?'

'Does that mean I got the job?'

'Oh yes, yes, Butterworth, you've got the job. You're part of the team now. Welcome to the Everlasting Club.'

Of course, he didn't mean that Butterworth was a *member* of the Everlasting Club. That was not the team he was now a part of. Butterworth was part of the team that worked for the club. He had now been Kingsley's chauffeur for three months and it was true he had never encountered any racism in that time. Nobody had noticed his colour enough to comment on it, and in fact, people hardly noticed him at all. He took his orders from Kingsley. Mostly he just ferried his boss around but he would also occasionally pick up people at airports, deposit them at their hotels, transfer them to the club, then some time later take them or their equivalents home.

These comings and goings took place at all hours of the day or night. He might drive a man in full evening dress to the club at nine in the morning. He might take someone home who looked as though he'd had a hard night, but it would be one o'clock in the afternoon. He found this a little decadent but kept his disapproval to himself.

His instinct about mopping up vomit had been perfectly correct, but this was usually accompanied by a fair-sized tip to ease the hardship. Sometimes he had to carry unconscious members out of the club. On a couple of occasions he had to carry them in. But he never went into the club itself. He had to pick up or deposit his charges on the threshold. The entrance hall was a kind of air-lock beyond which he could not go. It was as if his lungs could not cope with the rarefied air of the inner sanctum. That suited him fine. He suspected the club was no place for a God-fearing man like himself. The less he knew about what went on in there the better.

Sometimes his passengers were famous, their faces familiar from newspapers and television, but Butterworth was seldom able to identify them. He took a perverse pride in knowing that the person he was chauffeuring was a somebody, but not having the slightest idea who. The drunk in the back of the Mercedes might be a professional footballer, a night-club entertainer, a politician; it made no difference to him. They were all equal in God's and Butterworth's eyes.

Butterworth had to keep the car clean and do very basic maintenance on it, but for many hours each day it was as though he was employed to do nothing. In fact, he was paid to wait, to be ready. He would often sit at the wheel of the car, staring blankly into space.

That suited him fine, but Kingsley thought it looked bad. Couldn't he read or something? Butterworth said he'd be very happy to sit reading the Bible but Kingsley thought that looked even worse. So he gave Butterworth the promised club history. He could read that. Butterworth kept the book in the car but it was a long time before he got round to reading it.

It soon became apparent to Butterworth that he had not only landed a new job, he'd landed a new life. He now had no time for rum and cricket and a good smoke and good company. He certainly had no time to find himself a good Christian woman. But somehow it didn't matter. He enjoyed being detached from the world of normal working hours, of five-day weeks, lunch breaks and weekends off. His existence became entirely regulated by work. He worked and he slept, that was all. He became oddly content. The job offered him no serious challenge, demanded nothing from him that he wasn't capable of doing; until, that is, the arrival of Virgil.

He hadn't formed any strong opinion of Virgil when he picked him up from the airport. Forming opinions was no part of his job. Virgil had been civil to him and Butterworth shared Virgil's opinion that the business with the blindfold was pretty silly. Virgil probably didn't care where the Everlasting Club was situated, but if he'd really wanted to know, Butterworth would probably have told him, certainly if the tip was large enough. A large tip could corrupt even a godly man like him, at least on trivial things like that. But Butterworth had been corrupted on something not so trivial by a very large tip from Kingsley. In fact, he was now prepared to admit to himself that it wasn't so much a tip as a bribe. Either way it was dirty money.

Kingsley told Butterworth that Virgil was a very, very special guest of the Everlasting Club, one who merited very special treatment. Something new would be required of Butterworth, specifically he would be required to do a spot of 'acting'. This all sounded very difficult and very unwelcome to Butterworth; an unexpected disruption to the regulated order. But Kingsley had placed a roll of twenty pound notes in his hand and suddenly Butterworth couldn't see any harm in doing a little play-acting. His only worry then was that he might not be a good enough actor.

When he arrived at the hotel and interrupted Virgil in the middle of his sexual goings-on with Rose, Butterworth had, despite himself, started to form an opinion, one of fierce disapproval. Butterworth didn't consider himself a prude or a killjoy, sex was, after all, a perfectly godly activity, but there was something sickly and ugly about that scene in the hotel room, the smell in the air, the remains of wasted food everywhere. Butterworth had begun to realise he was involved with something distasteful, but he had no idea what.

The next part of the act was to take Virgil to the underground car park and that was where the hard work was to start for Butterworth. It wasn't as hard as what Kingsley had to do. Kingsley's part was to provoke Virgil into hitting him, then he had to do a stage fall and pretend to hurt his head on the concrete floor. Butterworth had watched this part of the show carefully and he wasn't at all sure that Kingsley had been acting. The noise his head made against the concrete was perfectly authentic. Then Butterworth's own act came into the spotlight. He had to convince Virgil that Kingsley was seriously injured and get him to take the car keys and drive away in the Mercedes.

Butterworth hadn't thought his performance was very convincing but it had obviously been good enough to convince Virgil, and the act had worked more or less as planned. At the time he'd had no idea what this plan was really all about and perhaps he hadn't wanted to. He realised his part in it was small and that Kingsley would be unlikely to tell him, a mere servant, what the greater scheme was. Kingsley had muttered something about an initiation but Butterworth couldn't see why Virgil needed to be initiated when none of the other new members he'd delivered to the club had ever needed it. And Kingsley had also said something about Rose taking him off on some kind of tour, putting some English flesh on his American bones. That too had meant nothing at the time, but now that everything had fallen into place it all seemed perfectly obvious.

Kingsley was not badly hurt. The crack of his head on the floor had been real enough, but the sound was more frightening than the injury. Butterworth administered a little light first aid, helped him into his Bentley and drove him back to the club. Kingsley was happy enough with events.

For Butterworth, the real bonus of the operation was that with the Mercedes purloined by Virgil he now became the full-time driver of Kingsley's Bentley. This was a delight for him, but it required a slight change in his working practices. The car was Kingsley's own, his pride and joy, and he was damned if he was going to let it be used to ferry armies of vomiting drunks to and from the club. So Butterworth only ever ferried one drunk: Kingsley. Consequently he spent even more of each day waiting, being ready, doing nothing. And Kingsley became more insistent that he shouldn't sit behind the wheel looking vacant.

This had two crucially important and unpleasant consequences.

The first was that Butterworth finally read the history of the Ever-lasting Club. It was an eye-opener. He didn't find it at all an enjoyable read. He was disgusted by much of it. He had already guessed that some untoward things went on behind the club's closed doors, but all this talk of wildness with whores and food and semen was worse than he could possibly have imagined. He was also deeply offended by the anti-religious sentiments. And he was thoroughly appalled by the loving detail in which Haarman's sex murders were described. He was so appalled that he couldn't bring himself to read every word of it. He couldn't see why anyone would want to write a book like that, much less read it. And he couldn't see what this apparent obsession with cannibalism was all about.

The second consequence was unpleasant in a completely different way. When Kingsley was inside the club, Butterworth had to park the Bentley as nearby as possible, but sometimes this was not very nearby at all. He would use a parking meter where possible, but sometimes he had to park illegally and watch and wait for a meter to come free, then grab it. He felt that scrabbling for a parking space was rather undignified for the driver of a Bentley but that was what driving in London required, and he could manoeuvre, reverse and park the Bentley with as much ease as some people parked their Minis.

And so it was that he was waiting on a double yellow line with his eye on a row of occupied parking meters. Then a car left its spot and he immediately, silkily, reversed the big Bentley into the now vacant meter bay. So easily did he accomplish it, he didn't even notice that a brand new red Mini had been lining itself up to drive forwards into the spot. Even when he did notice, he didn't think much of it. So he'd pinched somebody's place, so what? It was a jungle out there when it came to parking your car, dog eats dog.

The two people in the Mini saw it differently. There was a woman driver and a male passenger. They were young, expensively dressed with fancy haircuts, well-heeled but a bit too flashy. Their skins were white.

Whether the male passenger was motivated by chivalry or London traffic aggression or class hatred was not clear, but he decided his companion had been insulted and honour needed to be satisfied.

'You cunt!' he shouted in Butterworth's general direction without even looking at him.

Butterworth nodded at him, acknowledged his existence, making it clear that he had no intention of getting into an argument. It was then that the man noticed the colour of Butterworth's skin.

'You black cunt!' he shouted.

Butterworth nodded again and smiled in a dignified, condescending, provoking way, guaranteed to make things worse. It did.

'What's a black bastard like you doing with a car like that?'

Butterworth shook his head sadly as though humouring some poor, demented simpleton.

'Fucking dumb as well as everything else,' the man yelled. 'Why don't you get back to the jungle where you belong?'

Butterworth continued to smile. Then the girl shouted something. At first Butterworth thought perhaps she was embarrassed by her friend and simply wanted to put a stop to it, or perhaps she just wanted to drive on and not miss some other parking space. She shouted to her friend, though it was clearly meant for general consumption, 'Don't get into a fight with him, Chas. If he wins he'll put you in a fucking pot and eat you.'

That was when it all fell into place for Butterworth.

Why hadn't he realised before? It all fitted. It all made sense. Those references to the starving in his interview with Kingsley, those references in the history of the club. It was all glaringly, blindingly obvious to him now. Quite simply, the members of the Everlasting Club were cannibals.

Butterworth had heard about this sort of thing, societies who ate human flesh as a horrible parody of the Eucharist, in order to perpetuate themselves, like vampires. That was what was meant by the word 'everlasting', a club that tried to make itself immortal by eating the human body.

And how did they come by human flesh? Well, that was obvious now too. They made human sacrifices. They slaughtered young men. That was where Virgil came in. He was young, good-looking, a good example of the tribe, yet being American he was an outsider. He was being treated like a king, given free air tickets, hotel rooms, sex, fine English food. And at the end of it all he would be sacrificed on the altar of the Everlasting Club; and the members, those devils, would consume his body and his blood.

Butterworth crossed himself. He had only ever wanted a quiet life. He had wanted to serve God in a diligent but relaxed, unspectacular way. That was irrelevant now. His personal preferences counted for nothing. The moment finds the man, and Butterworth had been found. Virgil, in the name of all that was holy, needed to be saved, and Butterworth believed he was just the man to do it.

NINE

Mary Marcel and Leo were sitting in the wide first-class seats of the 747, LAX to London. Mary looked as though she might have walked out of a fashion feature on the discerningly chic older woman. Leo looked as though he had just walked out of the kitchen. Mary wore a Cardin hound's-tooth jacket, velvet trousers that buckled at the ankles, and some heavy, Aztec-influenced chunks of jewellery. Leo wore jeans, a T-shirt and baseball boots. His stubby hands were dirty. His hair flopped greasily over his wide forehead. Mary planted a reassuring kiss on his cheek.

'Here's a theory,' said Mary.

Leo looked at her uncertainly. He had not been reassured by the kiss.

'This theory says there are two kinds of people in the world; those who live to eat and those who eat to live. People who only eat to live are a dismal bunch and once they've eaten they're stuck with the problem of what to do with the rest of their lives. People who live to eat have a much easier time. Food is their life. Therefore, so long as their food is good, their lives are good. So long as they enjoy their meals, they enjoy their lives. Sounds simple, huh?'

Leo grimaced and then looked out of the window. He was being leaden and uncooperative.

'Sounds *too* simple maybe,' said Mary.

They had been served a meal that had depressed Leo. There had been a sodden selection of canapés with melon and lobster and caviar, then a fillet of turbot with champagne sauce and asparagus spears, and then there had been a terrible hazelnut meringue. The ingredients had probably been quite good when they started out, but they had been sacrificed on the altar of international cuisine, made bland and characterless, ruined as far as Leo was concerned. He could have done great things with those ingredients. He hated waste and it made him sad.

'Another theory, Leo,' said Mary, 'not one of mine. One of my

131

lovers used to say, probably still does, that the way people eat indicates the way they make love.'

Leo did not respond.

Mary continued, 'Some people are very easily satisfied; one nibble and they're through, and they can go a long time before they feel hungry again. Some people like a little but often. Some alternate between bingeing and starving.

'And some people are just insatiable. They can carry on all night, hour after hour, course after course. They're just plain greedy. You think, surely they can't manage another mouthful, but somehow they do. It's so important to find a lover who has the same sort of appetite as you do.'

Mary looked wistful, deep in reverie, savouring a memory of some previous lover, someone whose appetite matched her own better than Leo's did. Leo knew he'd bitten off more than he could chew with Mary Marcel.

'I wish you'd tell me why you're taking me to England,' said Leo for the third or fourth time.

Mary didn't answer. She pointedly picked up the in-flight magazine and began to read an article on Caribbean ways with seafood. Leo knew better than to insist. He knew Mary that well, at least. But he didn't know what he was doing on this plane to England. He was in a state of confusion, but that was a perfectly ordinary state for him to be in these days.

He still didn't know what the hell was going to happen to him. His fate was still in Frank's (and maybe Virgil's) hands. He hoped Mary was maybe taking him to England so they could all get together, talk things through and speed up the decision, but if so, he didn't understand why she wouldn't simply say that was what she was doing. Mary preferred to hint at dark, secret motives, at manoeuvrings and game plans that he was too obtuse to follow. He thought Mary sometimes tried too hard to be mysterious.

Leo was also worried about what might happen at Trimalchio's in his absence. Mary had been vague about how long they were going to be away; a few days, a week, maybe longer. With no Virgil and no Frank, and now no him, he feared the worst. The restaurant's standards would tumble. There'd be complaints and angry, dissatisfied customers, and there'd be nobody left to put things right. Oh sure there'd be a few waiters, a few competent assistant chefs, but they were nobodies really. A week was a long time in L.A. gastronomy and a culinary reputation could get ruined pretty damned quick.

Mary told him not to worry, not to be silly. The jerks who went to Trimalchio's these days only went for the name, and the name wasn't going anywhere. Leo was pretty hurt that she should say that.

He didn't argue with Mary, he couldn't, never had. When she told him she was taking him to London he knew he had no choice in the matter. That was why he was on this plane. That was why he was staring out of the window, staring at the soft, feathered surface of cloud beneath, feeling leaden, uncooperative and sad.

Mary was feeling anything but sad. She was remembering her lover, her theorist. She was finding the noise and vibration of the plane reassuring and erotic. The seat seemed to support and envelop her like a strong, well-engineered lover.

She had first met him a couple of years ago in the Los Angeles Museum of Contemporary Art. She didn't have much time or taste for art but she spent many hours in that gallery, enjoying the bright sheen of the floors, the clean space, the slow, over-reverent passage of the other visitors. There was a lightness, a stillness about the place. Nothing bad could ever happen to her there.

She knew right away that he was English and older than her. He must be, what, sixty years old, not really her type. Her ideal for this kind of liaison would have been a cute but disposable young man. She knew as well that he would approach her with some rather tired, obvious pick-up line. Because he was English and rich and had an aristocratic manner, a wolfish smile, a sweep of metallic white hair, a blazer, a college tie, immaculate white cuffs, he thought he could get away with murder. And as far as Mary was concerned, he could. He had about him an authentic, enticing whiff of sulphur that she found irresistible.

They fell into conversation in front of a stack of Warhol's Brillo Boxes. He was no less corny than she'd been expecting. He said modern art was all very well, but his real enthusiasm was for the female nude; Renoir, Matisse, Klimt. The rest of the afternoon was a foregone conclusion. She followed the script. She felt as though she was on a gently descending escalator.

His body turned out to be unexceptional, not especially well-shaped. He had an appendix scar, some stretch marks, some asymmetrical flourishes of reddish hair on his back. And he had, this she had not expected, a small blue tattoo on his left buttock, a tattoo of a snake eating its own tail. He was no cute young man, and she was to find that he was not disposable either.

He was vague about what he was doing in the States. He said

he was on a short business trip, the business unspecified. He said something about 'trade', 'the leisure industry', something about 'heritage'. She didn't much care what he did or was in the real world, but she cared about what he did for her in the private world of their rented hotel bed. He seemed to have an infinite capacity for pleasure, a formidable, unassuageable appetite. He was ruthless, voracious, omnivorous. He scared her and she liked it. She soon knew that he would be more to her than an afternoon's anonymous pleasure. She gave him power over her and she knew he would not use it wisely, nor did she want him to.

She realised that first afternoon that what they were offering each other was destined to last far into some as yet unrevealed future, quite separate from and quite other than her marriage to Frank, or from any other casual relationship she might have, from any other lovers she might take. Her lover visited America briefly, irregularly, but often, and each time they met it was always the same; frantic, eager and dangerous. The necessary hunger was always there.

There were strange, edgy games involving knives and blindfolds and pieces of ice, and sometimes there was a third person, a male friend of his or some woman he'd picked up off the street. She did things with him, let him do things to her, that she could never previously have imagined, things she now knew she'd been waiting for all her life. She could never have told Frank that she wanted them, indeed, with Frank she would not have wanted them at all. But with her anonymous Englishman everything was permitted and desired.

Of course, he did not stay totally anonymous. She discovered his name: Charles Radcliffe. She talked to him about her life, her husband, her son, her boredom. In return he would theorise, talk to her about abstractions, ideas, things outside herself. He would construct small confections based on logic and language and thought; on the economics of pleasure, woman as cook, woman as poisoner, cookery as an act of love, consumption as affirmation, eating disorders as expressions of female revolt, the relationship between weaning and aggression.

She knew Frank suspected nothing, but even if he'd discovered she was having an affair with Radcliffe she thought he'd be somehow impressed, flattered. The snob in him would be complimented that someone so cultured, so conspicuously 'old money' as Radcliffe had taken an interest in his wife.

Radcliffe was not a nice man and he made sure she knew it. He told her about his other sexual conquests and about some savage business deals he'd made with the weak and unwary, and he told her tales about lechery and gluttony and drunkenness, all that nonsense at his club. He told her about the Everlasting Club, about what they got up to and why and how. She was appalled. She found it juvenile and wicked and sick and disgusting and terribly exciting. She said she wanted to be part of it all.

The occasional Leos of this world were fun but ultimately, perhaps primarily, they were not satisfying or sustaining. They were snacks, junk food. They left her feeling hungry. Radcliffe was the real thing for her. He was a feast.

Finally he had taken her to England, to the Everlasting Club. It had required all sorts of subterfuge to enable her to get to England without Frank accompanying her. She had had to tell any number of lies about wanting to see her family, but she had succeeded.

At the Everlasting Club she had been treated royally. Men fussed over her, deferred to her, offered her drinks, cigarettes, lights, seats. Like Radcliffe, these men had for her a dangerous, brimstone air about them. She loved them. She felt at home. She was staggered by the food. Who would not be? She ate all manner of things she had never tasted before. She wondered where they got their chefs. She had drunk too much, eaten too much, been indiscreet, but that was fine. That was what a club ought to be for. It was what she had been looking for. It was what she'd always wanted.

After her first visit, Radcliffe asked her if she wanted to be a member. She hadn't even thought that women could join. She supposed women could only be guests at this all-male establishment. She interpreted the offer as some supreme act of affection, almost as a confession of love by Radcliffe. She said, 'Sure.' The England of gentlemen's clubs was a long way from the England she'd known in Dartford. Radcliffe told her how few women had ever been accepted into the Everlasting Club, how special this made her. But by now, thanks largely to him, she was accustomed to thinking of herself as special.

Since joining, she had only visited the club a couple of times, and that only after even more elaborate intrigue to deceive Frank. But now she was on a plane to England, flying to London to meet Radcliffe, her English lover, her theorist, and she was taking with her Leo, her other lover.

She turned to Leo and said, 'We're going to England to attend a surprise party.'

He shuffled in his seat, turned his back towards Mary, concentrated on the soft emptiness outside the plane window. Once again she wasn't making any sense. He could no longer tell when she was being serious and when she wasn't. If she wasn't going to talk sense to him, he wasn't going to talk to her at all.

He stayed alone with his thoughts. He thought about lobster and caviar, and about dogfish and monkfish, and about some new ideas he had for serving John Dory. And he thought of grilled swordfish with chervil and fennel leaves, and of tiger prawns and angel-fish and conger eels, and yes, he thought there probably was something terribly sexual in all this. And he knew that this was his career, his life, and he knew that it was all in jeopardy, in danger of curdling, separating, boiling dry. He knew he had it in him to be a great chef, and that he was in danger of becoming a great nothing. He had to work very hard to stop Mary seeing a big tear roll down his cheek.

Scenes from a History of the Everlasting Club.
Number Eight: A Word from an Author.

When I, Charles Radcliffe, was a boy it seemed to me that all religion was a form of magic, magic made decent and respectable. Jesus was a kind of master magician.

I would read the account of the feeding of the five thousand as it appeared in John and there was nothing metaphoric about it. Nothing was said of spiritual hunger. It said, still says, quite plainly that Jesus took the five loaves and two fishes and he magically produced enough food for five thousand people, real food to satisfy a real, bodily hunger. It wasn't just the bread of heaven.

And Jesus turned water into wine. That was a good trick but not an especially holy one. And healing the sick? Well, that may not be entirely magical, but what of raising himself and others from the dead? What is that but pure wizardry?

And there was much talk in the Bible of ghosts, even if it was a holy ghost. And surely there was something magical about a faith that preached resurrection and eternal life. What could be more magical and less natural than being immortal?

I became obsessed with transubstantiation. I read of Pope Innocent the Third who, at the Fourth Lateran Council, declared that the bread and wine of the Eucharist were literally the body and blood of Christ. The priest, I thought, became at that moment a magician, though only, of course, with God's help. And did he not also become a sort of butcher, a dealer in the ancient magic of blood and sacrifice?

I thought it was easy enough to turn bread and wine into flesh. You simply ate it. You digested it and it became a part of you. There was nothing very magical or miraculous there. But that was not what the priests were talking about. They were talking about a much better trick than that, much better magic.

I wondered if I was being blasphemous by thinking of Christianity in this way. I hoped not. I hoped I was simply contemplating the many mysteries of God. As I say, I was only a boy.

I worried about practicalities. Once the bread has been consecrated it must remain in the pyx, a small box used specifically for this purpose. What if a church mouse found its way to the altar, knocked over the pyx and ate some of the body of Christ? The mouse could not be guilty of anything, being ignorant and simply obeying its nature. But the theological consequences of the body of Christ being eaten by a rodent left me dizzy. And what if that mouse was eaten by a church cat? And what if there was a famine in the land and someone killed the cat for food and ate it . . . ?

I wondered about the process whereby the body of Christ became part of my own body. What if I was sick after eating a wafer? Would my vomit be holy? And if I didn't vomit and the wafer was digested then sooner or later it would pass out of me. Would any part of my excrement be part of the body of Christ? Or would some other miracle have taken place in the course of digestion and would the holy body have turned back to bread?

I worried too that some wafers might get stolen. Witches or devil-worshippers might find all kinds of satanic uses for them, essential in their black masses. Just imagine, our Lord's body being abused, ripped apart by the teeth of fiends.

I became an altar boy. One day I went into the church, saw that the pyx had not been knocked over and that there were no mouse droppings around. I opened the lid of the pyx to look at the wafers inside, unleavened medallions as light as air, imprinted with a cross. I looked more closely and saw that although the wafers looked untouched they were spotted with tiny red dots. It looked exactly like blood. If this bread was the body of Christ it made perfect sense that it was able to bleed, but it would not be bleeding unless somebody somewhere was defiling and assaulting the Lord. Who would have done such a thing? Blasphemers, heretics, devils, Jews.

It seemed to me that the Jews were most likely to be responsible. They had the motive. They had done this sort of thing before. Fortunately, the priest was able to explain that the dots of 'blood' on the wafers were a red bacillus that thrives on unleavened bread stored in warm places. I was relieved. It seemed to be a triumph for reason. It was not always thus. For centuries certain Jews were persecuted, tortured and killed for mutilating the body of Christ. The only evidence against them was a few wafers spotted with red bacillus. Thus are theological ideas made flesh.

I knew that God's love was not soft or easily given. I knew that the old forces were never far away. The old world of darkness was always almost with us, ready to manifest itself. There were witches who fornicated with demons, dead spirits who fornicated with the living, creatures who were half-man half-wolf, drinkers of blood, devils with two penises. Smoke drifts across the village, martyrs, the smell of burning, roast flesh.

The moral: never trust a pope who calls himself 'Innocent'.

I was only a boy. One's beliefs change over the years. One becomes less literal. One may no longer believe in gentle Jesus and yet one still hopes for eternal life. Certainly one continues to believe in ancient magic.

No pope has ever been invited to join the Everlasting Club, but we have no prejudice against Jews.

TEN

It was night. The cold air was brittle and there were no clouds. Butterworth sat at the wheel of the Bentley, his heart feeling too big for his chest, his stomach feeling hot and acidic. He was waiting for Kingsley to stumble out of the Everlasting Club. Butterworth carried with him a Bible, a crucifix and a two-foot length of lead pipe.

It was shortly after midnight when Kingsley emerged, distinctly early for him. He was unsteady. Something granular and orange had spilled down his jacket and no attempt had been made to wipe it off. He launched himself heavily through the open car door, and fell across the grey leather of the rear seat.

'Home, Butterworth!' he shouted, then relaxed into a soft, smiling stupor, but Butterworth had no intention of taking him home.

It was an hour and a half later when Kingsley woke up. He did not know where he was, although that, in itself, was no novelty. He looked out of the car window and saw grass and trees, no buildings, no streetlights. He was in some deserted rural place. He did not like it. Fortunately he was still seated in his own car, but that was little consolation. He remembered little of the earlier part of the evening but he could not believe he had asked Butterworth to bring him here. He became aware of an aching in his wrists and ankles, and looked down to discover he was tied up. Thick, frayed ropes were lashed and tangled around his hands and feet. The tying was inexpert but thoroughly effective.

He considered screaming for help but knew that nobody would come. In the end he said quietly and enquiringly, 'Are you there, Butterworth old man?' And suddenly Butterworth *was* there. He pulled the car door open. Kingsley was at first relieved to see Butterworth's large, familiar face, but it was wearing a deeply unfamiliar expression, an unholy mixture of anger, determination, hatred and piety.

'Could you be good enough to tell me precisely what's going

on?' Kingsley asked, his voice still showing his customary cheerful authority.

Butterworth grabbed him by the neck and yanked him raggedly out of the car. Kingsley's head and knees hit the ground. It was surprisingly soft, covered in pine needles; rustic indeed. But then he felt the hardness of Butterworth's highly polished brown shoes kicking him in the kidneys and temple.

'I say, Butterworth!' he yelled.

Butterworth towered over him. He was now holding a Bible and talking to himself urgently. Kingsley could not believe his eyes.

'What's the game, Butterworth?' Kingsley said.

'You want to know what's going on, do you?' said Butterworth.

'I do rather.'

'I can understand that,' said Butterworth. '*I* wanted to know what was going on too, but nobody told me. Why should they? After all, I'm only the serving class. I had to work it out for myself.'

'Is this some sort of practical joke?' Kingsley asked. 'Did some of the chaps put you up to it?'

'Chaps?' Butterworth repeated as though it was some new and obscene word he'd never encountered before.

'You're not drunk are you, Butterworth?'

'Don't judge me by your own standards.'

There was a passionate venom in Butterworth's manner that Kingsley had never seen before, would never have expected to find in the man. Kingsley found it as surprising as it was frightening.

'I know everything!' said Butterworth.

'Do you? Well, bully for you.'

Even as he said it, Kingsley was aware that Butterworth in his current mood would react adversely to flippancy. Butterworth kicked him again. Kingsley shouted out with pain.

'I know all about the Everlasting Club,' said Butterworth, allowing himself a small, sinister, triumphant smile.

'I doubt that very much,' said Kingsley.

'Of course, I'm not saying I know every single detail. I don't know all the petty little rules and regulations that I'm sure you're all really fond of. But I know the important thing, the *only* important thing.'

'You think so, do you?'

'Yes. I know that you eat human flesh,' said Butterworth.

Kingsley was silent. Real fear and panic filled him for the first time and drove out his drunkenness.

'Er . . . what makes you think that?'

'Stop playing,' said Butterworth. 'I don't care if you deny it or not. I'm not here to beat a confession out of you. Confession might be good for your soul, repentance might be even better, but that's not what I'm here for.'

'Is this supposed to be some form of blackmail? It won't work, you know. I'm not nearly as rich as you probably think I am.'

Butterworth shook his head. He looked offended by the mention of money.

'I really don't care how rich you are, or how rich you say you are. All I want to know is where you've got Virgil. Have you got him locked up in a dungeon somewhere, or what? Just tell me. I'll make sure he gets free, and maybe then I can think about freeing you too.'

'That's just not possible.'

'Anything's possible,' said Butterworth.

'Look, Butterworth, I haven't been such a bad employer to you, have I?'

Butterworth thought about it and looked unwilling to come to a conclusion.

'We can work this out, I'm sure,' said Kingsley. 'But the one thing I absolutely can't do is tell you where Virgil is. It would break all sorts of club rules. It's more than my life's worth.'

'But your life is worth so little.'

Butterworth put down the Bible. He reached into the car and brought out the piece of lead pipe. He hit Kingsley in the knees and shins half a dozen times. Kingsley squawked in high-pitched, disbelieving pain.

'Please, please,' said Kingsley, 'let me try to explain. All right, so we eat human flesh. Is that so terrible? It's certainly not unusual. It happens all the time. It's perfectly natural. It's been going on since time immemorial. It happens in all sorts of societies; societies that you and I might call primitive and heathen, but societies, in fact, which are far more in touch with spiritual truth than ours is. Eating human flesh is _holy_.'

Butterworth hit him a couple more times with the lead pipe, because of his blaspheming.

'I don't want to hear all this,' Butterworth said. 'Just you tell me where Virgil is. Save yourself some grief.'

'I can't tell you. I really can't.'

'You saying you don't know?'

'Of course I know, I'm the Chief Carver, but I can't tell.'

'Oh really? I think you can.'

It was a long night, and in the course of it, as he beat and tortured Kingsley, Butterworth frequently had to ask God for forgiveness. Just as any Christian must love the sinner and hate the sin, so Butterworth hated the pain he inflicted on poor Kingsley, but he knew it was in a good, and higher, cause. Butterworth discovered there was a fine art in keeping his victim conscious enough to be able still to feel pain. Too much violence brought oblivion and release, and that defeated the object of the exercise. It was all a matter of technique and Butterworth was a little surprised to see how easily the technique might be mastered.

It was nearly light, a thin watery dawn, and Kingsley's body was a mesh of bruises and weals before he finally named the place where Virgil could be found, a place that Rose had told him of in her daily phone call.

'I hope you're not lying to me,' said Butterworth. 'We'll drive there together and if I don't find Virgil, we can start all over again.'

Rose had to buy Virgil a new pair of trousers in Carlisle. The pair belonging to his Armani suit had started to hurt round the waist. Carlisle didn't have such a wide range of shopping options as L.A., but a simple pair of jeans were easy enough to obtain. Designer labels had even got as far as Carlisle, not that Virgil knew exactly where Carlisle was. The jeans she bought were on the large side, but Rose assured him he'd grow into them.

He was no longer sure how he felt about Rose. It wasn't altogether easy to like a woman who had abducted you, stolen your passport, made you eat when you weren't hungry and made you stay in shitty bed and breakfast dives. She may have been nice looking and she may have been easy enough to talk to, and she was certainly as wild as ever in bed, but Virgil knew she wouldn't be talking to him or bedding him if it weren't for the money she was getting from the Everlasting Club. That depressed him. He thought there were one or two things you shouldn't do for money, and sex was one of them.

And yet, and yet . . . Virgil hadn't made any desperate attempt to get away from Rose. He hadn't tried running to the police or to the American embassy, or tried phoning home for help. He'd thought about it but it all seemed like too much trouble. Most of the time he felt too drunk or too bloated to do anything. He was living in a haze induced by excesses of food, alcohol and sex. There were worse kinds of haze. In fact, it did occur to him that Rose might be putting some will-destroying substance in his food, not that Virgil ever had very much will to destroy. Besides, Rose did have a peculiar kind of integrity. When Virgil offered to pay her what she was getting from the Everlasting Club plus more besides, if only she'd let him go, she declined firmly. She'd made an agreement. A deal was a deal.

It did cross his mind that Rose might simply be insane. Maybe her story was untrue and she had kidnapped him for her own dubious ends. That would mean he was not being 'initiated' at all, and therefore there was no foreseeable end to this farce. But she didn't seem mad and she appeared to phone the club every day and report their whereabouts, so maybe he really was being initiated, whatever the hell that meant. And if, as she claimed, the plan was simply for her to feed and water him for a month, that month was very nearly at an end. What the hell happened next?

He dreaded to think about all the food he had consumed, digested and excreted over the past four weeks. Mother's milk was the least of it. He had become stuffed with 'English Fayre', with skate and ray and smelt and tench; with calf's head and ox tongue and bullock's heart and faggots; with endless local delicacies like Barnsley Chop and Cumberland Rum Nicky and Oxford John and Bedfordshire Clanger. He felt he was a very different man from the one who had first stepped off the plane and got into the car with Butterworth.

Finally, it looked like some small concession, Rose let Virgil go to the cinema. It was at some arts centre somewhere in the Midlands (wherever *that* was). The centre was not the kind of place Virgil could easily tolerate, being simultaneously worthy and Bohemian. Posters flapped from noticeboards, unplastered brick walls were painted a gleaming white. There was a counter selling dense, home-made wholefood.

They saw a triple bill of films, comprising of *Tom Jones*, *Babette's Feast* and *La Grande Bouffe*. Virgil might have known. He sat there in the dark, his eyes turned towards the screen, but his mind made no sense of the images. Projected scenes of seduction, cooking and gluttony moved disconnectedly before him. He felt ill. He felt, not for anything like the first time, that he'd had enough. He felt like a zombie. He tried to doze off but Rose would keep prodding him in the stomach so that he'd be awake for all the 'good bits'.

Hours later they emerged from the cinema. Virgil felt half-dead. Rose told him he needed a pick-me-up, so they made a trip to the bar. As Virgil drank some cold, weak, American-influenced lager, he noticed that a small group of people, almost an audience, was gathering down the far end of the bar. Rose took him by the elbow and they joined the group.

They turned out to be poetry lovers. An anorexic redhead was shuffling a bundle of typewritten sheets in preparation for a reading. She looked haunted and skeletal, a little demented. Virgil had the feeling he wasn't going to enjoy this very much. Nobody introduced her. She just stood up and began to read in a precise but fractured voice.

'I am gall,
I am heartburn,' she began.
'I am wormwood,
I am broth,
I am a Tuc cracker,
I am a Cheddar cheese,
I am sage.
I am the olive pit under your duvet,
I am peanut butter stuck to the roof of your mouth,
I am oatmeal,
I am All–Bran and hog's pudding and tripe.
I am a midnight feast,
I am a tuckshop,
I am your Christmas hamper,
your vacuum flask full of Horlicks.
I am the fly in your soup,
I am the grit in your oyster,
I am full–bodied,
I am blood.
I am wholemeal and granary and wheaten,
I am bloomer and rye.
I am eels and pies.
I am the set menu and the dish of the day.
I am the appetiser and the wedding feast.
I am the amputee's finger buffet.
I am bulimia,
I am food poisoning,
I am salmonella . . .'
'Oh my God,' said Virgil, not entirely to himself, 'this is all I need.'

He saw that the poetess no longer seemed to be reading from her manuscript. She seemed to be, oh no, improvising. Having hit her stride she might go on forever. Virgil slipped away from Rose, out of the bar, out of the arts centre. He had terrible stomach pains. Escape didn't even cross his mind. He climbed into the back of the Mercedes, swept food wrappers and crumbs off the back seat and gently lay down. He tried to adopt a foetal position but that made his stomach feel worse. He began to cry quietly. It was some time before Rose found him there.

'What's the matter, Virgil?' she asked, sliding into the front passenger seat.

'What the hell do you think?'

'I'm sorry,' she said, and she did sound sort of sorry to Virgil. 'Can I do anything to help?'

'Like what?'

'We could go and eat something.'

'Oh please.'

The tears streamed down Virgil's cheeks.

'How about oral sex?' Rose suggested. 'Or I could do something indecent with a bag of salted cashews while you watched.'

'No,' said Virgil, very softly and politely.

Rose looked at him sadly, genuinely sadly, with compassion. This was not the way she had imagined things would turn out.

'It's very nearly over,' she said. 'The month's very nearly up.'

'And then what?'

'Then I guess you're a member of the Everlasting Club.'

'And *then* what?'

'How should I know? Maybe then you can eat, drink and be merry for the rest of your life.'

'With some bunch of English assholes who I can't stand.'

'I'm really sorry, Virgil. Really.'

'Huh.'

They said nothing, and for a moment Virgil felt strangely at peace, as though he might fall into a blissful sleep. Then there was a rasp of tyres across the car park and a big car braked hard and stopped abruptly beside the Mercedes. Virgil opened his eyes but could see nothing from his foetal position. Rose looked round startled as the car door against which she was leaning suddenly opened. A man's black hand swept into the car and slapped her across the face, and a voice said, 'Jezebel!' It sounded like a voice Virgil knew, like Prince Charles maybe, like Butterworth, but Virgil didn't see how it could be. He thought he must be hallucinating. He was ready for hallucinations. But then sure enough Butterworth was peering into the back seat and saying, 'Everything's all right now, Virgil. I'm here and I've saved you.'

Half an hour later Butterworth and Virgil sat in the front seats of the Bentley. Rose and Kingsley were in the back, their hands and feet inexpertly tied with the same frayed rope. Rose was sniffling like some pink pet animal. Her mascara was running. Her jaw wobbled like soft rubber. She looked terminally miserable. From time to time she muttered that she was sorry, and complained that the rope was cutting into her ankles. Her regrets and her complaints fell on equally unsympathetic ears.

Butterworth's beating up of Kingsley had been discreet. Apart from a lot of dried blood below his left nostril he looked very little abused. The bruises and abrasions were all hidden by his clothes. His face inevitably wore a pained expression, but at the same time, perhaps because he felt there was little else Butterworth could do to hurt him, the pained expression was alloyed with a look of superior defiance.

'So let me get this straight,' said Virgil, 'I was going to be a human sacrifice for those suckers? They were going to kill me and eat me because they believe that eating people gives 'em some sort of immortality? I was being fattened up and stuffed by Rose, and Kingsley was going to do the carving? Is that it?'

'That's it,' said Butterworth.

Virgil laughed and shuddered simultaneously. How could you not find this absurd? How could you possibly believe all this shit? In fact, he'd have been perfectly happy to believe that Butterworth was some kind of headcase if it weren't for the fact that Kingsley, the prime mover of all this lunacy, was sitting there admitting that every word of it was true.

'How the hell could you think of slicing me up?' Virgil demanded of Kingsley.

'That's what a Chief Carver *does*. As I've always said, I'm a new boy at the Everlasting Club. Terrific honour and all that. You don't get made Chief Carver and then immediately start questioning all the rules, do you?'

'I don't know,' said Virgil. 'I've never been in that happy position.'

'It's a tradition, that's all,' said Kingsley.

'You've been eating people for three hundred and fifty years?'

'Not me personally . . .'

'You're a bunch of fucking maniacs. How the hell can you sit around a table and eat human flesh?'

'It's not so hard,' said Kingsley. 'You managed it.'

'WHAT?'

'You ate human flesh, Virgil,' he repeated. 'The dinner you had at the Everlasting Club. The sausages. I think you found them quite tasty.'

Virgil left the car and threw up for a while. When he returned he demanded, 'Why the fuck didya feed me human flesh?'

'We do it to all our guests. It gives us a kind of hold over them.'

Even Butterworth, who seemed to have a pretty strong stomach for the workings of Satan, looked a bit ill at this one, and Rose began to sob zestfully.

'And your father,' Kingsley said, 'he seemed to enjoy it too, like father, like son.'

'What's my father got to do with this? He's been to the Everlasting Club? He's in town?'

'Oh yes,' said Kingsley.

'Jesus,' said Virgil. Then a new train of thought shunted through his mind. 'My Dad was at the Everlasting Club eating human flesh? Another couple of days and he could have been eating *me!*'

Kingsley chuckled to himself. Virgil tried to hit him. Then he turned to Butterworth, looking lost and hopeless.

'I mean, what the fuck are we supposed to do about this?' he asked. 'Tell the police? I know your policemen are wonderful, but they're gonna think we're mad.'

'As fruitcakes,' Butterworth agreed.

'So what do we do?'

'I've been thinking about that,' said Butterworth. 'The important thing was to save you, and I've done that, but that doesn't solve everything. Running away isn't always the answer.'

'I'll buy that,' said Virgil, 'but what are we actually going to *do?*'

'I know what ought to be done,' said Butterworth.

'Yeah?'

'But it isn't a job for simple human agencies.'

'Huh?'

'We need to exorcise the Everlasting Club. We need to go back there, to that abominable place, and we need to drive a stake through its black, evil heart.'

Virgil held his head, trying to clear the fog inside.

'Are we talking figuratively here?' he enquired.

'We raze it,' said Butterworth. 'We do a little work with a few gallons of petrol. We torch the lot. It'll be a kind of purification.'

In the back of the Bentley, Rose and Kingsley exchanged fearful, panicky glances. Butterworth was sounding dangerously out of control, and they were at his mercy. Who knew what punishments he might devise and inflict on them in support of his holy war?

In the front of the Bentley, Virgil, befuddled by food, drink and whatever else Rose had been giving him, thought Butterworth was one of the more rational people he'd met in England. His plan sounded just fine to Virgil.

Scenes from a History of the Everlasting Club.

Number Nine: The Body Economic.

(A chapter Butterworth did not read)

Big fish eat little fish. That's life. That's the food chain. That's perfectly natural, and even if it were not natural, that is still the way it is.

Even the air that we breathe has been breathed already by someone else, has been part of someone else. A man dies. He returns to dust. His constituent parts return to the ecosystem, the solids and gases and vapours. They become part of the world. Before long we are breathing the man himself. We have breathed them all, breathed them in and breathed them out, Cortés and Fritz Haarmann and the Marquis de Sade.

And, by the same logic, we have eaten them too; worms, fish, kings, beggars; an old story, an old chain of being. And if that is not immortality, what is? A thousand years after a man's death we are still consuming his, admittedly somewhat changed, body. And we too shall be eaten; our atoms, our particles, our DNA. We have no choice but to be part of the cycle.

The body is in a state of partial flux. The body changes, re-forms itself. Skin is shed and replaced. Bones and hair and muscles are constantly remodelled. Certain organs at certain times can replenish themselves completely; the liver in childhood, for example. Others, the brain, the heart, are not so fortunate.

What is cannibalism? For some it is a mark of ultimate respect, a way of absorbing the strength and qualities of the one eaten. It is the kings, the warriors, the fine specimens, who get eaten, not the waifs and runts. We want to become like them. We want them to become part of us. We want their flesh to be our flesh.

For others it is the ultimate act of defilement. We have defeated you, destroyed you. We will finally reduce you to nothing. We will eat you, devour you, make you digestible, then shit you out. (Though it seems to us that that which defiles the eaten must also surely defile the eater.)

And yet even this defeated body, turned to faeces, becomes part of the same process, the same cycle. That which is excreted returns to the system. It becomes manure, fertiliser. Plants thrive in it and we eat the plants and thus we eat shit. It is all a process of degradation and reclamation. Everything turns to shit, then shit turns back into everything else. Shit is just an intermediate form.

Why do we love the smell of cooking yet hate the smell of shit? Is it perhaps because cookery is food transformed by art, whereas shit is food transformed by nature? It contains the smell of ourselves. Death is a stinking and messy business; that moment of death when the body no longer needs food or air, and when the bowels can no longer contain our excrement.

So, eat, drink and be merry, for tomorrow we might have no need of food. And even if we don't eat, don't drink, and aren't merry, we may die anyway. And even if we knew we weren't going to die tomorrow, that would still be no reason not to eat, drink and be merry.

We all make small stabs at immortality; via our deeds, our works, but primarily through our children. They contain our hopes, our nurturings, our genes; these things passed down from father to son by something more nebulous and urgent than a mere last will and testament.

We would like to believe in alchemy. We would like to believe that everything we touch turns to gold rather than to ashes, dust and faeces. We would like our children all to be golden boys and girls.

There is cannibalism in the jungle and in the desert, on the battlefield and in the prison camp, high in the Andes and on the raft of the *Medusa*, and also in the bedsits of those who kill for company. Sometimes it is celebration and sometimes it is desecration, sometimes for survival and sometimes just for the hell of it.

And sometimes it is a symbol.

Let us consider cannibalism as an analogy for a certain kind of economic transaction. Quite simply, the world is not sufficient. It is depressingly finite. It does not contain enough wealth, enough money, enough food. I am rich because you are poor. You are hungry because I am bloated. This is as natural as breathing.

Enough is not as good as a feast. Enough is never enough. Appetite is self-renewing. The urge to consume is an addiction. Fat cats gorge themselves. They doze in their offices, falling asleep over forecasts, projections, annual reports, dreaming of flow charts that record higher, more abstract dealings; the passage of love and cash, food chains and chains of command; a circulation. The money goes round and round, a relentless movement, a fidgeting, with no hint of stasis

151

or stability. Here and there are fatty deposits, spare tyres of wealth. Elsewhere there are famines, Malthusian shortages.

Empires form and flourish, then sicken and so die. The private enterprises, the small concerns, the minnows, are taken over, farmed, gobbled up, ingested. They become part of the larger body, which will also, with time, feel the ravages of age, become rotten, fall prey to the vultures, become so much manure. Money attracts money. The fat get fatter. Big fish eat little fish. Dog eats dog.

We expand or die, or both. Money feeds on itself, whets the appetite, creates a taste for transaction, for deal-making. It creates an insatiable, necessary hunger, a rich diet. Money lets us eat. Let us eat cake. Let us do business. Let's make a deal. Shall we join the others? Let's go into the dining-room.

ELEVEN

Frank woke from shadowy, convoluted nightmares into a blizzard of remorse. He was in a strange hotel room, tangled up in smooth, unfamiliar linen sheets. The borrowed dinner jacket hung on a chair, spattered with ambiguous liquids and solids. Frank was not the kind of man who could easily shrug off humiliation, particularly not when he had inflicted it upon himself. Drink had got the better of him, but that was no excuse. He had *let* drink get the better of him. He had fallen down before it. Where now was his dream of culture, civilisation and European values? He had revealed himself to be exactly the kind of schmuck he had fought all his life not to be. He was a hayseed, a hick from the sticks. He had been found out. He loathed himself and he loathed his ambitions, aspirations and pretentions. He should have stayed home. He should have stayed in the shallow little duck pond he knew. He should have stuck with California, with boring, wholesome food, with certainties. All his problems had been caused by trying to be something he wasn't. If he hadn't opened Trimalchio's, if he hadn't employed Leo, if he hadn't put Virgil in charge, if he hadn't come to England, if he hadn't accepted Kingsley's invitation . . .

He was supposed to be in England looking for his son in order to discuss business. He hadn't found Virgil which wasn't so surprising maybe, but the fact was he hadn't even tried. He'd just flown to England and got stinking drunk. He felt pretty worthless. Serious, successful, cultured businessmen did not find themselves apocalyptically hungover in strange countries, in strange hotel rooms.

There was a knock on the door, and before Frank could tell the person on the other side not to come in, that he wasn't receiving visitors, the door had opened and a man he only half-recognised from the Everlasting Club had entered. Frank pulled the sheets around himself protectively.

'Hello, Frank,' said the intruder. 'You remember me. My name's Charles Radcliffe.'

153

Frank nodded unconvincingly. Oh Jesus, was there not going to be any let-up? When a guy's made an asshole of himself, surely the least they could do was give him a day or two to live it down. He had barely woken up and already one of the club's big noises was here, to do what exactly? Humiliate him some more? To tell him precisely what kind of asshole he'd been? To demand his pound of flesh?

In fact, Radcliffe was in the process of opening his briefcase and taking out a small, squat tumbler and a half-pint bottle containing some grey, inert liquid.

'This will have you feeling better in no time,' he said to Frank.

He filled the tumbler and handed it over. The idea of putting anything in his mouth was repellent to Frank, caused strange heavings to begin in his insides, but Radcliffe's patrician manner was persuasive and Frank's desire for penance was considerable. So he accepted the dubious potion and swallowed it down, taking his medicine.

'There is quite a science to hangover cures,' said Radcliffe, 'to say nothing of folklore. But we could save that discussion for another time perhaps.'

'Yeah. Perhaps,' said Frank.

The drink settled in his stomach in a surprisingly benign manner. He could almost believe it was doing him some good. Radcliffe sat down on the edge of the bed, a little too close for Frank's tastes.

'About last night,' said Frank, 'I know what you're going to say. I made a fool of myself. I admit it, okay? And I'm ready to face the consequences.'

'What sort of consequences were you envisaging?' asked Radcliffe, in a tone that Frank found inappropriately breezy.

'Paying for the damage, or whatever.'

'The only damage was that which you inflicted on yourself.'

'Then maybe I should pay a club fine or something.'

'No,' said Radcliffe. 'You were a guest at the Everlasting Club. Guests don't pay for anything. Only members pay.'

Frank pressed the palm of his hand to his hot, pulsing forehead.

'Not much chance of me ever getting to be a member now, right?'

Radcliffe looked as though he was giving the matter some consideration. Frank thought surely this must be play-acting. And when he said, 'Well, I wouldn't necessarily rule it out,' Frank had to assume he was just being kind.

'How's business?' Radcliffe asked.

'Fine,' said Frank, dismissively. If this was Radcliffe's attempt to change the subject and make conversation he didn't need it.

'How many Golden Boys are there in the chain now?'

'About forty,' said Frank.

'Do you own your own leases?'

'Some. Why do you want . . . ?'

'Heavily mortgaged?'

'Hey,' said Frank, moving awkwardly under the sheet, 'this isn't my idea of the right time and place.'

Radcliffe ignored Frank's protests. He said, 'I know you used to have ambitions to extend your operations to England.'

'That was a very short-lived ambition and it was a long time ago.'

'There are people in the Everlasting Club who could help you realise your ambitions, whatever they are.'

It seemed to Frank that Radcliffe was talking about something other than just opening restaurants. He saw opium smokers, cock fights, group sex, sombre rituals involving semen and holy water. Or were these just the residue of the shadowy, convoluted nightmares from which he had recently woken?

'I don't have many ambitions left,' he said.

'I think you're being too modest.'

'No I'm not,' said Frank.

'We don't have much time . . .' said Radcliffe.

Frank automatically looked at his watch. True, it was late morning, but he could imagine no commitment, no appointment, for which he could possibly be late.

'No, I don't mean time in that sense,' said Radcliffe. 'I mean that life is short, far too short. We want to fill it up. We want more of it. But life in itself is nothing. A profoundly miserable life might seem very long indeed. A truly pleasurable life might flash by all too rapidly. To live to a "ripe" old age is fine so long as that life contains sufficient enjoyment. I believe there are certain techniques available for prolonging both life and pleasure.'

'Like healthy eating?' said Frank.

Radcliffe got up from his spot on the bed. Frank was glad. He relaxed slightly.

'Look,' said Frank, 'you know, I'd be in a whole lot better shape to get philosophical if I'd had a shower and a shave.'

'Perhaps I'm only really talking about money,' said Radcliffe. 'People, businesses, institutions, they come and go. Today's household name is tomorrow's obsolete product. But money just goes on and on. Money seems to be immortal. What's your gross worth?'

'Hey,' said Frank, with as much indignation as he could manage, which wasn't very much, 'I'm not comfortable with this. I'm in a strange hotel room, I've got no clothes on and some guy I don't know is asking me details about my gross worth.'

'That's right,' said Radcliffe, pressing on. 'And what would happen if you died tomorrow? Have you made provision? Who'd get control of the company? Virgil? And what if something happened to him? Or would Mary take the reins?'

'How do you know all this stuff? How do you know my son and wife's names?'

'Relax, Frank. I read a profile of you in a trade paper, that's all.'

That was possible. Frank had received enough publicity that someone might possibly have read and remembered the names of his son and wife. But did Radcliffe really look like the kind of guy who read trade papers of the American fast food industry? Everybody knew how devious the English were; perverse and duplicitous and vicious, and that was only their sex lives.

Now Radcliffe looked at his own watch. 'It *is* nearly lunchtime,' he said.

Frank groaned thinly. The hangover cure was working slowly, but he wasn't ready to think about food, not even ready to hear the word.

'I really don't think so,' he said.

'I insist that you be my guest.'

'No, really.'

'Be a sport, Frank.'

Frank shook his head sadly.

'You're right, of course,' said Radcliffe. 'There's no such thing as a free lunch, just as there's no such thing as free love. But sometimes it pays to say, hang the expense. The waiter delivers the bill. You don't even look at it. You simply snap down your credit card. Whatever the meal costs it's worth it.'

'I don't understand,' said Frank.

'You will. Over lunch. At the Everlasting Club.'

'Will they still let me in?' asked Frank.

'Of course.'

'This is pretty white of you guys.'

As he showered and shaved, experiencing the wet spikes of water on his torso and the scrape of the razor blade across his cheek, it did not escape Frank that this was still not much of a way to go about finding Virgil. Nothing was being solved by accepting lunch from

Radcliffe. Yet something told him it was the right thing to do. It somehow made sense to return to the dark, elaborate feastings and panellings of the Everlasting Club, back to those smells of Cuban cigars and roasting meat. It was a second chance. It was good to know he was still wanted there. This time he wouldn't blow it. Radcliffe didn't seem like such a bad guy after all, and he certainly had one hell of a cure for a hangover.

Frank dried himself with exaggerated vigour. He was starting to feel good. He looked at himself in the bathroom mirror. If he tautened his stomach muscles only slightly he still looked like a reasonable figure of a man. He was ready for the Everlasting Club.

Radcliffe, inevitably, had a spare, unstained dinner jacket in his car. This invitation to lunch was apparently no spur of the moment thing. Frank slipped on the jacket. If he said so himself, he was the kind of guy who could wear a tux. He let himself be blindfolded and sat a little rigidly in the passenger seat as Radcliffe drove to the Everlasting Club. Frank imagined a day when this blindfold would no longer be necessary, when he would drive boldly and directly to the club, head held high, eyes wide open, and he would march straight in, proudly and of right. But not today.

When the car stopped Radcliffe retightened the blindfold and guided Frank across the pavement, along the short gravel path, up the steps and through the front door into the club. Frank heard the door close behind him. Nothing happened for a while.

'Hey,' he said to Radcliffe, 'can I take this blindfold off now? Hey, did you hear me?'

He immediately realised that Radcliffe was no longer beside him. Where the hell had he gone, and why? Frank tore off the blindfold with some petulance and looked around the small hallway where he now stood alone. Three doors faced him. One, he knew, led to the bar, but there was something not quite right about this. When he had stood here before, a great wave of noise had pressed up against that door, noise from the bar, sounds of drinking, talking and partying. The thin door in front of him would not be enough to contain all that sound. Things had gone very dead in there. Maybe lunchtimes at the Everlasting Club were always quiet. Maybe there was another explanation.

Gingerly and with the hope that he wasn't breaking some obscure but all-important club rule, he tried the door to the bar. He would perhaps have felt happier if the door hadn't opened, but it did.

A part of him was already aware there would be nobody home,

and yet the awful emptiness on the other side of the door still threw him. The big room was completely devoid of people. The lights were down low. A couple of logs glowed uncertainly in the fireplace. Every table was vacant, and the whole place was still and gloomy and deserted. And recently deserted too. There were half-empty glasses on the tables and on the bar, cigars and cigarettes were stubbed out in the ashtrays. It was as if everybody had simultaneously run away in fear and panic.

'What the fuck am I doing here?' Frank asked himself.

He walked a wide circuit around the dimly lit room. He peered carefully at the abandoned drinks and at the chairs that looked as though they'd been hastily pushed aside, but he didn't know what he was really looking for. Clues? But he didn't know what mystery he was trying to solve. Maybe there was a simple explanation. Maybe he'd arrived in the middle of a fire drill. Even he couldn't be convinced by such a mundane explanation, and that didn't explain Radcliffe's disappearance.

Frank did not know what to do. Should he pour himself a drink and wait patiently for something to happen or for someone to appear? Should he shout, 'Anybody there? Anybody serving at the bar?' But it was perfectly obvious nobody was.

He felt like an intruder, like a burglar. Radcliffe had set him up for this and then ditched him. Was it possible, therefore, that this was some sort of test? Perhaps in order to be accepted into the club he had to somehow do the right thing. He could not imagine what the right thing was, but presumably it wasn't helping yourself to free drinks. He decided to do nothing, just sit patiently, but his resolve did not last. This place gave him the creeps. Okay, maybe that meant he didn't belong there. He certainly didn't belong there totally alone. He got up and paced and sat down and then got up and paced again. This was ridiculous. This was really starting to piss him off. What was the point of hanging out in the bar? If he was going to pass some 'test' or other, he surely wasn't going to do it there. He was going to do some exploring. He knew that mightn't be the right thing to do either. Nobody wanted a club member who stuck his nose in where it didn't belong, but equally, a guy who sat nervously in the bar being a nerd must be even less attractive as a potential new boy.

There was a long, darkened corridor that led out of the bar. Frank remembered walking down it on the way to the dining-room. Then it had seemed spacious and inviting. Today a dark threat hung over it. Still, Frank was ready to face dark threats. He entered the corridor.

There were doors leading off it at intervals. Frank knocked on them, even called out weakly, 'Anybody home?' But he didn't have the nerve to open any of the doors and look inside.

Frank was lost and bewildered. Last time he was here everything had been so friendly and welcoming. He'd wanted to be part of it all. So why did it now seem so bleak and forbidding? He felt not only the absence of people and conviviality, but also the presence of something truly sinister and threatening.

He walked to the end of the corridor, turned a corner, and thought he detected the smell of cooking. He couldn't identify it completely. Was it cauliflower mingled with lime? But this was surely a good sign, a sign of life. If he could track down the kitchens he could surely find people, chefs hard at work preparing some of the hundreds of dishes that the Everlasting Club must get through in the course of a day.

But he didn't find any kitchen, didn't even know where to start looking. After a while the cooking smell was no longer detectable and he was left wondering if he'd imagined it. Then he thought he smelled petrol, but he knew that was impossible. Then he thought he heard footsteps, then he decided he was hallucinating.

He did however, at last, find the dining-room. He saw the two big panelled doors that he'd passed through on his way in to dinner. Then they had been open and somehow festive, but now they were firmly shut. Frank decided he'd had enough of jerking around. He'd had enough of being polite and knocking softly on doors. He was going in.

He turned one door handle, determined yet casual, as though there was nothing to it, certainly as though there could be nothing to fear on the other side. Then the door opened and he looked inside and he realised he could have been wrong.

The room looked at first as though it was as dark and dead as the rest of the building. The only light came from a couple of candles that flickered in candle-holders along the walls. The effect was disturbingly churchy. He wouldn't have been surprised to hear organ music. He could just make out the refectory table at the room's centre. He went in, not entirely certain why he did so, and in due course his eyes got used to the darkness and then he could see something on the table. It was white and it had curves and a moment later he knew it was a body; female, naked, and utterly still.

He got very close to the table and began to scrutinise the body, not that it required much scrutinising. He knew precisely whose body it was. He reached out as though to touch the bare right arm. He shivered. His mouth had no saliva. His legs had developed a tremble. He feared the worst, that the flesh might be stone cold, that it might be a corpse on that table. He drew back his hand. He couldn't bring himself to touch and find out. He said very quietly, 'Mary.'

He leaned over his wife's body. He saw the soft, comfortable, familiar breasts, breasts with which he had become rather less familiar in the last few years, but it was the sort of thing you didn't forget. He looked at the face. The eyes and lips were painted. The cheeks were dusted with powder. Then he thought, or was it perhaps just a flicker of the candlelight, he saw a gentle movement, a twitch at the corner of the mouth. He wanted to scream. And then, in an instant, the face was suddenly mobile, exploding in a fit of laughter that could no longer be contained. The body leapt into life, sat up, and Mary screeched, 'Surprise! Surprise!'

The dining-room exploded into light and noise. A couple of dozen revellers, all men, all dressed in dinner jackets, burst through the door, popping champagne corks as they came. Streamers jetted through the air, balloons bounced up to the ceiling. There was cheering and barrages of laughter and Mary stood on the table and danced naked for a short while until someone threw her a robe.

Frank, speechless, gasping, utterly at sea, found himself at the centre of a raucous, backslapping huddle, having champagne poured over him by men he didn't know. Somewhere, not far away, a Glen Miller record started to play very loudly, and everyone wanted to shake Frank's hand. A posse of waiters arrived delivering platters and tureens of elaborately arranged food. Simultaneous renditions of 'For he's a jolly good fellow' and 'Happy Birthday to You' clashed with each other and with the Glen Miller record. Frank could only say, 'But it's not my birthday.'

Various toasts were drunk to Frank's continuing good health, to his capacity for drink, to his business acumen, to his power as a sire. Mary ruffled his hair and gave him an unusually wet kiss. And then, and this was when Frank thought he might have lost his wits completely, Leo appeared bearing a tray of sausages. He looked drunk and hesitant, but nevertheless, he was very warm towards Frank and told the room that nobody had ever had a better employer.

'Some surprise, eh, Frank?' said Mary, but she was gone before he could answer. He wouldn't have denied it. This certainly wasn't the surprise party he'd been expecting.

Despite all the bonhomie and the frequent eruptions of good cheer, nobody was actually talking to Frank. He found this galling. It was supposed to be his party, after all. So he grabbed Radcliffe by the arm and pulled him into a corner. Radcliffe was not a man accustomed to being pulled into corners. Frank unhanded him hastily and smoothed the arm of his jacket, afraid he might have broken another club rule. Radcliffe turned a sedate ear towards Frank.

'Look,' said Frank, urgently, 'I don't understand this. Does this mean I'm one of you?'

Radcliffe looked at him slyly.

'Do you think you know what it means to be one of us?' he asked.

'Well sure. That is, I think I do.'

'I think not,' said Radcliffe, 'but certainly this is the occasion on which you are likely to find out.'

'Oh well, fine then,' said Frank, understanding nothing.

Radcliffe darted away. The dozens of questions stacking up in Frank's mind would have to wait. He looked around for someone else to talk to; no good. Nobody seemed to want to talk to him, not even Leo; especially not Leo. Frank got himself another drink. At least the waiters weren't avoiding him. It was pretty good champagne. He quickly drank a couple of glasses.

At which point Virgil and Butterworth burst into the room brandishing cigarette lighters and carrying what looked like giant cans of cooking oil, and Virgil yelled, 'One false move and you're all fried.'

Right from the beginning it had felt a little wrong to Virgil. He and Butterworth could hardly believe their luck in arriving at the Everlasting Club to find it dark and deserted. Their plan, Butterworth's plan, was at best unsophisticated. He knew where the club's tradesmen's entrance was, so he and Virgil, dressed up as delivery men, had arrived carrying a few giant cans of cooking oil; supplies for the kitchen. But the cans did not contain cooking oil. They contained petrol. Once inside the club the idea was that they should run amok, shout a lot, cause panic, splash petrol on every available surface, wave cigarette lighters around, beat off anyone who tried to stop them, and finally ignite the petrol, causing flames to run through the club like some heavenly, avenging wave.

Even to Virgil's less than clear mind this had seemed at first just a little extreme, but then again, in his present state he couldn't think of any other way to rid the world of those sick dudes, so he'd decided to go with the flow.

Virgil thought, in so far as he was capable of thinking, that the plan's main virtue was its element of surprise. Let's face it, he told himself, when you're sitting in your club, pie-eyed and stuffed full of food, you don't expect two maniacs in workman's overalls to appear out of nowhere and douse you in petrol. By the time any of the members had worked out what was happening he and Butterworth ought to be out of there, everyone being too concerned with fighting the fire to give chase.

That was the theory anyway. He could see that the plan contained a good deal of risk, and seemed to require considerable bravery on his part. He wasn't at all sure that he possessed that bravery, but Butterworth assured him that God was on his side and that the necessary bravery would be provided. Virgil took his word for it.

Butterworth also offered the opinion that once they'd set the petrol alight, it would be up to God to decide how many, if any, of the Everlasting Club's members survived. Virgil really wasn't too sure about all this God stuff, but before long it was too late. Butterworth was off and running, and a still confused, still drifting Virgil was being dragged along in his turbulent slipstream.

Butterworth developed an icy, righteous calm that didn't make Virgil feel very easy, nor was he impressed by the quantities of religious paraphernalia that Butterworth insisted on carrying with him. If God was really on their side, why did they need the lucky mascots?

There had been the problem of what to do with Kingsley and Rose. Butterworth felt he had imposed enough torture on Kingsley for the time being, and Rose, even he realised, had never been much more than a paid dupe. They were to be excused the worst excesses of Butterworth's wrath, nevertheless they had to be got out of the way for a while. Butterworth's solution was not one that Virgil would have expected from a good Christian. He stripped them naked, tied them very tightly together facing each other, then locked them in the boot of the Bentley. The car was then parked in a lonely lay-by somewhere outside Nottingham. Virgil almost protested that this was going too far, but he could tell that Butterworth was in no mood to listen to protests.

Thus Butterworth and Virgil arrived at the tradesmen's entrance of the Everlasting Club, ready to put the plan into effect, and were unable to believe their luck in finding the place dark and deserted.

But Virgil wasn't sure it had much to do with luck. How could it possibly be that a club which had run successfully and continuously for over three hundred years, happened to have fallen into a lull on the very day that he and Butterworth had come to destroy it? He had the profound feeling that some counterplan was shaping itself around them and that they might be ambushed at any moment. But they had padded about the dim, empty corridors of the Everlasting Club, penetrating deep into its panelled offices, and into the library and the club rooms, leaving a generous trail of petrol as they went, and they had seen no signs of life, much less of ambush. At one point Virgil thought he heard footsteps and a voice he recognised, but he concluded it was only his imagination.

It had just begun to occur to Virgil that they might be able to get the job done and make their exit without meeting obstacles or people, without needing any God-given bravery. They would be able to turn the place into an inferno without putting themselves at any risk. Since the place was empty they would destroy the building without inflicting any casualties, and although that didn't have the element of ritualistic destruction Butterworth wanted, Virgil would probably have settled for it.

They had distributed nearly all their petrol and were about to turn back when all hell broke loose. They were in one of the club rooms at the time. They heard footsteps outside, perfectly real this time. They heard a door open, a silence, and then shouts of 'Surprise! Surprise!' and the generalised sounds of guys whooping it up. Virgil remembered enough of the geography of the club to know that the commotion was coming from the dining-room. He pictured a group of people at the table, cannibals tucking into human flesh, gnawing on elbows and feet and thigh bones. Butterworth began to pray.

'Let's get out of here,' said Virgil, his bravery quite absent. 'Very, very fast.'

Butterworth started reluctantly to move, then stopped.

'No,' he said. 'We don't have to run any longer. Let's face them.'

'You're crazy,' said Virgil. 'We can still get out of here without anybody seeing us. We can light the petrol as we go, and we're home free.'

'It's not enough,' said Butterworth. 'I need to speak to them. They need to know why they're going to die.'

Virgil knew this was madness. He wanted to run away. Yet, he couldn't deny it, there was something actually persuasive and charismatic about Butterworth by now, and despite Virgil's caution and cowardice he found himself agreeing with Butterworth.

Heads high, cigarette lighters in one hand, almost empty petrol cans in the other, they burst into the dining-room and Virgil yelled, 'One false move and you're all fried.' And then, a moment later, he said, 'Oh, hi Mom. Hi Dad. Hi Leo.'

Some time later they were in a high-ceilinged, echoless, velvet-curtained room somewhere deep in the Everlasting Club; Radcliffe, Butterworth, Leo, and the Marcel family – father, mother and son. All but Radcliffe sat in a semi-circle on tall, ladder-back chairs. Drinks had been served. The surprise party was over. Butterworth and Virgil had brought it to an abrupt conclusion. They had been persuaded to put away their cigarette lighters, Virgil quite easily since he was a good enough son not to want to see his mother and father go up in flames, Butterworth rather less easily. Even now, teams of staff were at work in the club trying to rid rooms and corridors of the smell and stain of petrol.

'I don't want to sound like a member of the master race,' said Radcliffe, 'but you really were incredibly stupid, Butterworth, to believe we literally eat one another at the Everlasting Club. This is England. We are decent, civilised men, and cannibalism is a *metaphor*. I'm rather surprised you didn't grasp that, Butterworth. After all, your Bible is rather full of metaphors.'

Radcliffe stood before his audience. He was confident, in control. He had the voice of authority and command and of money.

'Yes, the Everlasting Club is concerned with a form of perpetuation, but not the sort of perpetuation that comes from consuming the muscles and organs of human beings. That would be naïve. We are not naïve. None of us at the Everlasting Club is naïve. None of us believes in immortality, neither in the religious nor the physical sense. Merely to live forever seems to us a banal scheme, like dull science fiction.

'We wish to perpetuate ourselves through actions, deeds, ideas, through wealth and a certain order of financial transaction. Call it power, call it manipulation. In the end we are businessmen, the superior sort, our appetites whetted by the complexities and the thrill of organisation and interaction. The "fast buck" does not interest us. Am I making myself clear?'

Radcliffe looked about the room, his line of vision deliberately above the heads of his listeners. Frank Marcel shifted his weight from one buttock to the other and said, 'No you're not. Not really. Like you could begin by explaining what I'm doing here. And what are my wife and son doing here? And Leo. Why the surprise party? Why here? How come Mary danced naked on the table?'

'And what about me?' Virgil demanded. 'Why was I kidnapped by Rose?'

'You weren't kidnapped,' said Radcliffe dismissively. 'You simply received a little corporate hospitality.'

'Oh sure.'

Radcliffe turned his back on the group. He was not there to discuss anything. He steeled himself, adopted an even more lordly posture, turned back to them, his face showing disdain. He was not to be argued with. He was not about to give up the floor.

He continued, 'Are we then, drawing some apparently cheap comparison between cannibalism and capitalism? Well, yes and no. It is a dog eat dog world, and big fish certainly eat little fish. These two old saws describe the problem, but not unproblematically.

'Imagine a pack of starving dogs, or of starving peasants if you prefer. The food runs out. At first they may survive on what little fat they have, but sooner or later, however much they resist, however unwilling they are, they will be forced to eat each other. Some therefore achieve a brief survival, but once their fellow dogs are eaten, the survivors are once again starving. Dog eats dog eats dog until finally there is only one dog left, a top dog, a top peasant, who has eaten himself into a corner and into oblivion, who must now perish, having nothing else on which to feed.

'Now, we ask ourselves, does this sound like a persuasive or desirable economic model?'

Radcliffe paused as though to give the slower members of class a chance to raise their hands and answer the question. Virgil, his head clearer than for some time, thought he was about to explode with rage. This was even more crazy than all the other crazy bullshit he'd been through. A lecture on models of economic activity he did not need; not now, not ever.

Radcliffe said, 'Well, no, I agree, it does not, because that kind of economic cannibalism destroys both the commodity and the market.'

He bowed his head slightly, as if ready to accept a little light applause, the conjurer who has performed a minor illusion and is now ready to move on to grander things.

'So let us consider the food chain,' said Radcliffe. 'It is a necessary, continuing, self-perpetuating system. Big fish eat little fish but they do not destroy the whole population of minnows. They allow growth, development. They ensure the survival of some of the small fry.

'The savage believes that by digesting the flesh of his brave but defeated adversary he will become stronger. He takes on the quality of his prey. Likewise, when a tribe eats its ancestors, it attempts to enfold and recycle those cultural traits which make it stronger, more fit.

'We at the Everlasting Club believe in this too. And it is in this precise, limited and metaphoric sense that we are indeed cannibalistic.'

There were blank faces in the room, suspicions of mania, of darker revelations, of death and decay, of mayhem that might be far from metaphoric. Though not from Mary. She was serene, regal, self-possessed.

'We know we cannot feed on ourselves. We look backwards to our traditions, and about us for fresh prey. We are hungry for new potential, for profit. We always need new blood. That is why you are here. That is why you have been delivered to us.'

At first it was not clear who Radcliffe was addressing. Virgil wondered if that word 'delivery' somehow meant he was still on the menu, that he was the fresh meat. Even Butterworth feared he might have made some terrible move from exorcist to sacrificial victim. Deliver us from evil. But slowly it became clear that Radcliffe was addressing only Frank.

'We want to absorb you,' Radcliffe said. 'We want your business. We want the Golden Boy chain of restaurants. We want Trimalchio's. We want Leo to be head chef at the Everlasting Club.'

'Oh come on,' said Virgil. Could this really be what it was all about? Could all these indirections have only brought him here, to a take-over bid for his father's company from some shadowy English consortium?

Mary smiled radiantly, triumphantly, as though she was responsible, as if it was all her idea. Frank didn't understand. He realised now that he hadn't understood, or even known, Mary for years. He hadn't a clue what was going on in her mind. The only thing he did know was that the bitch was enjoying this, enjoying his confusion and panic.

'You know I don't want to sell,' said Frank.

'Of course we know that,' said Radcliffe. 'Nobody wants to be swallowed up. But the cannibalism metaphor only goes so far, Frank. We aren't, after all, going to carve you up. We aren't going to chew you up and spit out the bones. We are going to pay you good money, the going rate and a little more. There will be generous consultancy fees for you, a seat on the board for Mary, a sinecure for Virgil if required. There will be expense accounts and free travel and company perks. We will make you a very rich man. It all makes economic sense.'

'Look,' said Frank, 'it may come as a surprise to you that I'm not in this solely for the money. You're not the first outfit that's come to me trying to buy the Golden Boys. But frankly, I can't think of one good reason for selling.'

'I can,' said Mary, 'and you can too if you really put your mind to it.'

Frank Marcel had long experience of never really listening to his wife, of believing she could have nothing worthwhile to say. Now, however, something told him that he'd better listen to her. The prospect was new and unsettling. He was also unsettled by the way Mary and Radcliffe kept looking at each other. There was something intimate and secretive about it. It made him feel sick in his stomach.

'Ultimately you're going to sell to Radcliffe's consortium,' said Mary, 'because I want you to.'

Frank was about to splutter something about that being the dumbest thing he'd heard anybody say in a very long time, but Mary didn't give him the chance to interrupt.

'I can see I'll have to give you chapter and verse on this,' she said. 'The bottom line is that if you don't sell to Radcliffe, I'll sue you for divorce. Think about the consequences of that.'

'Is that what this is about? You want a divorce?'

'No, I don't actually,' she said. 'It suits me pretty well to be married to you, but I want you to sell the Golden Boys to Radcliffe, and if you don't I'll file for divorce and take you for every penny you've got.

'I know what you used to get up to on all those business trips. You weren't the most faithful of husbands, Frank. And the courts would love to hear how vital I've been to your business success. I'll get at least half your assets. The alimony I'll demand will kill you. Then there'll be massive legal costs, masses of bad publicity. I can ruin you, Frank. By the time I'm finished with you, you won't be able to afford *not* to sell.

'Also, of course, I happen to know what Leo used to get up to in the kitchen at Trimalchio's. How much money do you think it might take to keep me quiet on that one?'

'You'd do that to me?' Frank asked. 'Why?'

Mary gave a kind of shrug that said it didn't really matter why, on the other hand she wasn't going to spare his feelings by not telling him.

'Is it you and Radcliffe?' Frank demanded. 'Are you an item or something?'

'Oh Frank, don't be so unimaginative.'

'Then why?'

'Because I hate you, Frank,' she said.

Frank's face looked soft and blank, like something partly defrosted.

'You *will* be selling, Frank,' Mary said.

'On the bright side,' said Radcliffe, 'we'll also make you a life member of the Everlasting Club.'

Scenes from a History of the Everlasting Club.
Number Ten: A Kind of Divinity.

June 1772, an upper room in a waterfront house in Marseilles. On a narrow but clean bed, the eighteen-year-old Marianne Laverne feels as though her guts are being turned inside out by cruel, invisible hands. She is sweating. Her pulse trots and gallops erratically. As the evening progresses, what began as a painful but commonplace stomach-ache becomes ever more ferocious and debilitating. She needs constantly to urinate, but when she tries, it is like trying to piss flame. Soon she is vomiting blood and bile and what look like flakes of her stomach wall.

A doctor is called. It seems to him, as to everyone else, that Marianne must surely die. She has all the symptoms of arsenic poisoning. How, for the love of God, did she come to take arsenic? Marianne is initially as baffled as everyone else. How could she have taken it? All she has eaten all day are a few bonbons given her by a client.

She spent the morning in an apartment in the Rue des Capucins. A good-looking, well-dressed man called Latour, servant to a nobleman, had invited her and two other girls to entertain his master. He explained that the master had specific, eccentric tastes, but that he would pay very well. She was happy to go with him. She had been surprised by the master's youth and good looks. She had expected an old, ruined aristocrat. Instead, he had broad, strong features and fair hair. He wore an elegant grey coat and silk breeches. He carried a sword and a gold-topped cane.

Marianne had been led into a bedroom, stripped naked, pushed down on a bed and given a whipping by the master. Latour had watched without emotion. Then Latour had left and the master produced a box of sweets which he said would produce flatulence, a necessary accompaniment to the act of buggery he intended to perform on her.

She protested. She felt a girl had to protest before submitting. She said it was unnatural, a crime against God, and punishable on earth by the death penalty. The master was not pleased but he did not insist. Nevertheless she swallowed a number of bonbons. He produced a second whip, spiked this time, and invited her to use it on him. She was reluctant. She tried, but half-heartedly. He became angry, told her she was stupid and useless. It was then that she felt the first stirrings of pain in her stomach.

She had been told to leave the room and wait outside. Latour and an older woman she had not seen before took her place in the bedroom. There were the sounds of someone being thoroughly thrashed, then the two other girls went in. Marianne heard more whippings and then the noise of more orthodox sexual congress. Finally Marianne was needed again. She was whipped a little, then the nobleman buggered her, while he himself was buggered by his servant.

It was all over by lunchtime. Little in the morning's activities had surprised Marianne. She received six *livres* for her half day's work, and if it hadn't been for her stomach-ache, she would have felt on top of the world. Six hours later she feels as though she is dying.

Marianne does not die. She lives to tell the tale. The medical and legal professions are in close contact and she must tell all, tell tales of debauchery, poisoning and sodomy. She claims she took no part in the sodomy, that it was all between the two men. The law is coercive and she doesn't need very much coercing. After all, he tried to poison her, kill her. She is asked to reveal the name of her nobleman. She seems to recall that the servant referred to him both as Comte and Marquis, but she is in no doubt about the name: de Sade.

Despite all the efforts of police throughout the area, de Sade and Latour are not caught. However, they are tried *in absentia*, found guilty of poisoning and sodomy, and sentenced to death, no ordinary death. They are to appear at the cathedral of Ste Marie-Majeur, dressed as penitents, nooses round their necks, candles in their hands. They are to kneel before the cathedral doors and pray for forgiveness before being taken off for execution. De Sade is to be beheaded, Latour hanged, as fits their station as master and servant. Their corpses are not to be allowed to pollute conse-crated ground, so they are to be burned, and the ashes scattered by the winds.

All of which is rather theoretical, since by the time the sentence is passed de Sade is living in Nice under the protection of the kingdom of Sardinia, beyond the reach of French law.

The sweets did not, in fact, contain arsenic. They contained Spanish fly: cantharides, blister beetles dried and powdered, an aphrodisiac introduced into Western Europe by crusaders returning from their holy war. It seems unlikely that de Sade really intended to poison Marianne Laverne. More probably he made up the bonbons himself and miscalculated their strength. Genuine Spanish fly seems always to have been a dangerous substance. When applied to the skin it causes blistering. Consumed in quantity it can destroy the lining of the alimentary canal. Scholars differ as to whether its aphrodisiac properties are real or imagined, but presumably the risks attached to its use are part of its attraction.

A whiff of danger, an element of risk, may add savour to sexual activity, but Spanish fly seems to us to be taking things too far. There are safer, and scarcely less exotic, aphrodisiacs to be sampled: truffles, toad venom, chrysanthemum flowers soaked in wine, myrrh, ambergris.

The ancient Chinese considered deer, beavers, seals and lizards to be prolifically sexually active, so they ate the phalli of those creatures as aphrodisiacs. They wanted to have the same qualities as the animals they ate.

Consider the mandrake, Circe's plant. It grows by the gallows, fed on human sperm, the ejaculations of the hanged. Below the ground its gnarled white root takes on human shape, the shape of a man who screams as he is pulled out of the earth. The mandrake is considered to be an aphrodisiac strong enough to arouse the dead.

Somewhere in all this is a materialist impulse. If one possesses the appropriate aphrodisiac then one need possess nothing else. Good looks, charm, sexual finesse are superfluous. All one needs is the opportunity to administer the aphrodisiac. But most aphrodisiacs are not cheap, not easily come by. One needs money to be able to afford rhino horn or truffles, and many will testify that money itself is the greatest aphrodisiac of all.

The divine Marquis was invited to join the Everlasting Club in 1784 but alas had to decline membership owing to prior commitments. He was not able to make his visit until the mid-1790s when, members reported, he was in poor health and far from the life and soul of the party that everyone had hoped for.

A book, too, may be a sort of aphrodisiac, and the simple truth about the Marquis de Sade is that in the real world he was not a very successful sadist. In life he administered a few beatings and a couple of poisonings, but it was tame stuff. It was only in his writings that he became the monster he wanted to be. Bodies used as tables and chairs, as platters for scalding hot food. Juliette's daughter roasted alive by Noirceuil. Every man is a tyrant in his bedroom, and in his kitchen, and in his imagination, and in his writings.

TWELVE

Everything in the restaurant was bleached and gleaming. The white table-cloths and the pastel walls and the cream lacquer-work looked clean and washed-out as though in an overexposed photograph. Charming, efficient, incorporeal waiters moved back and forth, serving and clearing and refilling glasses with a ghostly lack of intrusion.

'Have you ever been to this place before?' Frank asked. 'I see it's had some pretty good reviews.'

Virgil shook his head. It was lunchtime. Frank and Virgil occupied a corner table in this fashionable L.A. eaterie, and they were beginning their starter. A number of tiny quails had been dissected and sautéed, and were lying in front of Frank and Virgil on octagonal white plates edged with sprigs of thyme and blackberries, with a sauce that hinted at white wine, brandy, leeks, cayenne and basil.

'Have you seen much of Mom?' Virgil asked.

He wanted to show that he didn't have time for fripperies like discussing fashionable restaurants. He had no time for small talk. Virgil looked good these days. His hair was washed, his complexion less nocturnal, his cheek-bones less angular.

'Yeah, I've seen her,' said Frank, his mood souring, the very mention of her name enough to ruin a good meal.

'So you two aren't getting divorced.'

'Ask her. She's the one who makes the decisions. She tells me I can't afford to divorce her. She's going to cost me a bundle either way.'

'That's okay, isn't it?' said Virgil. 'You've *got* a bundle since you sold the Golden Boys.'

'The way she's spending money I'm not going to have it for long. She says she needs some time to work things out. So far she's worked out that she needs a house of her own and a top-of-the-range Porsche.'

'But it's still cheaper than a divorce?'

'So far,' said Frank, 'but things can change. I mean, can you believe

173

that woman? She sold out her own husband. You know, sometimes I think she was fucking that guy Radcliffe, though I don't see how or where, and of course she denies it. If I could prove it I'd sue the ass off her.'

'But you'd still wind up making a settlement, and she'd probably put in a counter-claim, and either way the lawyers are going to be into you. Yeah, I see how it makes sense to stay married.'

'And,' said Frank, 'all the time she was a goddam member of the Everlasting Club and she never told me. Can you believe that?'

'There's a lot about this that I don't believe.'

Frank glared down at his plate. He chased a piece of quail around it with his fork, finally catching it with his fingers, putting it in his mouth and crunching drily on a wing.

'You think this is meant to taste like this?' he asked Virgil.

'It's fine,' said his son, unenthusiastically.

'It's not as good as Leo would have cooked.'

'Of course it's not as good as Leo would have cooked. That goes without saying.'

'Have you been to Trimalchio's lately?' Frank asked.

'Yeah. It wasn't so bad.'

'They made many changes?'

'Some. They've changed the décor a little and given the staff a kind of uniform. And they've changed the menu, made it longer, made it more English, put on a few English dishes.'

'Oh my God, what are they trying to do, destroy the place?'

'I don't know, Dad. But it's not our problem, is it?'

'No, but . . .'

A waiter appeared and spirited away their empty plates. Seconds later two sorbets were delivered. Frank waved them away.

'It's okay, really, we'll go straight on to the main course. Our palates aren't in any need of cleansing.'

The waiter gave the merest bow of supplication and was gone.

'What kind of car you driving these days?' Frank asked.

'A Volvo.'

'A what?'

'I know it's not exactly my style, but I'm changing my style. I decided I've had enough flashy cars. I've had enough of conspicuous consumption.'

'What the hell does that mean?'

'It doesn't matter.'

'Next you're going to tell me you're getting a job.'

'Not a job exactly, but I've got something lined up.'

'Huh?'

'I'm involved with an aid programme, fighting world hunger.'

'A charity?'

'Yeah.'

'What are you doing for them?'

'Initially I'm going to be a kind of figurehead and fund-raiser. You know, "My name's Virgil Marcel, the Golden Boy. For years I've been helping to feed America. Now I'm going to feed the world." That kind of thing.'

'Charity dinners?' Frank asked. 'TV commercials?'

'At first, sure. But I made it clear I'd only be involved if they let me do some work in the field.'

'Where's the field?' Frank asked.

'Asia, Africa, South America. You know, Dad, half the world.'

Frank nodded. He was not going to argue with Virgil about hunger in the Third World. He wasn't going to knock charity work, and you had to be glad that Virgil was off his ass and doing something with his life. But he still didn't understand the Volvo.

The main course appeared; thick, pink triangles of shark, anointed with chilli butter, served with a tangle of rocket, tarragon, flat-leaved parsley and nasturtium flowers.

'This looks better,' said Frank. 'Enjoy.'

Virgil ate a mouthful or two of the meal.

'So what do you do with yourself these days, Dad? Now that you don't have to run a chain of restaurants?'

'Damned if I know, Virgil. I mean I sure as hell don't have any time on my hands, but I don't seem to do so very much. I play a little golf, I meet people for lunch, I chase the ladies, catch plenty too. I guess they find my money sexy. But you know, I always did those things anyway. I don't know how I ever found time to run a business.

'You know, even though I'm sore as hell with your mother for stabbing me in the back, a lot of the time I think she did me a favour. I'm a lot happier now than when I was working. Maybe it was the right time for the business to get swallowed up by somebody else, let them have all the headaches. Maybe I should write and thank her.'

'Have you been to England? Have you been to "your club"?' Virgil couldn't say it without sneering.

'A couple of times, sure.'

'Don't tell me you enjoyed it.'

'You bet.'

Virgil's disapproval drifted across the table like a bad smell.

'Come on, Virgil,' said Frank, 'if I ever taught you anything it was a) how to have a good time, and b) not to sneer at anybody *else*'s idea of a good time.'

'That's not what I'm sneering at.'

'Okay,' Frank said, 'so you made a fool of yourself with that chauffeur, with the gasoline. I can see how that would be pretty hard to live down. But nobody holds it against you. The guys at the club have forgotten it already. They're good guys.'

'Whatever else they may be, they're not good guys.'

'Hey,' Frank said suddenly, 'do you have any idea what happened to that girl you were running around with?'

'I wasn't running around,' said Virgil. 'I was kidnapped.'

'Whatever.'

'No, I don't know what happened to her. I don't want to know.'

'You spent a whole month together. You must have had something in common.'

'We had in common that we were both being manipulated by "your club".'

'There are worse ways of being manipulated. Ask your mother.'

They ate in silence. Virgil hated the food. It was too delicate, too prissy. He felt a need for French fries, hash browns, refried beans, something solid, substantial, impolite. He felt as though he'd need another meal after this one.

He had a fierce, poorly differentiated anger against his father, a diffuse sense of grievance. His father shouldn't have sold the Golden Boys and Trimalchio's. He shouldn't have split up from Mary. He shouldn't have let Leo go. He certainly shouldn't have joined the Everlasting Club. Maybe all he was saying was that his father shouldn't be the person he was. He'd have preferred it if his mother had been somebody else as well, but it was his father who took most of the flak.

Finally Virgil said, 'You know, like they used to say in the old Perry Mason shows, there's one thing I still don't understand.'

'Only one?' said Frank.

'It's this. Okay, so the Everlasting Club aren't cannibals, right? They never were, never will be. It was just a dumb idea that Butterworth jumped to, and that I was dumb enough to believe. The only kind of cannibalism they're into is financial, okay?'

'There's no need to state the obvious, Virgil.'

176

'Okay, if that's the case, how come Kingsley didn't know it?'

'Kingsley?' Frank repeated.

'Butterworth tortured him, right? I sat in the car with him, asked him a lot of questions. He could have said Butterworth was crazy. He could have said it was all about a business take-over. How come he didn't? He could have saved himself a beating. But he never denied that the Everlasting Club practised cannibalism. He even said you and I had eaten human flesh.'

'He did?' said Frank.

'Well yeah, but if it was all about take-over deals then obviously he was lying, but what I mean is, surely by the time Butterworth had him strung up in the back of the Bentley he could have had no possible reason for wanting to carry on with the cannibalism story, unless . . . Look, I don't know what this means or why it should be, but I came to the conclusion that Kingsley believed the same as Butterworth. He really thought the Everlasting Club were cannibals. I wonder why.'

THIRTEEN

The room was profoundly, though not austerely masculine; oak and old leather, cigar smoke and brandy fumes, still-lifes of pheasants and silver bream, volumes of history and gastronomy in glass-fronted cabinets; all lit by shadowy electric light. Radcliffe moved about his office with unhurried purpose, took a mouthful of Madeira from his glass, then slowly, carefully, removed his clothes.

Mary lay on the floor, her back on a sliver of Persian rug, her bare feet on the cold, dark, wooden floorboards. She was naked and in very good shape. Her slim body would have looked good in far harsher lights than this. Lately she had been tautening her flesh through diet and exercise, and had tanned her skin lightly back home in the Californian sun. In the grey, watery daylight of England she could look almost too good, too studied.

Radcliffe fucked her, briskly, briefly, with passion and precision. It was intense yet effortless. Radcliffe knew what needed to be done for their mutual gratification. There was no hint of performance; no delay, no teasing. It was skilled and thoroughly efficient. But this was merely an hors-d'oeuvre. As they dressed, Radcliffe said, 'I think we're ready now.'

He held the curled receiver of an old-fashioned telephone some way from his mouth, dialled a two-digit number and said clippedly into the mouthpiece, 'Ah, Kingsley, you said you wanted to see me. Yes, come along to my office now, please.'

The call had come as a surprise to Kingsley, as perhaps he had always known it would. It was true he had asked to speak to Radcliffe and was as mentally prepared as he would ever be, yet, by a typical and familiar instinct Radcliffe had caught him off guard, at a moment when he was in his own office, having overeaten, when he was on the point of falling asleep. He brushed sleep from him as best he could, straightened his clothing and demeanour, and went to Radcliffe's office, trying not to feel like a schoolboy on his way to the headmaster's study, but not quite succeeding.

He knocked on Radcliffe's door, firmly and purposefully, if any-thing a little too loudly. He did not intend to sound petulant. Radcliffe called for him to enter. Kingsley was further disorientated by Mary's presence. He had imagined he would be speaking to Radcliffe alone and in confidence, that was what he wanted. But it wasn't Mary's mere presence that unsettled him, it was her appearance. Whereas Radcliffe looked utterly composed and well-groomed, Mary looked, well, as though she'd very recently been pleasured on the floor. Her hair was dishevelled, her feet were still bare, her silk dress was not hanging quite as it should, and she sat somewhat askew on the buttoned Chesterfield. And yes, there was something in the room, nothing so unsubtle as an odour, but an unmistakable aura of recent sex. None of this was going to make Kingsley's task any easier.

'Make yourself comfortable,' said Radcliffe to Kingsley. 'Drink?'

'No thank you,' Kingsley replied.

'Would you like to sit down?'

Kingsley hesitated. If he stood while Radcliffe sat then he would feel even more like a schoolboy. But if he sat while Radcliffe stood, or, worse still, *paced* then he would feel like the victim of an interrogation. He decided to sit on the very edge of a seat, a leather campaign chair, some way from Mary, not very far from Radcliffe's desk.

'Look,' he said slowly, 'I don't want to make a big *thing* of this, but there's no point beating around, basically I don't think I want to be Chief Carver any more.'

Radcliffe showed no surprise.

'I'm sorry to hear that,' he said, though he didn't sound at all sorry to Kingsley. 'Why's that?'

'Well look,' Kingsley continued, 'perhaps what I'm actually saying is that I think it might be for the best if I resigned from the Everlasting Club altogether.'

'Again I have to ask why.'

Kingsley knew there was no way to be delicate or diplomatic about this, that delicacy and diplomacy would be somehow inappropriate and destructive.

'It's because of all this business with Butterworth,' he said feel-ingly. 'And with, pardon me Mrs Marcel, with the Marcels. It's all made me think that perhaps . . . perhaps I don't share the same ideals as the Everlasting Club. By which I mean that I came here in search of, well, for want of a better word, let's call it *excess*. The old Dionysian spirit seems to me to be a pretty damn good thing.

It refreshes civilisation, makes us whole, all that sort of thing. That was why I joined the Everlasting Club. I thought I was going to be in touch with, call me a fool, the old gods, the dark forces. A little human sacrifice, well, why not? Now I discover that the club is little more than an elaborate and, if you'll forgive me, a rather silly way of making business contacts, like the Freemasons or something. I'm sorry but I was wanting more.'

Radcliffe appeared to have been listening without attention or sympathy. He said, 'Perhaps you hoped for too much. Perhaps the world does not run on your Greek ideals. You may have discovered that people indulge in "excess" not to experience any Dionysian tremor, but rather to cement some business deal or other. If you're suggesting that this is a comparatively banal form of human interaction I think I would probably have to agree with you. Alas, that's how the world is.'

'I don't know that I'm all that interested in how the world is,' said Kingsley.

He felt suddenly articulate. He had things to get off his chest, important things to say. Yes, he knew Radcliffe would be more articulate still, would remain suave and supple of mind. He would undoubtedly have the last word, but for the moment, at least, Kingsley felt forthright, even persuasive.

'The Butterworth incident still rankles,' he said. 'It still makes me very angry in all sorts of different ways. I did not join this club to be made a fool of. I did not join in order to be beaten up by my chauffeur, stripped naked, tied to some young woman and locked in the boot of my own car.'

'No,' said Mary, 'I don't suppose you did.'

Memories of pain and humiliation returned to Kingsley, making his face feel red and fat, making him want to disappear, but also making him bloody furious. The simple memory of pain was slipping away, but the memory of humiliation was still all too fresh. He looked at Radcliffe and, unless he was very much mistaken, Radcliffe was suppressing laughter at his predicament.

'You made me Chief Carver, you know,' said Kingsley. 'I didn't ask for the job. Having given it to me I think the very least you might have done was give me a little respect.'

'We do respect you,' said Radcliffe.

Mary nodded in affirmation.

'Then why did you lie to me?'

'Did we actually lie?' asked Radcliffe.

'Yes you did. Why did you make me believe all this cannibal nonsense?'

'I don't think we *made* you believe anything.'

'All this stuff about Virgil being the sacrificial victim proves to have been so much hot air.'

'It was not hot air,' said Radcliffe. 'Virgil played a very important role.'

'Yes, but in a petty take-over bid.'

'Partly, yes. It's true that Virgil was invited to England as a bait for his father. That was Mary's suggestion. She knew that if Virgil came to England and then some crisis was engineered at Trimalchio's restaurant, Frank would be sure to come here pursuing him. And as you have seen, she was absolutely correct.'

'Yes, I can possibly see that,' said Kingsley, 'but why did you tell *me* that you were fattening up Virgil with a view to eating him?'

'We had to tell you that,' said Mary.

'I don't understand.'

'We had to tell you that,' said Radcliffe, 'so that you wouldn't suspect what was really going on.'

'You see, this is precisely my point. This is precisely what I'm objecting to. It seems to me that as Chief Carver I was more than entitled to know what was really going on in the Everlasting Club.'

'No,' said Radcliffe. 'It was important that you *didn't* know.'

Kingsley was speechless. He was confused and insulted. All his feelings of articulateness had gone. He was no longer having the conversation he had wanted to have. He no longer knew what he was doing there. He certainly wished Mary wasn't present.

'It was a shame we had to get rid of Butterworth,' Radcliffe said. 'He was capable enough. He was not wholly unintelligent. He was thoughtful, resourceful. One might well ask why he is condemned to survey the classified columns looking for work as a driver, while someone like you, someone not noticeably more capable or gifted or socially useful, continues to live off the fat of the land.'

'I say,' said Kingsley, 'there's absolutely no need to get abusive.'

'I was not abusing you,' said Radcliffe. 'I think I was stating a rather obvious fact.'

'You really are a plump little thing, aren't you, Kingsley?' said Mary in an amused drawl, as though noticing this for the first time.

Kingsley was partly offended but mostly astounded. You just didn't say that sort of thing to people. He had never tried to deny that he was overweight. It was hardly surprising given a sedentary life and a taste for gluttony. But he did not wish to argue with Mary Marcel, and he felt, in any case, that he was being sidetracked.

'You're like a little stuffed pig,' Mary added.

Kingsley started to speak but Radcliffe interrupted.

'Virgil was a decoy as well as bait,' said Radcliffe. 'He created a diversion. We knew that if you thought we were fattening up Virgil, it would never cross your mind that we were really fattening up you.'

Mary looked at Kingsley flirtatiously. She appeared, he could hardly believe it, to be winking at him. He began to think that she was probably naked under that thin sheath of a silk dress, and immediately he knew that was not what he ought to be thinking about.

'I don't understand,' he said, and he tried to laugh.

It was supposed to be a dismissive laugh, one of disbelief, but it came out a little too hearty and high-pitched, with a dry undertone of panic.

'*Who* was fattening me? I mean why? I don't . . .'

'You see, Kingsley, we never planned to eat Virgil,' said Radcliffe. 'We always planned to eat *you*. That's what we do with Chief Carvers. That's what Chief Carvers are *for*. The fact that we conduct a few sharp business deals doesn't mean that we don't enjoy a little light cannibalism.'

Kingsley's face became waxy and inert, incapable of expression. He felt intensely aware of every part of his body, yet he could move none of them.

'It was all true,' he muttered shakily.

He tried to get to his feet. He looked around the room, looking for what? An escape? An exit? He knew it was useless, and besides, Radcliffe was standing between him and the door.

'I know,' he said. 'This is a joke, a part of the initiation, isn't it?' But he did not believe the words he said.

'It's what you wanted,' said Mary. 'The old gods, the dark forces.'

She was mocking him but he could tell she wasn't joking. This was no hoax, prank or initiation. Radcliffe's hand reached inside his jacket. By now Kingsley was paralysed with terror. His mind was flooded, his body redundant. He expected to see Radcliffe produce something with a thick, curved handle, encrusted with rubies and turquoise, with Aztec markings, and with a long blade caked in dry, centuries-old blood.

Instead Radcliffe produced a small, squat revolver. He fired one